GRAY SEA RUNNING

A DAN CONNOR MYSTERY

R. J. MCMILLEN

SHOGUN PRESS

PRAISE FOR THE DAN CONNOR MYSTERIES

"Fabulous! McMillen makes the stark islands off western Canada a character as vivid and compelling as her main protagonists. If you pick up this book, prepare to lose a weekend." – Kelly Hayes-Raitt, author of *Living Large in Limbo*.

"Authentic characters, terrific dialogue . . . Highly recommended for mystery buffs . . ."
   – Caroline Woodward, author of *Light Years*.

"A pure pleasure to read" – Roberta Rich, author of the international bestselling *The Midwife of Venice* and The *Harem Midwife*.

"McMillen is a solid plotter and there are no extraneous details . . . That, along with some interesting characters, makes for a terrific weekend book. This is a perfect cottage hostess gift." Margaret Cannon, *Globe and Mail*.

"This book will keep you guessing at the ending right up to the final chapter and then leave you panting for a sequel." – Antonio Rambles, author of *The Mirasol Redemption*.

ALSO BY THE AUTHOR

Dark Moon Walking

Black Tide Rising

Green River Falling

This book is dedicated to the indigenous people of Canada

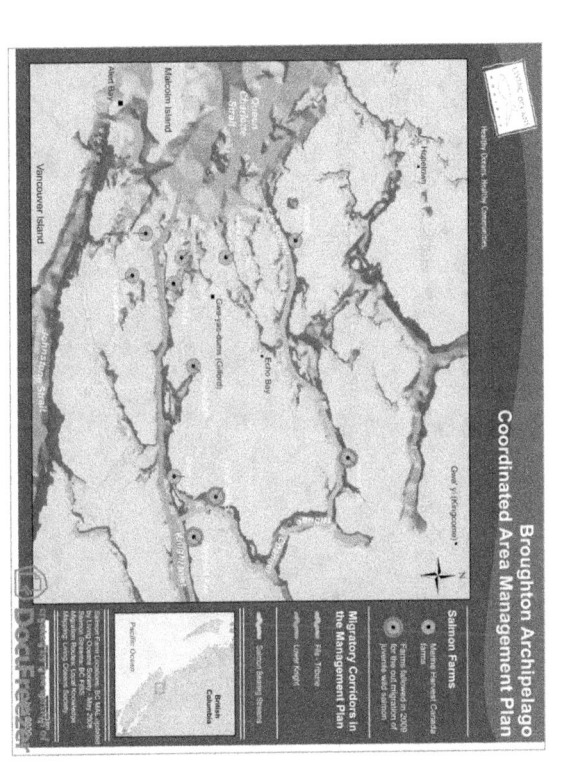

Broughton Archipelago
Coordinated Area Management Plan

1

The floats of the North Island Marina were crowded as Dan Connor walked down the dock, sailboats and powerboats jostling for space, some tied two or three deep. Even though it was getting late the fish-cleaning tables were still busy and the smell of fresh fish grilling on barbeques suggested those tables had been busy for a considerable time. The salmon fishing season had only been open for a week, but there was no shortage of eager fishermen ready to try their luck with the big Coho and Chinook that had made the area famous.

Connor was tired, his brain numb from spending the last three days in meetings, listening to endless discussions of administrative details that he was not the least interested in. New protocols and procedures. Inter-jurisdictional notifications. Personnel transfers. Reporting requirements. All of it considered of utmost importance by the brass and none of it in any way helpful to him or any of the other guys out there in the real world. The only reason he had been there was because he was a 'lone wolf', a term the North Island Commander had coined to describe the fact that Dan was not assigned to a particular detachment but instead could be sent to any of the remote communities that dotted the coast and were only accessible by boat or seaplane.

Dan had never been able to figure out why sitting on his butt all day listening to people talk was more tiring than hours of hiking up a steep mountain, but it was, at least for him, although he knew that most – and maybe all – the others around the table would not agree. Now he was looking forward to a couple of days off and he planned to spend both of them out on the water with Claire.

He smiled as he thought of her. The relationship had grown slowly, both of them wary of commitment and both carrying scars from a previous marriage. Hell, his 'scar' had been an open wound when he and Claire first met, and he still wasn't sure it had completely healed, although her presence in his life had certainly proved to be good medicine.

He glanced at the sky. The weather was unpredictable up here near the northern tip of Vancouver Island, but he couldn't see any sign of an approaching disturbance. With a little luck the next day would dawn bright and clear, a repeat of this one, and the two of them could spend the time relaxing together.

He stopped at the top of the ramp that led down to the floats in order to allow a woman who was walking a large dog to make her way up. It was the dog that caught his attention first. Tall and sleek with a thin, elegant head and long flowing hair, it looked as if it would be more at home strolling around the ring at the Westminster dog show than walking up a swaying wooden ramp at a dock in Port McNeill.

As the pair passed, Dan caught a whiff of expensive perfume and switched his attention to the woman. Her long red hair was twisted into a smooth knot at the back of her neck, and she wore a pale yellow silk shirt and dark green tailored linen pants. Not likely to be a fisherman's wife, Dan thought as he watched her pass. Not dressed like that. Both the woman and her dog looked expensive and out of place. The chain around her neck and the bracelet on her wrist were almost certainly gold and the way her earrings caught the light as she inclined her head in regal acknowledgement of his courtesy said they were probably diamonds. Even the leash she was using was finely braided leather.

Dan shook his head and continued on down to the float. Life at a marina never failed to entertain, particularly one like this that catered to not only local boaters but also – at least during the cruising season - to tourists and serious cruisers who were heading through the Inside Passage.

"Nice ass, huh?"

A thin, rasping voice caught his attention. Old Willie Pete had been a fixture on the float for so many years not even the harbormaster could remember a time when he hadn't been there. His boat was almost as decrepit as he was, and there were bets as to whether Willie or the boat would go first.

"Too rich for you and me Willie," Dan said, smiling as he nodded to the old man. "Neither one of us could afford the upkeep."

Willie cackled. "Ain't that the truth. Getting so I cain't afford to keep meself never mind some high-priced woman and her fancy dog."

Dan laughed and raised his hand in acknowledgement as he continued down the float.

When he first arranged to have *Dreamspeaker* moored on "B" float near the outer end of the breakwater, it was because he wanted to be able to leave at any time without disturbing the whole marina. He hadn't thought about the long walk needed to get to and from the parking lot. As it happened that proved to be a good thing because it meant that he had gotten to know all the regulars in the marina and they, in turn, knew him. A few years ago, with the pain of his wife's death fresh in his mind, he would not have wanted that. Now he not only enjoyed it, but he found it useful in his police work. The "kelp vine" was a great source of both solid information and random gossip and he had no qualms about cultivating it.

He stepped onto the stern grid of his boat and climbed up to the aft deck. *Dreamspeaker* was a converted fish packer, fifty-seven feet long with an eighteen-foot beam, and she still had some of her original gear. Dan used the big winches to help raise and lower crab traps while he was in the marina, and to set shrimp traps when he was in deep water. Neither he nor Claire was fond of cooking, but fresh seafood was something they both loved and living on the ocean meant it was easy to get. It hadn't taken long for both them to learn how to prepare it.

Knowing Claire would be home later that evening, Dan had set a crab trap before he left for his meetings. As he activated the winch to haul up the trap, he looked out over the bay to where a large yacht lay at anchor. It was hard to estimate her size, but he guessed she was well over one hundred feet of spotless white fiberglass. That had to be where the woman he had seen came from. The flag on the stern was the red and white maple leaf of Canada, but he was too far away to read the name and homeport. The yacht hadn't been there this morning when he left and he thought it was probably just anchoring overnight and would leave in the morning.

He dumped the contents of the crab trap onto the deck and watched as half a dozen Dungeness scuttled around his feet. He picked out the four biggest males and threw the rest back. An old woman on the dock down in Campbell River had taught him an easy way to clean them and it took him less than two minutes to get them ready for the pot. Now he could relax with a beer and wait for Claire's arrival.

It was a little after seven when Claire's boat turned the point and slid up alongside. Dan went out and helped her tie up the lines.

"Hungry?" he asked as she climbed over the railing and dropped lightly down onto the deck.

"Starving," she replied, eyeing the empty crab trap. "Did you catch anything?"

"Four big Dungeness caught and cooked," he answered with a smile, pulling her to him. "Even bought some French bread at the store on the way down here."

"Wow, I'm impressed! How about I have a quick shower while you open the wine?"

She turned and started towards the cabin, then stopped as she caught sight of the anchored yacht.

"Good grief, that's huge. Where's it from?"

"No idea. It arrived sometime today. It wasn't here when I left this morning."

"Huh. Probably on its way to Alaska."

The sound of an engine starting caught her attention and she turned and watched as a large, streamlined powerboat curved away from the neighboring float and headed out towards the yacht. "That must be their dinghy. It's as big as my boat – and what on earth is that they have in there with them? It looks like a small horse!"

Dan followed her gaze. "It's a dog. There was a woman walking it along the wharf as I was coming down."

"Guess you'd need a boat that big to have a dog like that aboard. I wonder what kind it is?" She turned back towards the cabin again. "See you in five minutes," she said as she disappeared inside.

They ate out on the aft deck at a folding table Dan had covered with newspaper. They didn't bother with plates or utensils, but simply set out the cooked crab along with the loaf of bread and a dish of butter Dan had melted in the microwave. When they were finished he threw the shells back into the water, put the paper in the garbage, and poured them both another glass of Chardonnay.

It was getting late and they sat quietly side-by-side, legs stretched out in front of them, and watched the light slowly fade and the ocean darken. An evening breeze came up, and then died away again. Boats came in off the water. The sound of laughter and muted conversation drifted over the floats and gulls flew in to roost along the rocks on the breakwater, their cries of greeting slowly quieting as night claimed the bay. A thin slice of moon rose above the mountains to the east and a scattering of stars appeared, but the air carried the first scent of rain.

Twilight deepened into night and still they sat looking out over the marina and the water beyond, occasionally murmuring in a desultory fashion but mostly enjoying a comfortable silence. It was Dan who finally broke the spell.

"We should probably be calling it a night."

"Mmmmm."

"Mmmmm?"

"It's too nice out here." Claire's voice was sleepy.

"Not for long. It's going to rain."

"No it's not."

"Yeah, it is. Look over there. See that black patch?"

Claire opened one eye.

"Where?"

Dan pointed to the southeast where the stars were disappearing one by one, swallowed by a dark mass of cloud.

"Well hell." She straightened up in her chair. "I was hoping we could enjoy some sunshine tomorrow."

Dan stood up and leaned down over her.

"I can think of a great way to enjoy the dark tonight," he said as he lifted his eyebrows and leered at her.

Claire laughed. "A great romantic you are not – although I must admit you do have other redeeming qualities." She put both her hands on his chest and pushed him away. "Help me up. My foot's gone to sleep."

"And you call me unromantic?" Dan reached down and scooped her out of the chair.

He was almost to the door when the phone rang.

2

Early morning bloomed gently in the small cove that opened along the shore of Clio Channel. A thin sea mist danced lightly on the water, the cedars along the shore lifted their dark skirts in the breeze and the iodine tang of kelp drifted on the cool air. Walker let his canoe drift with the slowing current as his eyes followed the flight of a gull against the lightening sky. He was in no hurry, content to wait for the surface ripples and eddies to show him when the ebb had turned to flood.

Further north, up on the mid-coast where he had lived for the past nine years, he would not have needed their guidance. He would have known the movement of the tides and currents by the height of the sun or the position of the moon, by the smell of the beach as the water rose and fell, by the sound of the waves as they moved along the shore.

But this was new territory for him, over a hundred and fifty miles south on the other side of Queen Charlotte Sound, and the patterns of the land and the ocean were different here. It would take him time to learn the sounds and the scents and to become familiar with the rhythm of the tides.

He had not wanted to leave the home he had made for himself up there in the maze of islands and channels that clung to the western edge of the continent. Hadn't wanted to leave the few folks he had met in that remote archipelago, although he had been surprised to realize he was looking forward to being closer to his home village, the place where he had spent his childhood and where many of his relatives still lived. He had Dan Connor and Claire to thank for that. Their friendship had somehow restored his faith in people – or perhaps it was simply that they had somehow restored his faith in himself. Neither of them had hesitated to offer him both friendship and respect even when – at least at the time he had first met Dan down in the city – he had deserved neither. He smiled as he thought of the pair, Claire with her tangle of short, blonde hair and her love of the sea, and Dan with his constantly questioning mind hidden behind a lazy smile.

It was he, Walker, who had first introduced them more than three years ago and although he hadn't seen them often since then, it was often enough that he had seen their relationship grow and strengthen until inexplicably, unexpectedly, it had swelled to embrace him as well. He knew it was their open acceptance that had given him the strength to leave the solitary life he had carved out for himself and edge back towards a world filled with the complexities and responsibilities of family and relationships.

Not that he had chosen to move voluntarily. If it hadn't been for a floating resort with its huge flotilla of noisy power boats and raucous customers moving into a neighboring bay, and a fish farm with its attendant traffic setting up in another, he would still be there.

A disturbance rippled through the water and he looked up to see a black dorsal fin carving through the waves. The orcas were coming to join the hunt. Like him, they knew the salmon would be following the current. Soon the narrows would be filled with racing water and hundreds of the powerful silver fish would spill out into the channel.

Walker had built his life around the salmon. They were what had allowed him to survive since his return to the coast after a failed attempt at living in the city all those years ago. They had given him his independence, even his life, and their movements formed the measure of his days. They had always been the lifeblood of his people, a gift from U'melth the Raven, and in turn they gave themselves back to the people. Each year they returned, their bodies strong and fat from their years in the ocean, and the people received them with thanks and rejoicing.

As the great fish swam up into the fast running water of the rivers they fed everyone and everything along their path. The strongest among them fought their way upstream through the rapids and struggled up the falls until they reached the shallow pools of their birth where they would spawn and die. Even in death they continued to give life, nourishing the land and all that grew on it, feeding the eagles and the bears, the osprey and the mink, and even the earth itself. All of them depended on the salmon, and the salmon had always been there for them, but now things were changing. No longer did massive schools of shining fish fill the coves and bays each summer, crowding together so closely that the water seemed to change into solid silver. No longer did thousands leap from the water in the early light of dawn, the first rays of the sun glinting on their scales. No longer did hundreds offer themselves freely to the people. Now the people had to seek them out.

There were many, including Walker, who blamed the fish farms with their overcrowded pens of alien fish. They had sprung up in coves and bays all along the coast, killing the ocean floor beneath them with a lethal mixture of excess food and waste laced with antibiotics. The fish they farmed there were mostly destined for processing plants and no one seemed to care if they were infested with sea lice and other parasites, but Walker had seen for himself what those lice did to the wild salmon smolts that had to swim through the murky water to get from the rivers of their birth out to the vast ocean beyond. Not many of them survived.

An absence of sound called him back to the moment and Walker turned his canoe towards the narrows. The current had stilled. It no longer held his canoe in its embrace and his paddle slid easily through the quiet water. Above him an eagle curved its wings, slowing its descent towards a tall spruce. Closer to the beach a seal lifted its sleek dark head above the surface. A second orca joined the first and the pair moved in towards to the shore, dorsal fins gliding in tandem through the water. The air grew heavy, filled with expectancy, charged with anticipation. It was as if the earth itself was holding its breath.

The spell was broken by the roar of powerful engines as a Coast Guard Search and Rescue boat burst out of the narrow passage. Within seconds it heeled sharply to starboard and disappeared around the point, leaving behind a heavy wake. Minutes later it was followed by a second vessel, this one a police boat travelling equally fast, and the resulting collision of heaving waves churned the water into a frenzy.

Walker fought to keep his canoe upright, and once he had it steady he sat back and watched as the last of the wake subsided, replaced by the first ripples of the building flood current. He was alone. The seal and the orcas had disappeared. Even the eagle had flown off, no longer able to see its prey through the disturbed water. Peace had returned to the cove, but for Walker the memory of the two speeding vessels remained. He had seen that same combination twice before and both times it had presaged bad news. Reaching down, he replaced his fishing gear into the cedar basket below his seat, turned the canoe away from the narrows and followed the wake left by the speeding boats: a clear path leading towards the cove where he had made his new home.

3

It took Harold Manuel a long time to realize he was a prisoner.

The day had started out like any other, in fact better than some. He had woken early, gone outside to greet the morning and offer thanks to the Creator and then joined his wife, Debra, for breakfast. The outboard motor he had worked on for two days started on the first pull and the ebb tide made his passage down the river into Banks inlet fast and easy. He would arrive at the fish farm in plenty of time to start his shift.

Working on the farm was not something he particularly enjoyed, but it got him out on the water and the pay was good. He knew many of his people were opposed to what he did, but a job was a job and he had a family to provide for – a growing family he reminded himself, smiling as he remembered Debra's announcement three weeks earlier of her first pregnancy. The money he brought home not only fed and clothed them, but also contributed to the welfare of his community, and now that he had been able to find Billy Jules work at the same farm, there was a new sense of hope filling the air. Just last week work had started on a new totem pole, the first in many, many years, and everyone in the village had turned out to celebrate.

Harold had just finished unloading the first barge of fish food totes when his boss appeared. He had never felt really comfortable around Anderson, but he couldn't explain just why that was. The man had never been rude – he did his job and mostly left the workers to their own devices – yet there was something about him that bothered Harold and as he watched Anderson approach he realized he didn't really trust him.

"Harold." Anderson didn't waste time with greetings or idle conversation. "I just got a call from the office over in Port Hardy. One of the loaders didn't show up and they need someone to help load the barge. They asked for you."

Harold felt a small thrill of unexpected pleasure. They had asked for him! The knowledge made him feel good and even though it would make for a long day he was happy to do it. It would mean more time on the water, something he always enjoyed, and there would be some extra money in it. He might even get a chance to talk to Billy, who had been working over there for more than a week now, ever since Anderson had sent him to help on some maintenance work in the warehouse.

"Okay," he said as he swung himself up onto the now empty deck.

There was no one around when the barge arrived back at the dock in Port Hardy and the captain and crew took off for lunch as soon as it was tied up, but there was a stack of totes sitting up on the wharf waiting to be loaded. Harold started the winch and began lifting them down. He knew how they were supposed to go – he had unloaded enough of them over the past weeks – and he jockeyed them carefully into place. He was lifting the third tote when a man approached him.

Harold had never seen him before, but then he hadn't been over this side of the water much. The guy looked official. He was wearing a cap with the company logo and seemed to know his way around as he walked up to the barge and signaled Harold to stop what he was doing.

"You Harold Manuel?" he asked.

Harold nodded. "Yeah," he said. "Why?"

"The guys up at the office said I should talk to you. We've got a problem with a shipment that went to the wrong place. They dropped it off in Port McNeill instead of here. We need your help get it on a truck."

Harold looked at the totes still stacked on the wharf. "Still got a couple of hours work here to load these," he said.

The man shrugged his shoulders. "You can do them later. This is more important and it won't take long."

It was Harold's turn to shrug. "Fine by me," he said as he turned off the winch and clambered up onto the wharf. The longer the day the more the money, and the long hours of daylight at this time of year meant getting home before dark would be no problem.

The man led the way to a blue pick-up truck parked on the street behind the office. He didn't offer his name and they drove in silence, which was fine as far as Harold was concerned. He had never been comfortable talking with white people, and this guy was very white. He had removed his cap and his hair was the color of fresh snow.

They drove to a house painted almost the same color as the pick-up truck. The front yard was full of weeds, but the cement driveway was swept clean. There was no sign of any totes - or of anything else for that matter. The place looked empty.

"Inside," the man said glancing at Harold as if he could read his mind. He opened the garage door and they drove in.

There was nothing in the garage either.

"Put it downstairs to keep it safe," the man said as he unlocked a door and led the way down a flight of stairs.

The room he led Harold into was bare except for an old iron bed pushed against one wall, a metal folding chair and a long table. Four plastic containers about the size of ice-cream buckets sat on one end, and two open cardboard boxes sat on the other.

"This is it?" Harold couldn't figure out what he was supposed to do. It didn't make sense. Why bring him all the way here to carry up four ice-cream buckets? He moved closer to the table and noticed that one of the containers was open. It was filled with pale green pills.

His question was answered by the metallic clang of a heavy lock being turned and Harold turned to see the man had closed a door made of wrought-iron bars. It looked like the bars of a cell.

"Like I said, it shouldn't take you long. Just fill all those little bags and you'll be done."

He turned away and closed a second door. This one was made of solid wood and just before he heard a key turn in the lock, Harold thought he heard a laugh. After that there was only silence.

4

It was close to noon when Arne Hjorth finally got the engine of his boat to start. He pulled himself up, using the battery shelf and the edge of the hatch to help his arthritic knees straighten out. Harry had been right last night in the pub when he said they were all getting too old. Hell, he only had to look at the engine to see that. Once it would have gleamed, the metal lovingly cleaned and polished, the hoses stout and flexible, the walls surrounding it bright with new paint. Now everything was filthy and rusted so badly it was scarcely recognizable. Arne gave a grunt of bitter laughter. Like me, he thought as he slammed the hatch in place and flipped on the switch for the pump that held back the leaks. They were two of a kind, this old boat and him. These days he had to pee so often it seemed like he had sprung a leak himself and every morning when he dragged himself out of bed he felt as if every joint in his body had rusted out.

Yet they kept going, he and the *Silver Lady*. They had spent their lives together out there on the water, matching wits with the gods, dodging the storms, battling the waves, chasing the silver treasure. And they had won goddamn it!

They had won. They had beaten the gods at their game – Aegir, Loki, Thor, all of them – but they hadn't beaten the government. They hadn't beaten the department of fisheries who let in the fish farms, who in turn had stolen the beautiful treasure they were supposed to protect.

He went up forward and released the line that held *Silver Lady* to the mooring buoy. Just a few years ago she had been tied to the wharf, safe inside the protecting arm of the breakwater, but he could no longer afford to keep her there. Now he could barely afford the rope to tie her up let alone the moorage.

But they weren't done yet. Harry had been wrong about that. Arne was not ready to give up. He and his Lady would go down fighting.

5

As he listened to the phone's insistent chime, Dan felt every nerve and muscle in his body tense and the fatigue he had felt earlier in the day returned. He lowered Claire's feet slowly back down onto the deck and closed his eyes in regret as he felt her slender body slide down his.

"I'm sorry babe, but I've got to get that."

Her hand briefly caressed his shoulder as she turned away.

"It's okay. I'll see you later," she said as she walked ahead of him through the salon and started down the stairs.

Dan watched her until she disappeared, and then continued on to the wheelhouse.

"Connor," he snapped as he lifted the phone to his ear.

"Dan." The voice at the other end of the line was unmistakable. Gary Markleson, North Island commander for the RCMP had a voice that sounded like crushed gravel. Dan had been listening to it for the past three days. "Where are you?"

"On the boat." Dan wasn't in the mood for chatting and Markleson knew where he was. They had talked about it earlier.

"You still planning on heading over to Tribune Channel tomorrow?"

Dan stared out into the increasingly dark night. What the hell was this about?

"Yeah, if the weather holds. Why?"

It sounded very much as if Markleson was about to cancel Dan's time off, but if that was the case Dan figured the man would be ordering, not asking. The Commander was not the type to beat around the bush when there was a job to be done.

There was silence for several seconds, followed by a quick inhalation of breath and a spate of coughing. Markleson had recently switched from cigarettes to a pipe, claiming that he was weaning himself away from tobacco.

"You need to quit that stuff," Dan said.

"Yeah, yeah. I'm working on it."

"So you gonna tell me why you're calling me at eleven o'clock at night? I'm guessing it's not to enquire about my health."

"What? Oh yeah. Sorry. We've got a report of a missing person. Young guy. His family thinks he was heading up this way."

Dan frowned as he stared blindly at the window.

"That's it? You called me in the middle of the night just to tell me some guy might have got himself lost somewhere around here? Couldn't that have waited – at least until morning? And why me? Get one of the guys in the office to look into it."

He probably shouldn't be talking to his boss like that, but over the past couple of years the two of them had become friends in a way that only Dan's 'lone wolf' status could allow.

There was another pause, but this time there was no

inhalation, no cough, and the voice, when Markleson spoke again, was softer. Slower.

"There's more to it than that. It's Pete's grandson. His folks say the kid was going to take a job at one of the fish farms over near Knight Inlet, but he hasn't called them for a week and the people on the farms say they haven't seen him."

Pete. That could only be Pete Clements, a retired RCMP officer who still lived in town. Pete had quit the force almost three years ago, just after Dan re-joined – remounted in RCMP speak. Dan had met him and his wife Jenny several times at various functions and had come to like them both. They had been married for almost forty years and they had planned to spend their retirement traveling the country in the motor home they had purchased specifically for that purpose, but five weeks after Pete's retirement Jenny had been diagnosed with cancer, and four months after that she was dead. It had hit Pete hard, but not as hard as the death of their son in a car accident three months later.

"I had heard his son was engaged when the accident happened, but I didn't know he had children." Dan said.

"He didn't. This is the daughter's son. Kathy and her husband live in Toronto. They don't get back here much – I think Pete and the husband had some kind of falling out a few years back – the guy's a government auditor or some-thing. Pretty up tight. From what I can gather the kid takes after his grandfather – doesn't like city life too much. Pete says he's an outdoor kind of guy – fishing, hiking, boating. That kind of stuff."

Dan closed his eyes. He was all too familiar with the anguish that went with losing someone you loved – the pain of losing his wife was always with him, usually just a pres-ence in the back of his mind although it still came back with searing intensity at times. To lose both a wife *and* a son had to be an unbearable agony – and now to hear your grandson was missing?

"A week isn't that long to get from Toronto to Vancouver Island. How old is this kid? He's probably hanging out with some buddies in Vancouver."

"No. He left home last month, called his folks from Nanaimo a week ago. Said he was heading up here that afternoon with some people he had met on the ferry. They haven't heard from him since."

Nanaimo to Port McNeill was a four-hour drive on a paved highway - maybe five hours if the weather or the traffic was bad or road repairs got in the way. Even with stops for meals and sightseeing it wouldn't have taken more than a day to cover the two hundred and twenty or so miles.

"You checked the hotels?"

"Yeah. I had Jarvis – he's that new guy you met at lunch yesterday – check them as far as Campbell River, and the Nanaimo detachment checked them the rest of the way. So far, we've got nothing. Same with the bank. He used his ATM card to take out some cash when he reached Nanaimo, but that's it. No credit card charges and he hasn't used his cell phone since he called his folks.

"We have a possible sighting in Telegraph Cove but it's pretty weak. Just some guy on the wharf who said a kid who looked a bit like Jimmy – that's the kid's name – was asking about a ride out to Minstrel Island, but you know how busy Telegraph Cove gets at this time of year – it's a zoo over there. The guy isn't certain and he could have seen anybody. None of the boats say they took anyone looking like Jimmy out that way."

Markleson was quiet for a long time before he continued.

"Minstrel Island hasn't heard of him and we've checked all the other places he could possibly stay out there – there aren't that many – and all of them were booked solid months ago. Nobody's seen him. We even contacted the marinas. Not a thing."

It didn't sound good and they both knew it, but neither of them was willing to say the words.

"So what do you want me to do?"

"Hell I don't know." Markleson sounded tired. "Just keep your eyes and ears open. You're going to be in the right area so if you run into anyone maybe ask them if they've seen him. I emailed you a photograph his mother sent. It was only taken a couple of months ago so it's pretty current."

It was a very vague request for a man who was used to giving clear orders, but Dan knew that Pete Clements and Gary Markleson had a long history together. This was not his boss issuing a command. This was a friend asking a favor.

"I'll do that," Dan said. "I'll call you if I find anything."

ON HIS WAY back from the wheelhouse, Dan looked in on Claire. She was already asleep, her breathing slow and steady and a slight flush staining her cheeks. A shaft of light from up on the float fell across the pillow and lit her blonde hair. Not only would it be cruel to wake her, but he was no longer in the mood for sex. Thinking of Pete with his dead wife and son had brought back the gut-wrenching anguish that Dan had been wrestling with for over four years: his own wife, Susan, lying on the dining room table in a pool of blood, murdered by a man Dan had been trying to track down at the time, a man who as far as he knew could still be on the loose.

The grief the memory brought with it now was still gut-wrenching, but it was not quite as intense as it had once been and Dan knew he had both time and Claire's presence in his life to thank for that. On the other hand, the guilt he felt was every bit as strong as the day it had happened, perhaps stronger.

Guilt. He let the word form in his brain, saw it appear in harsh, black letters on the inside of his eyelids. He had never allowed himself to fully acknowledge it before, never dealt with it. He had told himself at the time – had thought at the time, at least when he had been able to think at all – that it had been the agony of Susan's loss that had made him put in his resignation from the police force. That it had been the almost visceral pain that had driven him to buy the semi-converted fish packer and turn it into the boat he and Susan had once dreamed of owning and to sail her up into the remote mid-coast where he could lose himself in the wilderness of islands and inlets. But he knew now that had been only a part of it.

He had known the man he was chasing was a psychopath who would do his best to kill Dan first in order to eliminate the threat he posed, but the knowledge had only raised the stakes and fueled the adrenaline. He had even known the guy was cunning and twisted enough to use Susan as a way to get to him, but he had been too smug, too confident, and he had dismissed the danger. He figured he could get to the man first. Beat the odds and keep Susan from ever knowing how close the darkness could get. He had been wrong and she had paid the price.

He rubbed a hand over his face and went back out onto the aft deck. The stars had disappeared completely and a heavy blackness hung overhead. The wind had not yet picked up, but the sea was restless and the slap of rigging on the boats in the marina indicated a storm was on its way.

He had worked hard to avoid facing the truth. He quit the police force and isolated himself on the boat. Stayed away from any of the people he and Susan had associated with.

Avoided watching television and reading newspapers and refused to answer the phone. Even when he re-joined the RCMP a year later he kept his contact with anyone who might have known the story to an absolute minimum and dodged even the slightest hint of anything that could lead into a conversation about his background and history. He heard rumors of course; it had been impossible to avoid them completely, but he steadfastly refused to follow up on them.

Was he strong enough now to ask the questions he should have asked all those years ago? Had enough time passed? If the guy was still out there, walking around free, could Dan handle the knowledge?

He knew there had been an intensive manhunt at the time. The other members of his team hadn't said much when they'd been around him, wrapping him in a cocoon made up in part by camaraderie and in part by silence, but it was a foregone conclusion: cops looked after their own and he and Susan had been part of the family. If he really wanted to know, all he had to do was pick up the phone and ask Mike the question he had been avoiding for four-and-a-half years: had they caught the guy?

He went back inside, splashed cold water over his face and stared at his reflection in the mirror. His dark hair was streaked by the sun and the scar that ran across his cheek, courtesy of a drug-crazed woman he had tried to arrest two months into the job, stood out as a pale slash against weather-darkened skin. Hell, if Susan could see him now, she probably wouldn't be able to recognize him. He was not sure he recognized himself.

He had told himself that he had dealt with the demons set free by her murder, but the truth was he hadn't even come close. All he had done was to run away and hide and then when Claire appeared in his life simply convince himself that he had done the work necessary. That he was ready to move on. He shook his head in disgust. He had done nothing. He hadn't even made a serious attempt. One simple report of a missing person was all it had taken to let it all loose again.

He went to the galley and took a beer from the fridge. It was going to be a very long night. Sleep was no longer an option. It was time to do what he should have done long ago.

The salon was dark, lit only by the faint glow of the lights out on the dock, but the darkness suited his mood. He made his way over to the settee, sat down and tried to loosen the muscles in his shoulders that had tensed up with the first ring of the phone. He needed to look at all the memories head-on: his actions leading up to the murder, his reactions afterwards. Everything.

He would never be a whole man again until he faced it all, and a part of that was asking the question he had been avoiding for so long. For his own peace of mind he needed to know. Needed to hear the words. The problem was that he had waited so long it was no longer the only question. Now there was another one: would his relationship with Claire survive if he found out that the man who had murdered Susan was still out there?

He sighed and leaned his head back against the settee. He had dedicated his life to catching people who had committed crimes, but he had never thought there could be a crime of omission. It wasn't the kind of crime you could be prosecuted for, but he knew now it was a crime that carried its own guilty verdict. A crime that could result in imprisonment in a place far bleaker than a jail cell.

Even if he could come to terms with the things he had done there were still things he hadn't done that he needed to face, and tonight was the time to do it. The phone call to

Mike would have to wait until morning. That was something that needed to be handled in the clear light of day.

It was an hour later when the wind picked up. The rain started a half-hour after that. He didn't notice either. He was still sitting there when Claire got up in the morning, but sleep had finally come.

6

Dan woke stiff and aching from his few hours of sleep. He stood up and stretched, trying to work the kinks out of cramped muscles. It had been a tough night and one he would rather not repeat, but at least he felt he had made some progress. Hell, just recognizing that he had more work to do could be counted as progress. Hard to believe he could have been in denial so long – but wasn't that what the psychologists said men always did – compartmentalize and deny?

He sucked in a deep breath of air and the rich aroma of fresh coffee filled his nostrils. Claire was already at work in the galley, her face etched by the pale gray light that poured in through the windows. The clouds were still there but the rain seemed to have stopped and he couldn't hear much in the way of wind.

"Damn, that smells good," he said as he joined her. "You still want to head over to Tribune Channel?"

"May as well." Claire handed him a steaming cup. "If it's going to rain, we'll get just as wet here as there, and I would like to check on Sam and Roger."

Sam – the woman refused to answer to Samantha – and Roger were a couple in their late seventies who had spent their lives on the coast, making their living from collecting driftwood and using it to create unique furniture. Dan and Claire had met them several years before when they had been up near Milbanke Sound. Now arthritis and necessity had brought the two senior citizens down south, closer to civilization, but they still refused to move ashore.

"Good call," Dan answered. "They might even have seen that kid that's gone missing."

Claire looked at him over the rim of her cup. "Was that what the phone call last night was about?"

"Yeah. He's the son of a retired cop who's a friend of my boss. Seems his folks haven't heard from him in a while and they're getting worried."

"So they want you to look for him." It was a statement, not a question.

"Not officially. Markleson knew I planned on heading out there so he asked if I'd keep my eyes and ears open."

"And that's what kept you awake all night?"

Dan nodded. "In part. It got me thinking about some other stuff that needed thinking about, that's all."

He thought he had made some headway in coming to terms with his actions even though he knew there was more he had to do, but at least he had made his decision. He would phone Mike, but he would make the call after Claire had gone back up to Bull Harbour where she was currently working on a contract with the Ministry of Environment. That would give him a few days on his own to deal with whatever issues the answer brought with it. He knew that avoidance played a part in the decision, but . . .

"Maybe we'll see Walker when we're over there. If anyone's seen this kid, it would probably be him," Claire said.

"Walker? Why would we see Walker?" Dan's confusion was obvious. "He's miles away from here."

"Oh my God! I forgot to tell you. I saw him up in Bull Harbour. He's moved."

Dan stared at her. "Walker's moved?"

"Yes. He said it got too noisy and crowded up there. One of those floating resorts moved into Hakai Pass and then a fish farm set up in a cove just a couple of miles away. He said it was like living in the city – people coming and going all the time."

Dan nodded thoughtfully. "That would certainly create a problem for someone like Walker. Be a problem for me too for that matter – way too much noise and traffic with even one of them, let alone both. Even living in a marina is quieter than that. Where'd he move to?"

"I'm not sure. I didn't ask him and he didn't say, but it's around here somewhere."

"Maybe he went back to his village. I seem to recall him saying it's on one of the islands in the Broughtons so it could even be up there near where you are."

"No, I don't think so. It sounded as if he had found himself a little cove somewhere around here and set up camp like he did up north. He mentioned Knight Inlet a couple of times, and he said he'd been to visit a cousin up in Banks."

"Be good to see him again," Dan said as he switched on the computer and plotted their course.

Claire checked the weather channel while Dan warmed up the engines. When they were ready to leave he went out and let go the lines while Claire eased *Dreamspeaker* away from the float.

"That big yacht's still there," Dan said when he returned to the wheelhouse. "I figured it would be gone first thing."

"Probably need to walk the dog first," Claire answered, an

impish smile on her face as she swung the bow around the end of the breakwater and increased speed.

They took Cormorant Channel and made their way across to Joe Cove on Eden Island. They had been there before and both knew it well. The protected anchorage meant they wouldn't have to worry about *Dreamspeaker* dragging her anchor if they were delayed on some trip to explore the shoreline.

AS IT HAPPENED, they were delayed, but it wasn't because of exploring. The skies cleared and they found a deserted white sand beach, the only remainder of a shell midden at the site of an ancient native village. It enticed them into removing their clothes on the pretext of sunbathing. The sunbathing didn't last long, but it did lead to other more strenuous and enjoyable activities, which in turn led to a plunge in the ocean and then a hurried retreat up into the trees when they heard another boat approaching.

It was cool in the shade of the forest, and the two of them shivered and giggled like teenagers as they hopped, first on one leg and then on the other in their struggles to pull jeans up wet legs and work T-shirts down wet torsos. They stopped giggling when they realized the boat was a Search and Rescue vessel, travelling slowly, two coast guard officers standing beside the control console using binoculars to carefully scan the water and the shoreline.

"Do you think they're looking for that young man your boss phoned you about?" Claire asked, her voice reflecting her concern.

"Not unless they've found out something new since we came ashore," Dan answered. "They don't usually search like that until they know there's been an accident and someone's gone into the water. I'll go talk to them."

He stepped out of the trees and walked down to the beach, waving his hand to draw attention to himself. The coast guard boat slowed even more and came in close.

"You okay?" an officer asked.

"Yeah. I'm Dan Connor. I'm with the RCMP over in McNeill. Are you looking for a missing person or is this an accident?"

"Dan Connor? Yeah, they told us we might see you out here. It's an accident. Guy fell off one of those barges they use to bring the fish food in to the farms and he didn't come up."

"This over near Minstrel Island?"

"Not exactly, but it was close. Up in Tribune Channel, near Lacy Falls."

Dan shook his head. "Lacy Falls? Hell, I didn't even know they had a fish farm there. Those things are multiplying like rabbits."

He tried to picture the location in his mind. Tribune Channel was to the east of where they were. It curved around Gilford Island and flowed out through Nickoll Pass into Knight inlet both south and a little to the east of Minstrel Island. Minstrel Island was a place that Gary Markleson had mentioned when he was talking about Jimmy Fulton. Could this be the same fish farm that Pete's grandson had been headed to?

"You have a name for this guy?" he asked.

The officer reached down and picked up a clipboard. "Yeah. Colin Farnsworth. You know him?"

Dan let out the breath he had been holding. "No. Never heard of him. The missing guy we're looking for is Jimmy Fulton, but he was supposed to be heading out that same way."

THE COAST GUARD boat moved off and Claire came down the beach to join him.

"Did you hear that?" he asked her.

"Yes. Not the young man you're looking for, right?"

"Right," he answered. "Good news in a way, although it's always tough to hear of someone in trouble."

She nodded, her expressive face clearly reflecting regret, and he put his arm around her. She was still cool from her dip in the ocean and the time she had spent up in the shade of the forest.

"Feel like heading over to see if Sam and Roger are accepting visitors?" Dan asked. "If we take the dinghy we can be over there in half an hour or so and get back to the boat in time for dinner."

SAM AND ROGER had moored their boat at the Kwatsi Bay marina. Looking at it in the bright sunlight of an early July day, it wasn't hard to see why. Located in a tiny bay in Simoom Sound, it was almost completely surrounded by towering granite mountains with waterfalls cascading down the steep slopes. Bears wandered the shoreline and other than the family who owned the marina, a few visiting boaters and the old couple themselves, the place seemed to be inhabited only by wildlife.

Dan and Claire had both tried to convince the pair to at least move their boat closer to civilization, but they had steadfastly refused, saying that they had spent their lives living on their own and would not be happy being "in a crowd".

Roger was sitting out on deck when they arrived, carving a piece of driftwood.

"Dan! Claire! Well, this is a nice surprise. Come on aboard."

He put the driftwood aside and leaned forward to shout through the open hatch into the cabin. "Sam! Come see who's here!"

Sam joined them a few minutes later. Like Roger, she had aged since Dan and Claire had last seen her. Her hair was now completely white, her back a little more bent and her movements slower, but both she and Roger seemed to be in amazingly good shape and they were certainly in good spirits. They chatted together for a few minutes, and then Sam and Claire disappeared back inside to make a pot of tea.

"You doing any carving?" Roger asked. It had been their shared love of carving that had first brought the two men into contact. Dan had seen Roger collecting driftwood on a beach and had struck up a conversation with the man.

"No," Dan answered. "I'd like to, but I never seem to be able to find the time."

"Still with the police?"

"Yeah, but I'm based in Port McNeill now. You should stop by next time you're over there."

Roger looked at him in surprise. "You've moved off your boat?"

"No. I'm still onboard. They send me out whenever there's a problem on the water or one of the islands."

"Must be pretty busy with all the stuff that's going on these days." Roger shook his head and reached for his carving knife.

"What stuff's that?" Dan answered. "I haven't heard of much going on in the last little while."

"Well, I guess that's not too surprising. No offense, but the folks up there in Banks don't have much use for the police. Don't care too much for any white men for that matter although there's a few of us who have lived in the area for a while they talk to now and then. There's two of their men gone missing in the last couple of weeks. Seems both of them went out to work one morning and never came home."

Dan stared at him. "When was this?"

Roger shrugged. "First one was maybe a bit over a week ago. The other one was just a few days – Tuesday I think it was."

"You sure? I think I would have heard about them. In fact I would probably have been the one they sent to check it out."

"Guess the Banks folks never reported them."

Dan stared at him, momentarily made speechless by the statement. "Never reported them? Why wouldn't they report them?"

He couldn't even begin to make sense of what Roger was saying. A missing person was always reported. It was the first thing people did – usually too soon because the person returned home within a few hours only to be shocked that they had ever been reported missing in the first place.

"Ah, Banks folks keep to themselves," was all Roger said.

An image of Walker flashed through Dan's mind. Their relationship had changed in the last few years, morphed from the initial antagonism of two people on opposite sides of the law to a grudging respect that grew from shared adversity, and finally to an easy if distant friendship, but he knew there was still a cultural divide.

Would Walker tell him if he knew someone from the Banks village had gone missing or would he keep it to himself? He had certainly reached out to Dan before, first when Claire had disappeared, and then again the previous year when his friend Joel had been in trouble, but the circumstances had been very different. Claire was a white woman who was also a friend and there had been no one else to reach out to, while Joel had needed the intervention only someone inside the RCMP could provide. Would this situation be different?

Dan thought Roger was about to say more, but Sam and Claire returned with the tea and a plate of fresh scones and the conversation turned to the inevitable stories of boating misfortunes witnessed over the past season.

The arrival of two groups of kayakers, plus several small powerboats coming in from a day on the water reminded them that it was growing late. After promises to visit more often, Dan and Claire climbed back into their dinghy. As they were pulling away, Dan thought of a final question.

"Do you know where those two Banks men were heading for?"

Roger shook his head as he handed over the tie-up line. "I'm not sure. One of the fish farms is all they told me."

7

Arne Hjorth pointed *Silver Lady* into the tiny opening and nudged her between the rocks. He had discovered the cove years ago when he had been exploring in his dinghy. It was so small it was not even marked on the charts, and only a narrow-beamed boat like his *Lady* could squeeze in – and then only if the tide was right. It was certainly not big enough for any of the fish farms he hated so much to be established and once inside he was completely hidden from any passing boats. No one could find him here.

He had always loved small, private places – hollow tree trunks, caves, overgrown ditches, even the hollow centers of the haycocks left out to dry in the fields. As a child he had played hide-and-seek with his cousins and had been delighted when he realized they couldn't find him. In the end they refused to play with him at all, saying it was no fun, but that hadn't bothered him. The hiding places were his alone and they formed a private world where his father's drunken rages and heavy leather belt couldn't intrude. Where he felt safe.

Such a strange word that – safe. Where was safe?

Certainly not out on the ocean where the water would swallow you if you had even a moment's inattention or where the wind could flip you over if you misjudged the height or angle of a wave.

Certainly not on a boat in the harbor, where the wires and machinery rusted and the planking warped no matter how much love and attention you gave it.

Not even on the land where he had built his house with his own hands, board by board, each one smoothed with an old hand plane he had rescued from a junk pile. The house was gone now, bulldozed by the town council that said he had never applied for a building permit, and an inspector who said it had been condemned.

Condemned. There was another good word. He used to think it only applied to criminals: murderers who took the life of another man. He hadn't known it could apply to a house – or to a simple fisherman for that matter. One who wanted nothing more than to mind his own business and pull the silver treasure from the sea. But he knew now, and he knew who and what had done it.

He had been condemned by greed. By the owners of the fish farms who cared nothing for the sea or the life within it. They had forced him to give up his livelihood and spend his days scavenging the shore for crabs and seaweed and scraping oysters off the rocks like some homeless cur. Forced him to watch the boat he had shared his working life with slowly deteriorate to the point where, like him, she was reaching the end.

This was the only hiding place he had left. Where he was safe. Where he could almost believe he was free. He called it Holme after the village his mother had grown up in back in Norway.

8

Back onboard *Dreamspeaker*, Dan went up to the wheelhouse and called Markleson.

"You find Jimmy yet?"

"No," Markleson answered. "It's like he disappeared into a black hole. You?"

"Nothing. I showed his picture to the people that run that marina over in Kwatsi Bay but they haven't seen him. I did hear an interesting story though. It's about two other guys who have maybe disappeared around here in last the week or so."

"What the hell are you talking about? Except for Jimmy we haven't had a missing person report up here for almost a year, and as I recall that one turned out to be some guy who went off for a wild weekend with his new lady friend without remembering to tell his wife."

Dan took the phone out onto the side deck where he could watch a pod of dolphins play around the boat.

"Well 'report' may be the operative word here," he said. "The way I heard it, both men went missing from Tsa'wit, over there in Banks Inlet, and the folks in the village don't have too much faith in our abilities so they never called it in."

There was silence while Markleson absorbed what Dan had said and then he asked, "You think it's true?"

"Damned if I know. It doesn't seem like the kind of thing someone would make up. The guy that told me certainly thinks it's true and I tend to trust his judgement."

"Shit. So now we've got one guy in the water, probably drowned, Pete's son missing, and maybe a couple of guys from Banks as well? What the hell is going on?"

"Good question – and there's more. The guy that told me said both of the missing men were headed out to work at one of the fish farms. That's where Jimmy was supposed to be heading too, right?"

"Yeah." Markleson's speech had slowed down, softened. Dan could picture him sitting at his desk, papers scattered over every available surface, half-empty cups of cold coffee pushed to one side, a pipe and tobacco pouch within easy reach as he leaned back in his chair and stared out the window.

"And that guy the coastguard is looking for – what the hell was his name?" There was the sound of papers being shuffled. "Colin Farnsworth, that's it. He fell off one of those fish farms too."

"That's what the coast guard people told me," Dan answered. "At least they said he fell off a barge that was delivering fish food to a farm."

Silence fell again as both men thought about what they had learned. Claire's voice, calling from the galley, snapped Dan back to the present.

"That Claire?" Markleson had overheard her call. "Say hello from me. I'll phone you when I've got a better handle on all this."

THEY ATE dinner out on deck again. They had collected some mussels on the way back from Kwatsi Bay and Claire steamed them in a little white wine and added some stalks of sea asparagus on the side. As Dan nibbled on one of the crunchy green stems, he thought about the man who had first introduced him to the plant he now ate as often as he could find it. At the time, Walker had been berating him for his habit of eating canned and frozen food when, as Walker had put it, there was a 'restaurant' of fresh, free food out there for the taking.

"You think we could find Walker?" he asked.

"Walker?" Claire looked up from dunking a piece of bread in the mussel juice. "Not unless we get really lucky. We've never known where he lives even when we were further up the coast and I can't imagine it would be any easier here. Why?"

Dan repeated what Roger had said to him.

"If anyone knows exactly what happened, it would be Walker," he said as he finished the story.

"Why don't you just go to Tsa'wit and ask them?" Claire asked.

"That's not as easy as it sounds," Dan answered. "The band council over there has declared their village off-limits to visitors unless they apply for and receive permission, and that's a long process. Everything gets taken in there by boat, so getting an application and sending it in can take weeks – and that's only if they want to deal with it at all."

"Are you serious?" Claire was staring at him, her meal forgotten in front of her. "That's crazy – and surely it doesn't apply to the police."

"We could ignore it – and I'm sure we would if we knew there had been a murder, but for something like this . . . it would just cause trouble, and they probably wouldn't tell us anything anyway."

"But why? These are their people that have gone missing. Why wouldn't they ask for help?"

"They don't trust us, and I can't say I blame them. They've never signed a treaty, and they say they've never ceded their land so that makes them a sovereign nation. They look after themselves."

Claire stared at him in amazement. "I had no idea. Surely you don't agree with them?"

Dan's mouth twisted into a lop-sided smile and he turned and looked out across the bay. "I'm not sure," he said. "I guess I never really thought about it before, but there was a guy that spoke at the meeting last week – he was from the Aboriginal Justice program – and he said some things that got me thinking. Gave us some hard numbers."

He turned back to Claire, his voice tight with the same emotion he had felt when he first heard the speech.

"Did you know that our jails are filled with aboriginal people? Hell, I should know. I arrested a lot of them when I was down in the city – but I arrested a lot of white people too, and it wasn't until that guy started talking that I thought about how many of the Native folks I arrested were convicted and how many of the white guys got off." He shook his head. "I should have seen it a long time ago."

"Well there has to be a reason," Claire said. "Maybe Native people don't have the money to hire a decent lawyer, or maybe they can't get a job and they have to steal to eat . . ."

She was staring at him, her expression puzzled, and Dan knew his sudden change of mood had confused her. He wasn't surprised. His reaction to the talk had confused him too, although he doubted he would have felt nearly so strongly about it if it hadn't been for all the time he had spent with Walker. *And with Joel,* he reminded himself as he thought of the gentle Haida man he had met the previous year.

"No." He shook his head. "That's not it. Those things happen to white people too. Remember Joel? Do you think the police in Prince Rupert would have been so quick to pull in a white guy for questioning just because he was out in a canoe? They didn't check out anyone else and there were all kinds of people with canoes and kayaks in Kitsault and Prince Rupert. Joel was a suspect because he was Native."

His voice dropped until it was barely a whisper. "And the truth is, I would have done the same – at least I would have before I heard that talk. It's not fair, and it's not right."

"But the police thought all those people might have been killed with a paddle! Claire's hands were spread out in front of her, drawing the shape in the air as if to conjure up the real thing. "And Joel had a paddle."

"Doesn't matter," Dan answered. "Think about it. All they had was the possibility the weapon had been made out of a certain kind of wood and shaped somehow. It could have been an oar, a chair, a railing. Hell, it could have been a walking stick. Even that yew-wood cutting board I've got in the galley. Nothing pointed directly to a paddle, yet they went straight to Joel."

He shook his head. How come it was so clear to him now? He hadn't even thought about it last year when he'd been actually working on the case.

"But it doesn't make sense!" Claire was leaning forward, pleading with him. "Why would we put anyone in jail if they weren't guilty of a crime?"

"Ah, but they *are* guilty of a crime. The government makes the laws and they can make a crime out of anything they like. Being indigent. Being drunk. Taking drugs. Stealing a pack of cigarettes. It's not the crime that matters – or even being found guilty, although that's certainly a part of it. It's the sentencing. If you're white, you get off. If you're Native, you don't."

Her heard Claire's gasp of protest, but ignored it.

"Hell, indigenous people are only four percent of our population, yet they make up almost a quarter of our jail inmates. That's higher than the numbers for black people in South Africa during apartheid. We're using the jails like we did the residential schools: trying to solve the "Indian problem.""

He stood up, walked over to the railing and stood gazing out unseeingly over the bay. He felt both angry and helpless, with the weight of a guilt built by generations pressing down on him. His job brought him into contact with Native people almost every day. How could he hope to reconcile what he had learned with what was expected of him?

He didn't know how long he stood there, and he wasn't aware that Claire had moved until the touch of her hand on his arm pulled him back to the present. He looked down at her, grateful for the gentle warmth of her touch and for the sense of connection it gave him.

"So what are you going to do?" Her voice was quiet.

"I don't know." He smiled down at her. "I'll think of something." He could see she was worried and he kicked himself for dumping all his worries on her. None of this was her problem.

"Come on," he said, slipping his arm around her shoulders and pulling her close. "I think we've let dinner get cold, but the wine won't have suffered."

He led her back to the table and refilled their glasses. "Here's to us," he said as he toasted her. "And to sandy beaches."

As he heard her quiet laughter he felt the tension relax its grip on his body. In its place a surge of warmth spread through his blood and he offered up a silent prayer of gratitude for having this woman in his life.

They sat and sipped their wine as dusk settled on the bay,

first cloaking the trees and then sliding its dark veil over the water. The chatter of birds slowly stilled and soon the only sound they could hear was their own breathing and the occasional chuckle of water against the hull.

"We could take the dinghy out again tomorrow and go look for Walker." Claire's voice drifted out through the darkness.

Dan smiled and reached for her hand.

9

Dan and Claire were woken from sleep by the first rays of the sun. The water in the bay was calm, its surface barely ruffled with the morning breeze. As they climbed down into the dinghy they could hear the leaves rustling on the poplar trees along the shore and smell the resinous fragrance of balsam drifting on the air. For Dan, the scent carried with it a memory.

It had been over a year now since he had been out paddling with Walker and had cut his hand on a shell. Without hesitation Walker reached under the seat of the canoe and pulled out a small woven basket containing a sticky substance wrapped in a leaf. He handed it to Dan and told him to smear it onto the wound. It had been the resin of the balsam poplar, and it was so effective that before the day was over, Dan had forgotten the cut had even happened. It was months later when he discovered natural medicine practitioners referred to the balsam sap as the Balm of Gilead, a term straight out of the bible. He glanced down at his hand where the deep cut had been. There was not even the trace of a scar.

Before they had gone to bed the previous night, he and Claire had plotted out a meandering course that would take them through the least travelled passages and past the most inhospitable bays and coves in the area, all of them places where Walker might have chosen to create his new home. There was no way they could visit every one of them, but it was the best they could do in the time they had and they could talk with any boaters they came across to ask if they had seen Jimmy Fulton.

Their path took them first south and then west, but many of the coves they wanted to check out were blocked by fish farms. They altered course, knowing Walker would never consider living anywhere near one of them – after all, it was partly the presence of a fish farm that had caused him to move in the first place. Instead, they decided to head north to Broughton Island, but even there the little bay they had visited the previous year was no longer accessible.

"We're not going to find him around here. He's probably up in one of the inlets." Frustration colored Claire's voice.

"Well, there's no way we have time to check those," Dan replied. "If he's in Banks we wouldn't be welcome, and Knight is just too far and too long. Maybe we should just go to Sullivan Bay. It's not far and at least we could ask the people there if they've seen Jimmy before we head back."

Claire nodded her agreement. "It would be nice if we could find at least one empty bay where we could eat our lunch though."

Dan lifted his eyebrows and narrowed his eyes as he looked at her. "Especially if it had a sandy beach?"

She waved her hand dismissively, but he could see that she was smiling.

He turned the dinghy around and they made their way slowly east through Fife Sound and then north to Sullivan Bay. At this time of the year the resort was crowded. The marina was full and from the activity on the floats it looked as if all the float homes were in use. Even as they were wending their way past the long lines of moored vessels a helicopter settled on the upper deck of one of them.

Once the clatter of rotors had died away, the sound of talk and laughter filled the air and wafted out over the water from the floating village. The place was so busy, so alive, it made Dan wonder if perhaps marina business was benefitting from the reduction of available anchorages in nearby coves and bays caused by the increasing numbers of fish farms.

They tied the dinghy up in front of the store and Claire went inside to browse while Dan went in search of one of the dock staff. He finally found a young man wearing a Sullivan Bay T-shirt who was helping to tie up a sixty-foot trawler, its wooden hull and gleaming teak decks looking out of place amid the rows of shining white fiberglass and polished chrome.

While he waited for the boat to be secured, Dan checked out the other yachts tied to the float. Although all were somewhat similar, one looked very familiar and his suspicions were confirmed when a large dog padded out onto the foredeck to sit beside a red-haired woman lying in a lounge chair. This was the yacht that had been anchored off Port McNeill.

Just as Dan started to turn away, he saw the woman turn her head as a man appeared behind her. He was tall and slim, dressed in a white shirt and black jeans, and his long, dark hair was tied in a ponytail.

Dan's reaction was spontaneous and immediate. Adrenelin surged through his body and his muscles clenched as his mind flashed back four years to the *Snow Queen*, and to Harry Coombs and the men who had been chasing Claire. And it didn't stop there. It moved back further still, to the man he had been chasing when Susan was killed. That man too had been tall and slim, with dark hair worn in a ponytail.

Why hadn't his subconscious made that connection four years ago? Had his denial been that complete? And why now when there was no reason, other than a superficial similarity in appearance?

"Something I can help you with?"

The young man, whose nametag identified him as Kevin and whose hair had been artfully streaked and styled, had finished his task.

"I hope so." Dan struggled to force his mind back to the present. He pulled his badge out of his pocket and held it out.

"I was wondering if you've seen this guy around." With his other hand he held out a copy of Jimmy's photograph.

Kevin looked at him warily for a moment and then reached for the picture.

"Wow, man. Is he a bad guy?" he asked. "Whad'he do?"

"He didn't do anything," Dan answered. "He seems to be missing and his family is worried about him."

"Oh shit. That's seriously nasty, man." Kevin moved his head from side to side as he stared at the photo. He reminded Dan of a brightly feathered bantam rooster his neighbor had had when he was a kid.

"Doesn't look familiar, man, but I really can't be sure. You know how it is. There's a lot of people go through here at this time of year and I barely have time to look at any of them."

"Anyone else I could ask?"

Kevin shrugged. "Maybe check at the bar or the restaurant. Some of the chicks there might remember him."

"Thanks. I'll do that." Dan slid the photo back into the envelope and turned to go, but then turned back. "One more question. Have you heard anything about any men going missing? Native men?"

"Native men? You mean like Indians?" Kevin look of incredulity matched his tone of voice.

"Yes. Like Indians. Native men." Dan heard the sarcasm

in his response and he struggled to keep his voice level. Kevin's ignorance had triggered a surge of resentment that caught him completely by surprise. The sarcasm, like his response to the man on the yacht, were both reactions that were inappropriate and unacceptable given both his training and his profession and both worried him.

"They're actually Kwakwakawak'wa," he said, knowing that the term would mean nothing to the young man in front of him. "We used to call them Kwakiutl but there's different bands with different names. They live around here. This is their territory."

"Oh wow, we don't get many of them here. I don't think I've ever seen one." Kevin sounded as if he thought Natives were alien creatures from a distant planet, and the confusion on his face made him look even younger and more naïve than he had previously appeared.

"So you haven't heard anybody talking? No gossip of any kind?"

"No, man. No way. Nothing."

The kid looked so earnest Dan felt almost sorry for him, but the thought that Kevin would use this brief conversation to entertain his buddies for the next several days quickly took care of that.

Back up at the village he found Claire sitting on a bench between two hanging baskets filled with bright pink petunias and trailing fuschia.

"Wish I had a camera with me," he said as he smiled down at her. "You look beautiful."

She looked up at him but didn't return his smile.

"You need to talk to Belinda," she said. "She might have seen Jimmy."

10

Belinda Travers was a short, vivacious redhead with a mass of curls piled on top of her head and an infectious smile. She worked as a waitress in the restaurant and looked to be several years younger than Kevin, which Dan figured probably meant she was still in school. She wiggled her fingers at Claire when she saw them enter and pointed to an empty table by the window.

"What makes you think she saw Jimmy?" Dan asked as he slid onto a bench seat.

"I came in for a coffee and she asked me which boat I was on," Claire replied. "I explained that we were here looking for a young man who was missing and she asked his name. I told her it was Jimmy but I didn't know his last name, only that he had come from Toronto to work on one of the fish farms, and she got this weird look on her face. She asked me if I knew what Jimmy looked like so I told her you had a photo of him."

Dan nodded and watched as Belinda worked her way back towards them. It was obvious she was good at her job: she smiled and chatted as she took orders and cleared dishes and she seemed to know most of the clientele. By the time she arrived at their table, over five minutes had passed.

"Hi," she said, smiling brightly at Claire before turning to look at Dan. "I guess you must be Dan. Claire said you had a photo of a guy you're looking for?"

"I am, and I do," Dan answered. "And Claire said that she thought you might have met a guy named Jimmy recently?"

Belinda flashed a quick glance at Claire, and her smile faltered just a little before she answered. "Yeah. I did – at least he said his name was Jimmy, but he also said he'd call me and he didn't so who knows?" She shrugged her shoulders and hugged her tray to her chest. "Maybe he was just chatting me up?"

Her quick, forced grin was intended to show how little she cared, but it proved exactly the opposite, and her eyes held both hurt and confusion. Watching her, Dan figured there was an insecure little girl beneath the bright exterior and Jimmy was probably just one of a number of men she had been disappointed by, but then she straightened her shoulders and held out her hand for the photo. Tough too, he thought as he pulled it out of the envelope and handed it to her, watching her eyes widen as she looked down into Jimmy Fulton's face. The young man had been laughing into the camera when the photo was taken, not a care in the world, probably excited by the knowledge that he was headed for a new adventure.

Belinda's lips trembled as she stared down at the image and she blinked a couple of times before she looked up and handed the photo back.

"Is that the guy you met?" Dan kept his voice gentle as he watched the emotions play across her face. "Is that Jimmy?"

Belinda looked at him for a minute before she answered, her eyes bright with tears, but then she tossed her head and nodded. "Yeah," she said. "That's him. Is he really missing?"

"Yes, he is, but we're trying to find him. His mother said he was planning to work on a fish farm. Did he say anything about that to you?"

The girl shrugged. "He said he had a job lined up with one of them, but I didn't ask him which one it was. There are lots all around here so I figured it wasn't far. He was trying to find a ride with one of the boats – they come and go every day so he figured maybe one of them could just drop him off."

Another waitress, this one blonde and plump and about the same age as Belinda, came up to her and whispered something in her ear while she looked over towards the kitchen. Belinda nodded and turned back to Dan and Claire.

"I gotta go. I got an order ready. I sure hope you find him. He's a really nice guy."

She turned to leave, then turned back. "You should ask that lady with the dog. He was talking to her just before he left. She might know where he was going."

"The dog?" Dan wasn't sure he had heard her correctly. Surely she couldn't be talking about the woman he had seen walking some giant animal on the wharf at Port McNeill. The same woman he had seen just minutes ago on the deck of the large yacht. That would be quite a coincidence – and coincidence was not something he tended to put much faith in.

"Yeah, it's a weird looking thing – Jimmy said it's an Afghan Hound or something. It's huge. She told him they were bred to hunt stuff in the desert." Belinda looked out the window at the yachts crowded along the floats and the stretch of water beyond and laughed. "Not much desert here."

"Do you think it's the same woman," Claire asked as they left the restaurant.

"Gotta be," Dan answered. "How many dogs like that are you going to find on a boat – and she's here. She's on that same yacht we saw anchored back at Port McNeill. It's moored out at the end of one of the floats."

He left Claire to continue exploring the village while he retraced his steps. The woman and the dog had disappeared from the deck and the yacht sat quiet, apparently unoccupied. A flight of stairs led up from the wharf to an open gate in the bulwarks and Dan went up and rapped on the hull. There was no response.

After waiting several minutes he climbed the stairs and stepped through the gate. A covered side-deck ran the length of the ship and Dan walked aft, peering through the windows into a vast salon decorated entirely with angular chrome and white leather furniture that he thought looked both cold and uncomfortable, more like a showroom than a place to relax.

The yacht appeared to be totally deserted, although the glass doors leading from the deck into the salon were wide open. He knocked a second time, then leaned in and shouted, but it still remained eerily quiet. If there was anyone aboard, they must either be in a stateroom well forward in the bow, or perhaps on a lower deck, but it seemed odd there were no crew around.

Dan slid a card from his wallet and set it on a glass coffee table just inside the door. It was probably a waste of time. Experience told him it was unlikely anyone finding it would actually call him.

He glanced around once again at the immaculate salon. The glass was so clean it was almost invisible and the chrome gleamed. There had to be an army of staff on board to keep it looking the way it did, so where the hell were they?

He turned to leave and came face to face with the man he had seen out on the deck earlier. Dan hadn't heard him approach so there was no way of telling how long he had been standing there or where he had come from and he didn't speak now. Instead he simply stood, silent and still, no more than a foot away, his eyes hidden behind dark sunglasses.

"Hi. Sorry to intrude," Dan said, recovering from his surprise and holding out his hand. "I knocked but no one answered. Are you the owner?"

The man neither shook the proffered hand nor answered the question, but continued to stand there almost preternaturally still. Something about the way he held himself, seemingly relaxed yet somehow poised for action, suggested he might be a practitioner of martial arts and Dan wondered if perhaps he was Oriental. Certainly his hair was dark enough although the color of his skin pointed more towards South America or the Middle East. In any case he didn't appear to understand English, and after a few seconds had passed Dan took a slow step back and reached into the salon where his card lay on the table. He picked it up and held it out.

"Dan Connor. I'm with the RCMP. The police. I need to speak with the owner."

There was a flicker of movement behind the dark glasses.

"The owner is not available."

So he did speak English – and excellent English at that.

"Well it's actually his wife I want to talk to. Is she around?"

"He does not have a wife."

Dan sighed. He was already beginning to tire of this game.

"But there is a woman aboard. A woman with a dog. I saw her out on the foredeck about an hour ago. Who is she?"

There was a shrug and the faintest suggestion of a sneer. "She is a friend of the owner."

"Then I need to talk to this friend."

The sneer became more pronounced. "She is not here."

The two men stared silently at each other, locked into an unspoken challenge, each waiting to see if the other would flinch. It was Dan who moved first. There was nothing to be gained by forcing the issue. He leaned back and returned his card to the table. There was something going on here and he needed to figure out what it was, but that would have to wait. He had no reason to force his way in and he had neither the support nor the equipment – nor a valid excuse he reminded himself – to take on the man in front of him, although they were both well aware that he would dearly love to do just that.

"The owner needs to call me. Please make sure he does," he said as he pushed his way past his unknown enemy and climbed back down onto the float.

"DID SHE KNOW WHERE JIMMY WENT?" Claire asked when Dan returned from his futile search.

"She wasn't there," he answered. "I don't suppose you saw her and her dog come up this way?"

She shook her head, a puzzled look on her face. Like Dan, she knew that there was really nowhere else the woman could have gone. Even if she had decided to visit another of the yachts, the dog should have been clearly visible out on deck or on the float.

"Perhaps they went out on that big launch they use as a dinghy. That has to be at least thirty feet long, maybe more, but it would be a whole lot easier to explore the area in that than with the yacht."

Dan nodded. It seemed to be the only feasible explanation, but it meant that the woman could be gone for hours – or even days. The 'dinghy' was big enough to have several berths, although he didn't think she looked like someone who would enjoy anything less than the kind of comfort and convenience provided by the yacht.

"No use waiting for her. I left my card so maybe someone will call. It's not likely they took Jimmy anywhere – they don't look like the kind of people who would pick up a hitchhiker and I doubt they would want to hang around a fish farm."

As they passed the yacht on their way out, Dan saw the same man standing out on the deck. He couldn't be sure, but he thought the guy was watching them.

11

On the other side of Vancouver Island, halfway up the coast off the entrance to Esperanza Inlet, a fish boat ploughed through a heavy swell. The weather in the area had been good for the past two days, but the swell was the result of a storm that had recently pounded the shores of Japan, almost five thousand miles to the west. The boat bucked and twisted as it quartered the sea, angling up the smooth face of the wave only to teeter precariously on the crest before starting its plunge down into the trough. It was a fishing troller with a length of just thirty-nine feet, small in comparison with the steel monsters that now dominated the fishing industry. Big business had replaced the independent fishermen that once made a good living on the sea and few small boats remained.

The old-growth fir planks and the oak ribs that formed the hull of the Betty Jean did not show up well on radar, but her metal rigging and the radar reflector mounted on the mast made her clearly visible on the coastguard satellite system. She had logged into Canadian Marine Traffic Control when she first appeared off Cape Flattery and started north across the Strait of Juan de Fuca towards Carmanah Point in the early hours of the morning. Registered in the United States with a homeport of Sitka, Alaska, she had been regularly recorded in transit through the area over the past several years as she followed the diminishing numbers of wild salmon on their return to the rivers of their birth.

More than one hundred and twenty-five miles north, off the entrance to Esperanza Inlet, the boat changed course and headed in. The captain, a man by the name of Tommy Estrada, again called up Marine Traffic Control and informed them of the course change as was required, adding that they were headed into Zeballos to take on fuel. That too had happened many times in the past. A small boat heading up as far as Alaska had to cover large distances between refueling stations and this one had come all the way from the Columbia River.

The new position was once again logged into Marine Traffic and the technicians there turned their attention to other things: there were nine freighters anchored off Vancouver Harbour waiting their turn to load or unload goods, three more waiting at Roberts Bank for coal and wheat, three inbound in the Strait of Juan de Fuca and two outbound in that same body of water. If that wasn't enough to keep the overworked staff busy, there were also two cruise ships headed down the Inside Passage plus all the regular tug, tow and barge combinations and the ferries that crisscrossed the waters between the mainland and the myriad offshore islands. No one even tried to count the recreational boats that dotted the screens like a virulent rash.

Even if the technicians had been paying close attention it was doubtful they would have noticed the insignificant splash made by the small inflatable lowered off the stern of the Betty Jean as she entered calmer waters. Within minutes the dinghy became just another local boat moving up and down the inlet, another couple of guys out for a day of fishing in one of the best salmon fishing spots in the area. By the time the old troller turned into Zeballos Inlet, the dinghy had already disappeared into the narrow sliver of water the charts identified as Port Eliza.

An hour and a half later, sitting lower in the water now that she had a full load of fuel and fresh water in her tanks, the Betty Jean headed back out. She barely slowed as she picked up the same two men and lifted the inflatable out of the water. It was a little heavier than it had been when they launched it, and they carefully removed six packages, each one tightly wrapped and sealed in black plastic, and placed them into the hold.

The Betty Jean continued on her course and when she had rounded the point and was once again feeling the swells of the Pacific under her keel, the captain changed his heading and set a course for the Scott Islands off the northern tip of Vancouver Island. From there he would angle across to Rivers Inlet and then enter Fitz Hugh Sound and the calmer waters of the Inside Passage on his way to Alaska.

Later that same day another inflatable with two men aboard plus their fishing gear and a couple of coolers presumably to hold their catch, returned to Zeballos. A heavyset man with short blond hair operated the boat, but it was the much smaller dark-haired passenger who directed its course.

They loaded it onto a trailer pulled by a blue pickup truck and by midnight, driving slowly over the rough, gravel roads, the truck and its tow arrived in Port McNeill and was backed into the driveway of a house located high on the hill above the town. The two men unhitched the trailer and pushed it into the garage. Before the door was closed, the dark-haired man walked out to the end of the driveway and stared into the night, his eyes scanning the houses lining the quiet street. After a couple of minutes he turned and walked back inside, the garage door rolled down again and the lights were turned off. The house returned to silence, like all the other houses around it.

12

Walker sat quietly across from the old man and waited for him to speak. The man had come a long distance in order to find him, first by boat from his home in Tsa'wit, far up the long tongue of water the white man's charts called Banks Inlet, and then on foot once he reached the town of 'Yalis on Cormorant Island. He had shuffled along the beach in front of the village and asked one of the men he found there for directions, saying that he was looking for Walker. He had been greeted warmly and directed to the house of Walker's aunt, who offered him a cup of tea and then told him how to find her son, Harold, who was perhaps the only person in the village who knew where Walker was currently living. The old man had thanked her and made his way slowly up to the top of the hill as he had been instructed.

Almost an hour later he located Harold's house and found Harold in the driveway working on his truck. The two men exchanged greetings and chatted for a while and then the old man asked Harold if he could please take a message to Walker. Harold listened to the request and then drove them both back to his mother's house to ask her opinion. Both Harold and his mother knew that Walker did not like visitors and even though Harold knew where Walker lived, he himself did not go there uninvited.

Harold's mother listened to the old man's explanation, and when she nodded her approval Harold left the two of them sitting in her kitchen with a pot of tea on the table in front of them and went down to the marina where he kept his boat. He fired up the engine, made his way out to the tiny cove where Walker had built a rough cabin out of driftwood, and gave him the message. Walker agreed to talk to the old man, but he refused a ride back to Alert Bay: he never went anywhere without his canoe. He would make his own way there.

It had all taken several days, but the old man showed no sign of impatience. He would speak in his own time. Walker waited with equal patience, and when that time finally came, the old man's voice was as thin as the breeze that rustled the branches of the poplar trees.

"I am troubled, my nephew," he said, and Walker smiled as he heard the traditional honorific. 'There are evil things happening. The balance has been broken." He paused and looked out across the beach, his eyes staring blindly at the ocean beyond. "These men that have gone missing. They were good men. Hard workers. They honored our traditions. They knew the ocean and her ways. They have travelled on her waters since they were children. It does not seem possible they would both lose their way."

"When did they go missing, Grandfather," asked Walker, offering back the respect he had received. "Were they together?"

"No," replied the old man. "They went alone. The first disappeared perhaps one of the white man's weeks ago. The other less than that."

"Do you know where they were going?"

"They both had work on one of those places that farm fish. There are many of those things here and I do not know which one they were working for."

"Have you spoken to their families? Perhaps they would know."

The old man smiled. "Yes, but it was a job, nothing more. These things were not important to them so they did not ask. We do not have farms. Mother earth gives us all we need. A farm that grows some kind of strange fish is not something we understand.

Walker nodded. "What is it you would like me to do Grandfather?"

"The farms belong to the white man. I have been told that you have a friend, a white man, who is with the white man's police. My people say that he is a good man, and that he has helped us before."

Walker let his gaze wander across the cluttered shoreline of the village: the rocky breakwater that enclosed the marina, the tangled rigging of the fishing boats, the wooden houses jutting out over the water on crumbling pilings, the ferry dock that linked Cormorant Island to the bigger island to the west, and then he looked out over the restless ocean beyond.

The old man had to be talking about Dan Connor, someone Walker hadn't seen for over a year and someone this wise and gentle man had certainly never met, yet somehow news of Dan and his efforts on behalf of Walker's friend Joel had reached the remote and isolated community of Tsa'wit. How long had it taken, Walker wondered, for that news to travel down that wild, empty coastline; a hundred miles across Hecate Strait from Haida Gwaii, another seven hundred as the raven flies from Prince Rupert down to Banks Inlet, perhaps twenty thousand miles if it had also made its way up all the other inlets and out to the forty thousand or so islands that clung to that the western edge of Canada. Had news of how he and Dan Connor first met all those years ago down in the city also travelled that same route? He thought it probably had.

"Yes Grandfather. His name is Dan Connor and he is a good man. He honors and respects our people. I consider him to be my friend."

The words sounded strange in his mouth, but even as he said them he knew it was true. Dan Connor *was* his friend.

"We would be grateful if he would help us with this matter also."

The old man finished speaking. They were sitting on a low wall above the beach and the slanting rays of the sun shone on his face, burnishing it with copper light and etching the deep lines that marked his years with shadow. Sitting beside him, Walker thought he looked more like an ancient carving than a frail and elderly man. He looked as if he had been sculpted out of bronze, strong and powerful and as old as the land itself.

"I will ask him, Grandfather," Walker answered. "I think he will try."

The old man turned and looked at him. "Trying is all any of us can do, my nephew. It is enough. I thank you. Gilakas'la."

He reached for the carved stick he used as a cane and stood up. As if on cue, the boat that had brought him to the cove nosed around the rocks on the outer point of the bay.

WALKER WATCHED as the boat now carrying the old man disappeared back around the point and thought about what he needed to do. It seemed as if it should be an easy task to contact Dan Connor. Dan kept his boat tied up at the marina in Port McNeill, less than ten miles away from where Walker was sitting.

Almost everybody with a boat in Alert Bay – the town Walker's people called 'Yalis – would have a VHF radio, and would be happy to let him use it, but VHF was public and one of the favorite pastimes in the village was listening in to conversations between boats. Hot fishing spots were discovered that way. New romances were discovered that way. Infidelities and affairs were discovered that way. It provided endless entertainment and fueled the village gossip. If people were disappearing, it didn't seem wise to announce that Dan Connor was being asked to help find them.

Radiotelephone or satellite phone would be better, but it meant climbing up into the wheelhouse of one of the big fish boats tied to the floats behind the breakwater. Because of the damage he had done to his legs when he fell from the roof of a bank all those years ago Walker could not do that without assistance, and assistance meant any of the privacy gained would be lost.

Ham radio or SSB might be possible – he knew Dan had them both onboard his boat – but Walker didn't know how to use them and even if he did, few of the boats at the marina would have them. That left regular telephone lines – and Dan's boat, *Dreamspeaker,* was not equipped with a regular phone.

It was less than a mile from the beach up to his aunt's house but it took Walker well over an hour to get there. It would have taken considerably longer if he hadn't been offered a ride from a passing truck that took him over the steepest part of the road. While he could sit for hours in a canoe, his legs no longer allowed him to walk easily and even with the help of a driftwood branch he had picked up on the beach each step was agony.

Once at the house, he spent an hour with his aunt as both

courtesy and tradition demanded, then another hour with the two neighbors who dropped in to see who was visiting her. By the time he made the phone call to the police station in Port McNeill, the sun was very low in the west. It was only when the man who answered the phone asked him how Dan Connor could contact him that he realized he would either have to stay with his aunt until Dan called, or go and find the man himself.

Although he loved her dearly, staying with his aunt was not an option. It had been many years since he lived in a place completely surrounded by walls, the wind kept out by solid doors and windows, the sky blocked out by a roof. It was not something he had any desire to do again. That made his decision easy. It was what he should have done in the first place.

The beach was deserted when he slid his canoe back into the water, the troughs of the waves already dark with the shadows of night. If he returned to his cove, he would be on the water until well after midnight and he would still have a long trip ahead of him the next day. If he headed straight for Port McNeill he could get there by two or three o'clock in the morning. It would be a long paddle but nothing he wasn't used to, and there would be little if any other traffic out on the water. He had woken Dan Connor from his sleep in the stillest hours of the night more than once in the years they had known each other and he smiled as he thought about Dan's reaction when he did it yet again. Walker twisted his paddle to angle his canoe out into the bay.

13

Although it had been late when Dan and Claire got back to the marina in Port McNeill, Claire still had to leave early early the next morning and she and Dan shared a cup of coffee out on the aft deck as they watched the light return to the land. Two days together had not been enough for either of them, but she had a government contract to fulfill and Dan had his work to return to – and a phone call to make she reminded him before she kissed him goodbye.

Dan watched her boat disappear around the point and felt the first hint of aloneness. That was all he could call it. It wasn't loneliness, because he was used to his own company and enjoyed it, but Claire was a woman whose presence he enjoyed and he was becoming more and more aware of her absences.

It was still too early to call Mike, but he could stretch his legs and go up to the office to tell the desk guy the owner of *White Lightning* might be phoning. He had made an ostentatious show of checking the name and port of registry inscribed on the stern of the yacht right after he stepped down onto the float. Although it was information he needed to know, he knew the way he had done it was a reaction to his confrontation with the man on board and the knowledge bothered him.

He had thought he was past that kind of juvenile response. During his training he had been made very aware of just how vulnerable he was to it – and in turn of how vulnerable it made him - and with the help of the police psychologists he had worked hard at disciplining himself to control it. It was what had motivated him to take up martial arts after he graduated from the academy, a practice that demanded a calm, clear mind and that would punish such adolescent, hormonal behavior with an immediate and painful rebuke. He nodded to himself. It was time to get back to his judo practice.

He checked his watch and headed up the float. Mike tended to get in to his office late, so that call could wait. Once again Dan recognized there was a measure of avoidance in the decision, but he dismissed the thought. If the owner of the *White Lightning* actually phoned, he wanted to know about it, plus the police computers could access far more information than the one he used aboard *Dreamspeaker*. It might take a little playing around, but he should be able to get into the Ship's Registry files where he could check the registration number and find out who the owner was.

This early in the morning – it was not yet six o'clock although it had been light for well over an hour – the town lay quiet under a pale sky that was neither blue nor gray but some indistinguishable color that held a little of both. The streets were empty and the only person Dan saw on his walk up the hill to the station was a woman walking a small black dog.

The sight gave him an idea: was there a registry for dogs? Belinda had said that the dog belonging to the woman on the yacht was an Afghan. Surely there couldn't be too many of those around – in fact he couldn't remember ever seeing one before. If he could find an Afghan Hound registered in Vancouver where the yacht was registered, then perhaps he could track her that way.

He dismissed the thought almost as quickly as it had come. Just because the yacht was registered in Vancouver, it didn't mean the owner lived there. He could live anywhere, and Dan already knew the woman was not the owner's wife. The man with the ponytail had told him that.

He decided to take a detour into the park and spend half an hour performing stretches and working on a basic judo kata. By the time he arrived at the station he felt newly invigorated from his workout and his subsequent jog up the hill and he was covered with a fine sheen of sweat. He could feel the beginning of a few muscle twinges, but he felt good. He could still do it. If he got back to the daily routine he had kept before he moved onto the boat he would be back in shape in no time.

It was shift change when he arrived and the place was crowded. He knew most of the people he met as he moved through the hallways, although none of them well, and he was aware there was some resentment and mistrust. That was partly because he didn't appear to have the same constraints and requirements they did, but it was also because of his deliberate rejection of any overtures of friendship. Also, his free access to Markleson, the North Island Commander, who worked out of the same building, didn't help.

He acknowledged the few greetings he received and made his way to the front desk, where the desk sergeant, Albert Rediger, was already ensconced in a chair barely big enough to handle his bulk, a copy of the Saturday Globe and Mail spread out in front of him.

"Hi Al." Dan leaned his hip against the counter. "You had a call from the *White Lightning*?

Without glancing up, Al reached under the newspaper, pulled out the logbook and flipped through the pages.

"Never heard of it. What the hell is it? A new pub or something?"

"It's the name of a boat. I guess you'd have to call it a yacht. It was anchored out in the bay a couple of days ago. I asked the owner to call me."

"This owner got a name?"

"Not one I know, but he would have asked for me."

Al ran a tobacco-stained finger down the page. "Nothing here from any *White Lightning*," he said, "but some guy named Walker called. Asked for you but wouldn't leave any message."

"Walker?"

Dan could hardly believe he was hearing right. Walker was both the most elusive and reclusive person Dan had ever met and the man had no liking for either telephones or the police. Hell, Dan had just spent the last couple of days trying to find him – assuming this was the same person – but how many guys called Walker could there be?

"You record a phone number with that?" he asked.

"Yeah. It came from the reserve over there in Alert Bay. You think that might have been the guy you're interested in?"

"What?" Dan was still stunned by the idea that Walker had tried to contact him. "Oh! No, that's someone else. Walker's a friend."

Al shrugged and stuffed the logbook back under the newspaper. "Well, that's all I got. I hear from the *White Lightning* guy I'll give you a call."

Dan slapped him on the shoulder and started back down the hall. He had almost reached the door when Al called out to him.

"Hey Connor! What's a burial garment for a sailing ship? Six letters. Starts with 's'."

Dan smiled. Al was a devoted crossword fan. "Shroud," he shouted over his shoulder.

WALKER HAD CALLED HIM. It seemed so unlikely that Dan couldn't get it out of his mind. He could only remember two other times in all the years he had known the man that Walker had reached out to him, the most recent being the previous year when Walker's friend, Joel, had been in trouble. Was Joel in trouble again? That seemed unlikely. Joel was as reclusive as Walker, although for different reasons, and he had been proved completely innocent of the crimes he had been suspected of. Right now he was no doubt back on his little island in Haida Gwaii, talking to the ravens who were his constant companions.

It had been Joel and his ravens who had taught Dan there was more to the world that met the eye. Although everything he had learned up till then told him it was ridiculous, he had to acknowledge that not only had they helped him rescue Walker, they had helped him solve the case – and the paddle that had started it all was now mounted in the wheelhouse to remind him of that fact.

But why would Walker phone the police station? The man knew Dan lived aboard his boat and seldom went into the office. Why wouldn't he simply call *Dreamspeaker* on a radiophone – or by VHF for that matter? Alert Bay was only a few miles away across the strait so he would have no problem reaching Dan's boat.

There was an empty desk in the squad room and Dan sat down and dialed the number Al had given him. It rang for a long time before it was answered.

"Yes?" The voice was ancient, quavering and heavily

accented with the guttural vowels and slurred sibilants of the Kwakwala language.

"Hello, is Walker there please?" Dan asked.

"Walker?" There was a long pause, a sigh, then, "Him no here."

"Is he . . ." Dan started to ask when Walker might be back, but thought better of it. It was unlikely the woman knew Walker's plans even if he could make her understand. "Thank-you," he said. "Gilakas'la. I will call again later."

There was nothing more he could do. He would have to let Walker find him in his own way, at his own time.

MARKLESON ARRIVED in his office a little after eight o'clock by which time Dan had walked down to the coffee shop and picked up two large coffees and a couple of cinnamon buns to go. Markleson's eating habits were notoriously bad, and Dan hadn't eaten before he left the boat so he figured he might as well take the easy route and please his boss while curbing – or perhaps more accurately indulging - his own hunger pangs.

"You find out anything about those two guys from Banks Inlet who are supposed to have gone missing?" Dan asked as he cleared a space for his coffee among the accumulated piles of paper.

"Yes and no," Markleson answered, reaching for a bun. "I talked to the guys at the station over in Alert Bay. They hadn't heard anything, but a woman from the Aboriginal Justice office there and she said she had heard the same rumor. The problem is she hasn't been able to confirm it. She's working on it but it could take a while."

"How about the guy who fell off the barge? The coast-guard find him yet?"

"No. They've called off the search. It's a recovery now, not a rescue. Unless some boater finds him washed up on some beach we're never going to see him again. Pretty shitty way to go."

He took a bite of his cinnamon bun and washed it down with a gulp of coffee.

"So you got any good news for me? You find Jimmy?"

"Not exactly," Dan replied. "But I know where he was four days ago."

14

A rne Hjorth was troubled. Every day for the last six days he had climbed up the hill behind the cove to the rocky promontory at the top and looked down at the fish farm anchored in the bay on the other side of the channel. He had found a hollow in the rocks that provided a comfortable seat from which he could watch the comings and goings.

He checked his notebook again, hoping it would give him some answers to the things that were troubling him, although he knew it wouldn't help. He had kept meticulous notes, recording every new arrival and departure with both the time and a description of the vessels. If he was going to succeed he needed to understand the pattern.

Few of the fish farms in the Broughtons had accommodations for workers other than a small security staff that monitored the pens at night. Crew boats brought the men in each morning and took them back in the evening. The timing of their arrival and departure was not exact, but it was predictable enough that Arne was comfortable with it.

The barges that brought in the fish food weren't nearly as regular, although they too had a schedule. The fish in the farm Arne was watching were approaching maturity and even in the six days he had been there he had noted the increase in barge traffic. More food was coming in, and more of the foul-smelling totes containing dead fish were being off-loaded. He would have to make his move soon. If he waited too long the tenders would come in to start collecting the live fish to take to the processing plants. If that happened he would have to wait not only until they finished emptying the pens, but until they had re-stocked them again with smolt from the hatcheries.

None of that bothered him. He had expected it. It was the way all the fish farms operated and there were more than thirty of them in the Broughtons now. What he had not expected, and what was troubling him, was the fancy power-boat with its out-of-place passengers. A sleek and obviously private powerboat should not be at a fish farm. The boat had to be well over thirty feet long, maybe even thirty-five. Thirty-five feet of sculpted white fiberglass and smoked glass windows with several well-dressed men aboard.

The first time he saw it he thought it was simply a fluke, perhaps an inexperienced cruiser stopping to ask for directions, but it returned three days later and then again one evening. Not only that, but the men it carried acted strangely. It could possibly be an owner, perhaps with a partner and an assistant, but one of the men looked and acted more like a thug, and then why the odd times and the strange activity?

He checked his notebook again. He had not thought to keep track of the people. At a fish farm, people came and went – workers, divers, crew from the boats – they were always there, moving around, doing their jobs. They were too far away to identify as individuals so he simply tried to keep a rough record of the numbers, although even that wasn't something he placed much importance on as there was no way he could be sure he was counting them all. The barges were self-propelled and there might be crew up in the wheel-house or working in the engine room. The two security guards were only visible in the early morning and late at night, and it was hard to tell which of the men that arrived on the crew boats were divers and which maintained the pens. None of it really mattered anyway. All that mattered was that they were there, and that they came and went at certain times. But then he had seen the powerboat and everything changed.

15

Walker paddled over a dark sea. He had chosen to take Cormorant Channel towards Malcolm Island before turning southwest. It was a longer route, but it would take him over Haddington Reef, out of the path of any marine traffic, all of which avoided the shallow, rock-studded patch to the north of Haddington Island, and he would have the light on the outer end of the reef to guide him for part of the way. It meant he would not arrive at the marina in Port McNeill until the early hours of the morning, but that didn't bother him. He was used to paddling long hours, and he was used to paddling at night with only the stars and the movement of the water to guide him. It was the time he liked best.

Above him the moon cut a thin silver scimitar into the night sky and as often happened when he was out on an empty ocean, the rhythmic motion of his paddle took him to a different place, one where the worries of everyday life and the work required in order to maintain his existence in the mortal world faded along with the light of day.

The motion of the water and the patterns of moonlight tracing the waves soothed him, lulled him, linked him to the worlds of the sea and the sky. He became Salmon, sliding effortlessly through his domain, his body sleek and strong, and he could taste the ocean, feel it slide along his skin. He became Raven, wings outstretched, riding on unseen currents of air, and he could smell the night, feel it lift the tips of his feathers. Yet he was also Man, descendant of a thousand ancestors since the time of transformation, inheritor of his clan's regalia as well as their stories and dances, and he could hear his own heart beating, feel the blood coursing through his veins.

It was at times like this that he felt most at ease with his life and all it encompassed and he let his mind roam free, drifting out over the years and the places and the people who had played a part in his journey. He could remember his boyhood in the village, with the innocent laughter and games of friends. He could remember the long nights of the potlatch where the families all gathered and the smell of wood smoke drifted through the longhouse to mingle with the scent of salmon and bannock. He could remember the pounding of the drums calling him into the dances, and the shadows that played across the masks as the dancers moved around the floor, their capes lifting and swirling as they performed the dances passed down from generation to generation, reenacting the stories that defined his culture. They were the stories of creation and the transformation of the animal spirits into human form and they had taught him his relationship to the world.

It had been a time of happiness that had turned to a restless discontent as he approached adulthood. That discontent had led him down to the city, to the dismal basements and dank alleyways where so many others from so many other villages all congregated as they struggled to survive.

He had lost his way there, and like so many of those others he had grasped at alcohol and drugs in order to escape the fear and the memory of what he had given up. They hadn't worked, but instead had led him deeper into the underbelly of the city, into a world where he could almost convince himself that the houses he broke into belonged to an enemy that neither deserved nor needed what he stole.

He remembered the blanket of despair that drove him to riskier and riskier burglaries, and the feeling of vindication, of elation, when he realized that he had succeeded. When he was asked to help rob a bank the invitation came as an acknowledgement of his ability, of his prowess. It was something he hadn't known he needed, but he reveled in it. And then it had all come crashing down when the police arrived.

He knew there were many of his people who expected him to be bitter, who thought he should hate the white man's police for what they had done when they chased him down, but he didn't. He knew he had caused it all himself. Even when he was lying in his hospital bed, recovering from yet another surgery on his damaged hips and legs, he had known he had only himself to blame. In the long years afterwards, as he sat in the dreary common room of the jail and listened to the drone of whichever counselor or minister or social worker they had brought in, he promised himself that once he got out he would build a new life. Bitterness and regret would have no part of it.

He had succeeded. The life he had built might seem hard to some, but it was his and he was happy with it. Out on the water he felt like a whole man, content in both body and spirit, and he held no grudges.

He smiled as he thought about it. The man he was going to see had been one of the police officers who had arrived at the bank all those years ago. It had been Dan Connor who chased Walker out onto the roof, it had been Dan Connor who called an ambulance to collect him when he fell, and now it was Dan Connor who had become a friend. Perhaps his only friend, and someone he knew he could count on for help.

EVEN THOUGH IT was July and the days were both long and warm, the high peaks of the Coast Mountains were still covered with snow, and in the soft twilight that lingered between dusk and dawn they seemed to float above the world, anchored to the sky rather than the earth.

Dan had intended to get an early night, call Mike before breakfast and then let the events of a new day occupy him while his subconscious dealt with whatever answer his question received, but it hadn't worked. He had tossed and turned for a couple of hours, his mind filled with jumbled images of Susan, the dark-haired man on the yacht, Jimmy Fulton, and the blond woman with the dog, until finally he had given up any attempt at sleep. He got up, found a Stan Getz CD, took a beer out of the fridge and padded barefoot out onto the aft deck to let the night and the music quiet his brain. He was still there at two-thirty in the morning, the CD and the beer long finished, as he watched Walker's tiny vessel glide up to the swim grid.

"I see you're still keeping the same weird hours," Dan said as he walked over to the stern rail to watch Walker tie up his canoe and pull himself up onto the grid. Dan did not offer any assistance. He had learned several years ago that any such offers would be both unacknowledged and unwelcome.

"Looks like you're keeping the same ones," Walker replied a few minutes later as he lowered himself onto one of the bench seats and leaned back against the rail. "That's too bad. I was kind of looking forward to waking you up."

Dan smiled. "Good to see you too Walker. Is this a social visit or is there something you need help with?"

Walker didn't answer right away. He turned his head and looked out over the breakwater towards the dark waters of Broughton Strait and the darker mass of Malcolm Island beyond, his eyes lifting to follow the jagged peaks of the mountains over on the mainland. It was several minutes later when he looked back at Dan.

"I guess it's kind of both. The old man sent me here, but it's good to see you too."

It was Dan's turn to pause. Walker had always been reclusive, and while they had become more and more comfortable in the brief times they had shared each other's company over the past few years, Walker had never acknowledged any kind of friendship between them. To hear him do so now sparked an unexpected surge of warmth.

"Thanks," Dan mumbled, not quite sure how to respond to the gift Walker had offered, but pleased it had been given. Speaking quickly in order to hide his discomfort, he returned to safer ground. "What old man are you talking about?"

Walker smiled. "Never met him before," he answered. "Took him a long time to find me. He had to travel a long way. Went to Y'alis – that's Alert Bay to you – and searched out my family. Finally got my cousin to come out and get me."

"And?" Dan asked patiently. "What did he want?"

"Wanted me to come and ask you to help."

Dan stared at him. Walker was usually both laconic and direct. This unwillingness to get to the point was something new.

"Get me to help with what?"

Walker straightened up and leaned forward, his voice hardening as his eyes focused intently on Dan's face. "He wants you to find out what happened to the two Banks Inlet men who have gone missing."

16

Two hours sleep wasn't much, but it was better than nothing. It was almost four o'clock in the morning when Dan and Walker finished talking and Dan went in and sprawled, fully clothed, on his bed. He woke at six when the sun rose above the mountains to pour its light through the porthole. Rolling off the bed he made his way to the head, sluiced cold water over his face, ran his fingers through his hair and went out to check on Walker.

The man had refused Dan's offer of a bed, saying he preferred to sleep outside, and he was still sitting on the bench, his eyes closed although not, Dan suspected, asleep. Looking at him, Dan couldn't help but feel a surge of admiration. Life had not been easy for Walker, but he had faced every challenge head on and his difficulties had made him stronger. There was a purity, an honesty that ran through him like a strand of fine wire, impossible to bend and impossible to break. Dan on the other hand . . .

He wandered back through the salon and up to the wheelhouse. An array of telecommunications equipment stretched out in front of him, their dials and switches black, their silence somehow accusatory. All he had to do was pick one of them up and flip a switch. It was ridiculous to wait any longer, but just as he reached out to lift the satellite phone from its cradle, he heard Walker struggling to his feet out on the aft deck.

Later. He would make the phone call later. There was plenty of time and he had another urgent issue to deal with now that Walker had confirmed the two Banks men had gone missing.

"You like some breakfast before you leave?" he asked Walker, who was already sliding along the bench towards the stern.

"Nope. I'll get something on the way home."

"You want to tell me where home is these days? It's kind of hard to let you know what's happening when I can't find you."

Walker grinned as he lowered himself down the ladder to the swim grid. "You don't need to find me. I can find you, and I usually know what's happening before you do anyway."

For once, the glib answer did not make Dan smile.

"I've got a bad feeling about this one Walker. I think I might need your help with it."

Walker turned and gazed at him for a long moment before he twisted himself down into his canoe. His answer, when it came, floated quietly over the water.

"Knight Inlet," he said. "Up past Siwash Bay. Near the mouth of the river."

DAN WATCHED the battered canoe with its lone paddler disappear around the breakwater before he went back to the wheelhouse. The tiny vessel left barely a ripple in its wake.

Although Walker's information made it certain that two more men had disappeared it was still not Daan's case and until Gary Markleson assigned it to him there was nothing he could do. In fact, without an actual report from the families of the missing men, or an official notification from their band office, it was not really a case at all.

All the police had was one man – Jimmy Fulton - definitely missing, and a rumor that two others were also unaccounted for, but missing persons were not normally assigned a case number. The information would simply be sent out to every detachment along with the description. Only when enough time had passed without any result would there be any serious investigation, and even then it would not become urgent until and unless something else happened – some piece of evidence or a link to some other event that would catch the eye of an investigator.

But Dan didn't really care whether this was official or not. He was already pretty sure that this was about something more than three missing people. Three men did not simply go missing within the same short period of time in this remote area, all of them linked in some way to a fish farm. True, weird things happened and he couldn't completely deny the possibility of coincidence, but even as he thought about it he cautiously added a fourth person to the list.

The Coast Guard he had spoken with at the beach just a day or so ago had said that the guy they were searching for – Dan couldn't remember his name – had fallen off a fish farm, or at least off a barge that was tied up at a fish farm. It could have been an accident, and the Coast Guard seemed to think it was just that, but if so it was odd timing and the link with a fish farm was stretching the limits of anything Dan could consider normal. Something was going on and Dan very much wanted to figure out what that something was. Before Walker's nocturnal visit, with only the information Roger and Sam had given him, Dan had been concerned. Now, that concern had escalated to worry.

He turned on the computer and while he waited for it to go through its start-up routine he rifled through his stash of paper charts until he found the one that covered the area of the Broughton Archipelago. It wasn't a large stretch of water, more like a jumble of islands separated by a series of straits and inlets. It lay between the mainland of British Columbia and the northeast tip of Vancouver Island and it was bordered in the northwest by the open waters of Queen Charlotte Sound. A popular cruising destination in the summer, it was also the traditional home of Walker's people and where both Dan and Claire were living and working. Whatever was happening, it was uncomfortably close to home for all of them.

The computer screen came to life and Dan brought up a map of the various fish farms in the area. There were more than he had realized and using a red pen, he carefully marked the location of each one on the paper chart. When he had finished, the previously pristine depiction of yellow land and blue water looked as if it had been attacked by some kind of strange measles virus, red dots appearing everywhere.

He focused his attention on the area in and around Tribune Channel, where eleven of the red dots clustered on the northern end with several more on the eastern arm. Markleson had said Jimmy might have been heading for somewhere near Minstrel Island. Minstrel Island was close to the eastern end of Tribune. It was also the location the Coast Guard had mentioned as being near the place the man they were looking for had fallen into the water. It wasn't much to go on, but it was the only real reference he had. His eyes kept scanning the labyrinthine contours as he picked up the phone and dialed a number he now knew by heart.

Markleson answered on the first ring. "You better have

some good news for me," he growled. "So far this is not turning out to be a real banner day."

"Sorry to hear that, and I don't think I'm about to make it any better," Dan said. "You know those two guys from Banks I told you about?"

"The two you said *might* be missing even though no-one has reported anything about them?" Sarcasm and impatience vied for supremacy in Markleson's voice.

"That's the ones," Dan replied, deliberately ignoring the jibe. "But it's now official – more or less."

"More or less," Markleson repeated. "What the hell does that mean? Is it official or isn't it because if it isn't, I've got more than enough work here to keep me going for a month, maybe more, without running off on some goddamn wild goose chase. As of two hours ago I've got two kids in Port Hardy dead with suspected Fentanyl overdoses and a local guy we thought was clean picked up with a bag of China White."

Dan made a sound he hoped indicated sympathy, but drug-related issues in Port Hardy were not something that involved him. Unless . . .

No. He couldn't and wouldn't veer from what was his own concern.

"I don't think it's a wild goose chase," he said. "In fact I think it's probably something pretty big."

He explained Walker's visit, and the information the old man from Banks Inlet had provided as well as the request he had made. There was a moment of silence as Markleson digested what Dan had said.

"So what are the chances that either this old man, whoever the hell he is, or your friend Walker will make an official statement?"

Dan thought the tone had softened just a little. His boss was now sounding more resigned than annoyed.

"Somewhere north of zero," Dan answered. "You already know that. But it doesn't matter. They have no reason to make this up. These guys have gone missing."

"Well it matters to me!" Markleson's bark was back. "I'm the one that has to send in all these goddamn forms and reports, remember. Gonna have a real good time explaining to those pain-in-the-ass desk jerks down south why I assigned one of my guys to investigate a rumor."

"Might not be so hard when you add in Jimmy Fulton," Dan said.

This time his statement was received with a long silence.

"You figure they're linked?" Markleson finally answered.

"Gotta be. You said yourself no one has gone missing here for the last couple of years or more. Now we've got three in a bit more than a week– and that's not counting the fellow that fell off the barge."

"Farnsworth? That was an accident! The fish farm called the Coast Guard. Our guys in Alert Bay went out and talked to the people out there as well as the crew on the barge. The guy was hooking up a pallet of fish food totes and the winch cable knocked him off balance."

"You had a lot of accidents like that around here recently?" Dan asked.

As he waited for an answer he could hear the creak of Markleson's chair as the big man leaned back, the repeated flick of a what sounded like a cigarette lighter, and then an inhalation of breath that resulted in a fit of coughing.

"Goddamn it, I gotta quit this shit," Markleson wheezed once he was able to take a breath. "So I take it you want me to assign this 'sort-of' case to you?"

Dan smiled. "Yes. I do. Thanks Gary. I'll keep you posted."

"You're damn right you will. I'm not going to add writing up your reports to the list I'm looking at here." The rasping voice softened. "Be careful out there," it said. "I'm not liking the sound of this."

DAN WROTE down the case number Markleson had given him on the top of the chart he had used to identify the fish farm locations, then called Al Rediger at the front desk. Rediger was in charge of dealing with the public, but he had also been given the job of filing reports and he made it his business to know everything that was going on. That included all the current investigations.

"Hey Al," Dan said when the man came on the line. "You wouldn't happen to know which fish farm that fellow the Coast Guard were looking for was working at would you?"

"He fell off a barge, not a fish farm," Al answered, confirming his reputation as someone who kept very exact records. "But the barge was tied up at one of the farms out there in Tribune Channel. Hang on a second and I'll get you the details."

He was back in less than a minute with the information Dan had asked for.

"The guys over in Alert Bay have already taken statements from everybody. You want me to send you a copy?" he asked.

"Yeah, sure. That would be great," Dan said. "Thanks."

"No problem – hey, while I've got you on the line, you got a word for "Nautical wind catcher from Italy"? Five letters."

"Genoa," Dan answered, smiling. "It's a kind of sail."

17

So it was now official: there were three men missing. The two men from Banks Inlet had taken on both shape and substance and thanks to Walker their names were now listed in Dan's file. Harold Manuel and William Jules had joined Jimmy Fulton.

As he looked at the list, the concern Dan had been feeling grew into an urgent, living thing that coiled through his veins and thrummed on his nerve endings. Three men were out there somewhere and as far as Dan knew they might still be alive. Might be lost and hungry, or hurt and clinging to life on one of the islands. He wanted – no, *needed* – to find them.

But it was more than that. He could feel the adrenalin building in his bloodstream like a hunger - what the guys on his team down in the city had referred to as "the thrill of the chase", and it still grabbed him with the same force all these years later.

He leaned in towards the computer screen to read the report Al had forwarded to him, but even before he finished it he found himself reaching for the phone again. He wasn't sure what it was about the accident at the fish farm that bothered him so much other than the timing, but he wanted to talk to the Alert Bay detachment himself.

The dry words and superficial comments in the report were useless. They couldn't tell him the way the guy had looked and sounded when he was questioned, or whether he had seemed upset by what had happened. Had he been eager to get away or cooperative? Was he calm or jumpy? How long had he worked that run, and for that company? Had anything unusual happened before or after Farnsworth fell? Dan couldn't blame the officer taking the report. It was only preliminary, and referred to what was believed to be an accident, but he needed more.

Even though his call was answered promptly, he didn't get answers to any of his questions. There had been a shift change in Alert Bay the day before and the constable who had done the interviews was not on duty. In fact he was not even on the island. His grandfather had died and he had been granted a compassionate leave the previous evening and had caught the ferry over to Port McNeill. By now he would probably be down in Vancouver and he wasn't expected back for a week. A week was far too long for Dan to wait.

He searched the report again looking for the name of the company that owned the barge and went online to get the phone number for the local office. Maybe he could talk to the crew directly.

A woman answered his call and said the manager was down on the loading dock, but she would get him to phone back when he returned. Reluctant to wait, Dan asked her if she could give him the names and phone numbers of all the crew that were on the barge the day Farnsworth fell off. He expected her to refuse, but her reply was instantaneous.

"Well that's Reuben Crosbie's run. He was the captain

and he felt just awful about Colin. – we all did of course, and still do . . ."

Her voice tailed away and Dan thought she might be on the verge of tears, but she pulled herself together and continued her story.

"I saw Reuben when he came in afterwards and he looked just terrible, like he'd aged twenty years. His face was gray. I tried to talk to him – I mean accidents do happen sometimes and there's really nothing you can do about them – but he wouldn't even look at me. Just grabbed his coat and left."

"And he was the only other person on the barge?" Dan wasn't sure how many people it took to run something like that but it seemed like there would be more than just two.

"Oh no. There's always at least two crewmen. The other one would have been Paulie – Paul Benko. He and Colin always worked the weekend run."

"Worked?" Dan noted both her dismissive tone and her use of the past tense. "Has his schedule been changed?"

"You could say that," she answered, a note of disapproval creeping into her voice. "He's disappeared. Hasn't shown up since he arrived back that day and we don't know where he is. He's not answering his phone and his car's not at his house. Mark – that's my boss – figures he's skipped town. He was kind of a weird guy anyway, always talking about spirits and ghosts and alternate dimensions. Stuff like that. Probably got spooked when Colin fell off."

Dan interrupted her. "Have you reported him missing to the police?" he asked. If she had, he certainly hadn't heard anything about it and he was pretty sure Markleson would have told him.

"The police?" The woman sounded completely confused. "Why would I call the police? He's skipped town, that's all. Mark said when he looked in the window of Paulie's condo it looked like all his stuff was gone." Her tone changed. "It's happened before and I guess it will happen again. Guys come in looking for a job, think it's going to be real nice being out on the ocean and all that, then they find out it's not quite as good as they thought it would be. Mind you, most of them give us notice, but some of them just take off."

Her sniff of disapproval provided emphasis.

"It's hard work let me tell you. My son did it for a while. You're out there in all kinds of weather trying to handle those big totes, and that's not easy. And then there's the farms themselves. They stink! All those dead fish – morts they call them – in those containers! I'm surprised anyone stays long. Hell, I wouldn't stay myself except the pay is good and Mark's been a friend of the family for years."

"Sounds like a tough job," Dan said as he tried to absorb the flood of chatter. Was Paulie yet another missing person, or was there something else behind his disappearance?

"Is there a way I can get hold of Reuben Crosbie?" he asked. "I need to talk to somebody who was on that barge when Farnsworth fell off."

"Got his phone number right here," the woman said. "But I don't think you'll be able to reach him before the weekend. He's a real avid fisherman – wild fish, not those farmed things."

Dan heard another sniff of disgust before she continued.

"Usually takes his boat out as soon as he ties up the barge and doesn't get back until he's got another shift scheduled. Been like that ever since his wife died, and with Colin's accident and all I bet he took off even quicker than usual. He's probably way up around Hakai Pass by now. That's his favorite spot."

She gave Dan the number and he thanked her for her help. She sounded more like a mother than a secretary, but it took all kinds and up here in these small communities everyone knew everyone else. It made the need for the kind of tight-lipped formality normally found in the bigger centers almost non-existent. The resulting openness should have made investigations a little easier, but even with the information he had been given, he still wasn't any further ahead.

As PREDICTED, Reuben Crosbie didn't answer his phone and Dan left a message asking him to call when he returned. Now what? He went back to the report Al had sent him and noted the name of the fish farm. Maybe he would have better luck talking to some of the staff at their office. People that worked together often talked together.

That attempt turned into another brick wall with the receptionist proving to be much more the big city type: well trained to not give out any information at all. In fact her reply to his request was so predictable Dan could have recited the words himself.

"That would be the Personnel Manager, but I'm afraid he's not at his desk right now. Would you like to leave a message?"

Dan slammed the microphone back into its holder. No, he damn well would not like to leave a message. What he would like was to talk to someone who could give him something useful. Something relevant. Something that might help him figure out what the hell was going on. He had wasted well over two hours on phone calls already. It was time to act.

He thought about going over to the fish farm in the dinghy, but it was over thirty miles and while there might still be a full crew working when he arrived, that was far from a certainty. What was certain was that it would be late by the time he was ready to come back and if the weather changed he would be out there with no protection. He was not averse to risk-taking, but he wasn't crazy either. The prospect of having to spend a night huddled in the bottom of the dinghy or crouched under a tree was not appealing, especially when there was a good chance the people he wanted to talk to wouldn't be available anyway.

He peered out the window to check the sky. The sun that had been so much in evidence early in the morning was hidden behind scudding clouds and they seemed to be moving in from the southeast, a sure sign of bad weather. The big boat would make it a much slower trip, but also a much more comfortable one. He could anchor overnight and do the interviews first thing in the morning. Not only that, but it would give him a chance to get a good look at the farms as he went by. He had never really paid much attention to them.

IT FELT good to be doing something physical, but by the time he had the boat squared away, the engines warmed up, and the tie-up lines released, it was well into the afternoon and the first drops of rain were falling from a solid gray sky. As he rounded the end of the breakwater and felt a swell lift the hull, a wave broke against the bow and spray flew up onto the deck. The trip was going to be even slower than he had thought.

Two crew boats passed him as he was entering Fife Sound, both travelling fast and both headed west towards Vancouver Island. He wasn't sure what the shift schedule was on the farms, but he thought it likely these boats were taking daytime crew back home. That would leave just the security staff on board and as Farnsworth had fallen off early in the day it was probable no-one working security had seen it happen. As he watched the aluminum hulls carve wide wakes around a rocky point he realized that his decision to wait until morning to do the interviews had been a good one.

He slowed the boat as he approached the first fish farm, studying the design and trying to make sense of the various pieces of equipment he could see. It looked simple enough. An outside float formed a rectangular perimeter, and the inside area was subdivided into twelve pens by a series of narrow walkways. At one end, the outside float widened and a series of small buildings stretched across almost the full width. A couple of hoppers sat off to one side and pipes ran down from them and out along each float before disappearing into the water. In the middle of each pen another pipe rose up like a fountainhead with a rotating arm.

Although he was too far away to be sure, Dan thought the arms were scattering something on the water and he guessed it was fish food pellets when he saw flashes of silver roil the surface of the water. He couldn't see any sign of human presence, but he assumed at least a couple of workers were inside the building monitoring what was going on. His assumption was confirmed when a man stepped out of the doorway and lifted a pair of binoculars to his eyes, clearly checking out *Dreamspeaker* as she passed.

The next farm was much the same although it looked considerably older than the first: metal bins replaced the hoppers and there were no pipes sticking out of the water in the pens. A third consisted of circular pens, each separate but linked by a series of hoses and pipes. Two of the farms had a row of what looked like septic tanks lined up along an outside float. The third had a couple of big plastic totes. None had any active crew that he could see. He had definitely arrived too late. Mentally he kicked himself for wasting all that time on the phone. He should have known better.

He nosed *Dreamspeaker* into a protected cove and lowered

the anchor. He barely had it set when the radiophone pealed its shrill call.

"Where the hell are you?" Markleson's mood had obviously not improved over the last eight hours, but Dan no longer had the patience to humor him. His day hadn't been great either, and dealing with frustration had never been one of his strong points.

"I love you too," he said. "And I'm over in Tribune Channel trying to figure out what the hell is going on. Where are you?"

Even as he heard the words leave his mouth he knew he had gone too far. He and Markleson might have forged a casual and friendly relationship, but the man was still his boss. Dan braced himself for the rebuke he was sure was coming, but it never arrived. Instead there was a long silence. When it was broken, Markleson's voice was quieter.

"Sorry. It's been a tough day." There was another pause, followed by a sigh. "You were right. The fourth guy, Farnsworth, is part of the case."

"Farnsworth? The fourth guy?"

The reference to the fourth guy caught Dan by surprise. Up until now he had been the only one even thinking about a link between the three missing men and the man the coast guard had been searching for. Now it seemed that Markleson agreed with him.

"Yeah. They found him a few hours ago. A trawler snagged his body in their net."

Dan thought about Markleson's words for a few seconds, confused by the apparent contradiction. "Okay - but how does that make him part of the case?"

Markleson sighed. "The coroner just called. The guy was dead before he fell off the barge. He was murdered."

18

Murdered. The word echoed down the line and Dan felt it slice into his brain like a scalpel. He sucked in a lungful of air, felt it catch at the back of his throat, and let it out slowly.

Although he had refused to acknowledge it, murder had been what he suspected ever since Roger first told him about the two men missing from Banks Inlet. It was what he had been dreading, and yet at the same time what he had refused to accept, foolishly hoping there was some way all of these men were simply lost somewhere in this maze of islands and if he looked hard and long enough he could find them and bring them home. At some level he had known the hope was unrealistic, but he had wanted to maintain it as long as he could.

Ever since he had listened to Walker talk about them, Harold Manuel and William Jules had become real; two people whom Dan felt he knew. Flesh and blood. Alive. He did not want to think of them dead, but with the news of Colin Farnsworth's murder, he could no longer avoid that possibility.

Yet even now he sensed himself clinging to the hope that Jimmy Fulton was different. That Jimmy was still out there, a young man who had freed himself from the confines of a city he didn't like and who was exploring a new world, seeing new sights, meeting new people, perhaps even in a new relationship. It was still theoretically possible even if it was becoming increasingly unlikely.

But that would not explain Manuel and Jules. Walker had told him they were both comfortable with their lives. They were familiar with the area. They had families they went home to every night. Walker had also told him both men were important to their community and proud of their culture. They would have gone home if they could have.

He took another breath and brought himself back to the present.

"How?" he asked.

"Shot," Markleson replied. "Up close. Bullet hit his heart. Skin is pitted around the entry hole. The coroner figures powder burns."

"Shot?" Dan repeated. "I just read the report from the guys over in Alert Bay. Not one of the people they talked to mentioned hearing a noise. How the hell would they miss that?"

"I guess it's technically possible," Markleson said. "Coroner says it was a .25 and there was probably a lot of noise happening with the barge unloading and the crane working."

"Possible, but it's odd, and a .25 is not that common. Could have been an automatic I guess. That might have suppressed the sound enough that no one recognized it, and if it was a contact shot . . . "

Dan thought about it for a few moments. The last time he had seen a .25 – in fact the only time he had seen a .25 – had been more than twenty years ago when he had busted up a brawl in a nightclub in Gas Town, an old section of Vancouver. A female onlooker, the girlfriend of one of the men involved, had pulled it out of her purse and he had taken it from her. It had been an old Beretta 1919 semi-automatic with a wood grip and no grip safety. He hadn't seen another one since.

"Still, surely someone should have seen the weapon," he continued. "A guy with a gun would have been pretty hard to miss."

He knew he was rambling, thinking out loud, but they were all valid questions that needed an answer.

"Well at least there isn't a big pool of suspects," Markleson said. "According to the report there were only two other people on the barge at the time, plus seven workers on the farm – and three of them were divers who were down when it happened so it sounds like they're out of the picture. Shouldn't be too hard to figure out who did it."

"Yeah." Dan said as he let his mind drift back over his conversation with the chatty woman at the barge company. "Should be a piece of cake - except that one of the people who was on the barge has already disappeared, and the captain has taken off on a fishing trip to Hakai Pass where no-one can reach him."

This time the silence seemed to hang in the air for a long time and when Markleson spoke again he sounded tired.

"You want me to get the guys over there in Alert Bay to call you? Maybe whoever did the interviews picked up on something that didn't make it into the report. Happens sometimes, and they've got a couple of pretty new guys over there."

"Already checked," Dan answered. "Constable Stewart did the interviews. He must be one of the new ones. I've never met him, and I usually get to know all of the people over there pretty quickly. Doesn't matter anyway. He left that same evening. He's down on the mainland somewhere on compassionate leave. Won't be back for a week."

"Shit. This just keeps getting better and better. How about the people on the fish farm?"

"I'm planning on going there tomorrow. The receptionist at their office in Port Hardy couldn't or wouldn't give me anything. Said I had to talk to the personnel manager and he was out. I figured I might have better luck going out to the farm myself, but I have no idea if the same guys are even going to be there."

Dan listened to the faint hiss of atmospheric interference coming through the speaker as he stared out over the water. The air smelled of rain, and the dark cedars clinging to the shore seemed to absorb what little light the clouds allowed through. It was as if the cove itself was in mourning, saddened by the news of death. A small boat had gone by while Dan and Markleson were talking and its wake was now lapping gently against *Dreamspeaker*'s hull. It sounded like a woman sobbing.

Markleson finally brought him back to reality.

"Let me know what happens. They're pretty short-staffed both here and in Hardy right now – hell, we're short-staffed everywhere – but maybe I can shake one of the desk guys loose to track people down for you."

"Yeah, thanks." Dan knew that both detachments were making do with a minimum roster and with both the tourist and the boating high season in full swing he didn't have much hope either of them would be able to spare much time, but he appreciated the offer. It wasn't often that the North Island Commander would run interference with the head of a detachment.

He replaced the microphone in its cradle and went out on deck. Daylight had faded and as the damp air washed over his skin he could feel the same gloom that had crept into the cove envelop him. He had never thought he was the kind of man to be affected by the weather: it was what it was. You simply put on the appropriate clothing and dealt with it. But here, in the gray dusk of the day's end, it was as if he was joined with the earth itself in regret for a life lost.

He thought back to the time more than three years ago, when he and Walker had buried the body of a man they had found on a beach further up the coast. The man, who at the time had been Claire's boss, had been brutally murdered and Dan vividly recalled the feeling of closure, even of peace, he had felt as Walker chanted over the rough grave the two of them had created in the rocks. The memory was so powerful it made him wish Walker was here with him in the cove.

Briefly Dan wondered if he could come up with some kind of chant himself, but the thought of even trying brought with it an image so ludicrous that it made him smile. Not only would he look and sound incredibly stupid, it would be completely inappropriate. That was Walker's world, not his. Whatever spirits or powers Walker could call on – and Dan thought there were probably many – none of them would respond to his entreaties.

He straightened up and looked around, realizing as he did so that just thinking about the chant had lifted his mood – or maybe it had been the mental picture of himself standing out on the deck chanting which had cheered him up. Whatever it had been, his bout with melancholy had ended and he was ready to focus on what needed to be done.

A QUICK GLANCE at the sky told him that it was getting late: gray had deepened to black and absorbed the outline of the land. He had wasted a lot of time with his introspection. He would spend half an hour or so on one of his judo katas and then study the report Al Rediger had sent him. He needed to

have the names and stories straight when he got to the fish
farm in the morning.

HE WOKE EARLY and drank his coffee on the aft deck as he
watched daylight blend softly into the night sky. It was much
too early for the dayshift to be in place at the fish farm, but
he felt restless. He didn't want to stay on the boat for any
longer than he had to. He needed to be doing something.

Perhaps it was the frustration he had felt the day before,
but by six o'clock he was in the inflatable making his way
south through Nickoll Pass and into Knight Inlet. It meant he
would have to almost circumnavigate Gilford Island in order
to reach the farm, but he had all day to do it. As long as he
arrived before mid-afternoon the daytime crew would still
be there.

He kept the engine revs low and stayed as close to the
shore as he could, nosing the bow into each tiny indentation,
entering every cove, searching for anything that might lead
him to the missing men. It was probably a waste of both time
and fuel: his chances of finding anything were so slight they
might as well be non-existent, but he didn't care. It was something he felt compelled to do and at least it provided him
with some feeling of satisfaction, some reassurance that he
was doing everything possible.

In the five hours before he arrived at the fish farm he
found many things. He found two shoes, both runners and
both for a left foot, albeit different sizes and styles. He found
a life jacket, its zipper corroded from a long stay in the ocean
and with what he took to be Japanese or Chinese characters
stenciled on the back. He found seemingly endless amounts
of plastic bags and boxes and so many bottles he gave up
counting them. He even found an old Styrofoam cooler,
battered and discolored and covered with barnacles, but

there was nothing that pointed to any of the missing men. It wasn't until he reached the last cove, a tiny opening within sight of the farm, that he found anything that might belong to either Harold Manuel or William Jules.

It was the color of the fabric that caught his eye, a deep red with black markings. As he maneuvered his way in close enough to pull it out of the crevice in the rocks, he realized it was a bandana and it had something wrapped inside. The something turned out to be a circular band, about an inch wide and perhaps three inches in diameter, woven out of strips of smooth bark or root. He had seen one similar just recently on Walker's arm. It was a cedar bracelet, but this one had a tight roll of clear plastic bags stuffed into the center.

19

Arne Hjorth scrambled down the rocky bank to the shore below, his fingers seeking out the indentations he knew were there, his toes reaching blindly for the ledges and outcroppings that would support him. He had climbed up and down this bank so often he could do it with his eyes closed.

He didn't know if the dog he had seen was still swimming, or even if it was still alive, but before he had lost sight of it in the darkness its head had still been above water. He didn't think he would have been able to see it at all if he hadn't been up so high, looking down on the surface of the water with the moon at his back. The dog's head had a strange shape, long and narrow, and while the face itself was so pale it seemed to almost glow in the dim light, it had long dark hair hanging down from just above its eyes. The hair floated out on the waves and distorted what small part of the head was above the water, making it all but invisible, but the moon reflected off the eyes as the animal drifted towards him. They seemed to be pleading with him, begging him for help.

Arne had never had a dog. He hadn't even thought about it. Dogs weren't something that fit into a fisherman's life. Even now when he no longer fished – except for himself when the goddamn fish police weren't looking – he had no place in his life for a dog. How would he feed it? Hell, he could barely feed himself. No, it wasn't any desire for a dog that drove him down to the shore and into the cold water. It was something else entirely.

He felt an odd kind of kinship with this animal. An animal that those people on that fancy boat had simply discarded for some reason he could even not begin to understand. If he hadn't seen them do it he wouldn't have believed it. Surely you didn't discard a living thing, something you had taken into your life – although now that he thought about it, society had done a pretty good job of discarding him.

The dog didn't appear to do anything wrong. It was sniffing at one of the totes of fish food Arne had seen delivered earlier in the day. Maybe the tote had been damaged because they hadn't emptied it into the hopper the way they usually did and Arne thought the dog might have had its nose stuck into an opening in the plastic. That made sense because he knew the food the farms used had a strong smell. It was mostly made from fishmeal and fish oil and Arne had read somewhere it was dangerous for dogs to eat it because of the high protein level.

In any case, he heard one of the men yell something and then watched him walk over and kick the dog so hard its yelp of pain carried clearly across the water. The man then turned and gestured to his partner who went over, grabbed the dog by the collar, and heaved it over the railing.

Arne heard a sharp noise right afterwards and he thought at first it might have been a gunshot, but it was too dark to see if either of the men had a gun, and it didn't seem likely anyway. Why would someone shoot at a dog in the water? In fact why would anyone on a boat or a fish farm have a gun in the first place? It didn't make any sense. He was just letting his imagination run away with him. Probably it was from some equipement banging on the fish farm.

He waded into the dark water, clinging to the jagged line of rocks that ran out into the ocean from the west side of the cove. The dog hadn't looked like it could swim well and the current here was strong. It would push the animal in towards the shore and then suck it around the outer end of the point. If Arne could reach it there, he might be able to pull it in.

He had to put his face right down onto the top of the water in order to see it, but the dog was still there, maybe twenty feet out, only visible as a dark distortion on the surface. Every now and then it moved its head and there was a tiny splash as a paw came out of the water in an apparent attempt either to stay afloat or to swim towards the safety of land. Arne moved out as far as he possibly could, feeling the bottom slope away under his feet, shuddering as the cold water crept up his legs and wincing as the barnacles tore his fingertips where they gripped the rocks. When he reached the furthest tip of the rocks he stretched out his free arm as far as he possibly could and grabbed a handful of floating hair.

It took all his strength to pull the dog in. It was bigger than it had looked and it had the same long hair he had seen on its head all over its body. Soaking wet, Arne figured the damn thing must weigh nearly a hundred pounds, maybe more, and it was too weak to help itself. Even when he managed to pull it in far enough that it should have been able to stand, its legs kept collapsing and he had to hold it up with one arm under its belly and the other hand clutching a bunch of the hair on its shoulder. By the time he made it to the shore Arne was as exhausted as the dog and probably almost as cold.

The two of them lay sprawled on the gravel until Arne had caught his breath. He was shivering, but he knew that was a good thing. It meant that while he was cold and uncomfortable, he wasn't suffering from hypothermia – at least not yet although he needed to change into something dry as his wet clothes were rapidly sapping what little heat he had left. He reached out a hand to pat the dog. It hadn't moved from where he had deposited it and it looked dead except for the eyes. The eyes followed Arne's every move.

Arne pushed himself to his feet and went over to the dinghy he had tied to a piece of driftwood further along the beach. He had dry clothes onboard the *Silver Lady*, and he kept some old towels and blankets stowed under his bunk. He could use those to dry the dog off and make it a bed. He would have liked to take the animal over to the boat but there was no way he could get it up onto the deck. It would have to stay where it was. As he pushed his oars into the water he heard the dog give a low whimper.

"It's okay," he heard himself say, the sound of his own voice surprising him after so much time alone. "I'll be back."

20

Walker steered his canoe along the shore, easing it in amongst the rocks, letting it drift over the long kelp fronds undulating gently on the surface. He had already filled a basket with sgyuu, the black seaweed the Japanese called nori, and had another half-filled with purple sea urchins. That was more than enough to feed him for the next several days and back at his cabin he also had the herring roe he had collected last week from the kelp fronds in front of the cove, and the salmon he had already dried. Food was never a problem.

What was a problem for him – what was bothering him - was something else entirely. This was the second time he had reached out to Dan Connor to ask for help with his own people and it didn't seem right. Last year it had been for a friend, Joel. This year it was for two men from Banks Inlet. They were two men he didn't know personally, but they were still his people and he could not refuse the request the old man had made. He knew there was no way he could have helped any of them without involving Dan, so why should he feel uncomfortable about doing so?

It wasn't as if Dan had objected in any way: it was part of his job and he seemed quite willing, even happy to do it, but what troubled Walker was that he was the one doing the asking. Asking was not something that came easily to him. He had spent too long and worked too hard on gaining his independence.

But if he was honest with himself, he had to admit it was even more than that. It was also pride, a kind of pride he had struggled to overcome, that he thought he had conquered, but which had crept back again while he wasn't looking.

Pride in who he was, in what he had achieved, in his culture, in his heritage – all that was fine, but this was different. It was a kind of pride that whispered in his ear and told him that he was too good to ask for help. He had not recognized it until now and he did not like it. It was the kind of pride that had gotten him into trouble when he was young.

He thought about the old man. An old man who was chief of his people and yet willing, in spite of his age, to leave his home to seek help from a stranger when one of them was in trouble. An old man who was certainly proud of who he was, and deservedly so, but who had no problem asking for what was needed when he himself did not have the means to accomplish the task at hand.

WALKER WAS SO busy with his self-analysis his brain didn't register the momentary glimpse of shape and movement seen through the narrow opening to a tiny cove until he was almost past it. Even then, he wasn't sure what it was he had seen. Curious, he dug in his paddle, turned the canoe, and nosed it slowly past the rocks.

The scene inside the cove was like nothing he could have imagined. A man huddled on the shore, his back hunched as if he were trying to hide something from view – or maybe trying to protect something although nothing was visible. He was thin and angular, almost emaciated, and his body looked awkward. Thin colorless hair hung in wisps across his shoulders and down his back, but it was cut short at the front where it looked as if it had been hacked off with a blunt knife. The man's face, as he watched Walker's approach, was almost as pale as the hair.

This apparition was too old to be the young white man Dan had mentioned was missing, and it certainly wasn't anyone from the village in Banks Inlet. Although the man did bear a faint resemblance to a few of the people Walker had seen over on Malcolm Island where a group of Scandinavians had settled several generations ago, But what was he doing here?

What looked like a pile of dirty rags was heaped on the gravel beside him, along with a battered saucepan and a couple of plastic bowls. An old blue tarpaulin was stretched between the branches of two trees to create a rough shelter. As Walker approached, the man leaned further over the pile of rags and put out his hand in a protective gesture.

"She's mine. I found her."

The voice reminded Walker of the rasping calls of the Night Herons that roosted in his cove. The words were faltering, the cadence odd, but he could hear the strength of determination in them.

Walker nodded. He had no idea what the man was talking about, but it was obvious he was either crazy or very frightened, maybe both. For perhaps the first time in his life, Walker wished he were the kind of person who could put others at ease, but that was impossible. He was who he was. His appearance alone turned most people off and conversation was not his style. Still, he had to say something. The man was looking more terrified by the second.

"Morning," he said. As a conversation starter it was

totally inadequate, but it was the best he could come up with. "I'm Walker. I live up the inlet a bit."

He nodded vaguely towards the south. He wasn't surprised when the man didn't answer.

"You live here?" Walker tried again, thinking that perhaps a question might elicit a response, but it seemed to do the opposite as the guy hunched even lower.

"Too bad Dan wasn't there." The thought surprised Walker. He couldn't recall ever wanting the presence of anyone else before, but this was something he had no skill at. Meeting people was Dan's strength, not his.

He made yet another attempt. "I guess I'm a neighbor."

There was still no response, but the pale eyes slid sideways and as Walker followed them he saw an ancient fish boat nestled in behind the curving rock wall of the cove. From the peeling paint and the rusting tackle it looked like it might have been there for a long time. In fact it looked about ready to sink.

"You from the fish farm?"

The rasping voice caught Walker by surprise and he turned back to see the man lifting the bowl up to the pile of rags. As he watched a black nose slid out from between a couple of layers of cloth and a pink tongue flicked out to lap up whatever was being offered.

"No," Walker replied, and then added, because he simply had to know, "That a dog in there?"

The man looked down and nodded, his hand hidden inside the pile of rags.

"They didn't want her," he said. "They threw her away."

21

The fish farm was in full operation when Dan arrived. A self-propelled barge, perhaps the same one that Farnsworth had been on or at least one very similar, was unloading several large bales wrapped in white plastic. Dan figured those were the fish food totes he had heard so much about, and as he approached he could see two men using a small crane to jockey one of them into position above a hopper.

As Dan brought the inflatable up to the float a heavyset man wearing an orange life jacket with the name of the company stenciled across the front and R. Johnson printed in black marker on one sleeve strode over and waved him off.

Reg Johnson was the name of one of the men listed on the interview form and if this was indeed the same man, he didn't look happy to have company. Under the weathered skin there was a flush of anger.

"You can't tie up there. This is private."

Dan reached into his pocket and pulled out his credentials. "Police. I need to speak to whoever is in charge here."

"Hell, we've already talked to you guys." Johnson leaned

forward and spat into the water. "I can't tell you any more than I've already told them."

Dan ignored the protest. "You were here when Colin Farnsworth fell off the barge?" he asked.

Johnson scowled and shrugged his shoulders. "Yeah, if that was his name, but so what? I didn't see it. I was over on the other side." He inclined his head towards the far side of the float where two other men were working on a piece of equipment. His words were clipped, and his belligerent tone was emphasized by arms folded across his chest and an aggressive scowl.

"Did you hear anything?" Dan asked.

"Heard a couple of guys shouting, that's all. It's noisy around here when they're unloading. You've got the crane working, and the guys are yelling instructions, and those barges have engines damn near as big as the tugs. They make a hell of a racket."

"It doesn't sound that noisy right now," Dan said, turning to look at the barge.

"They're almost done. They're not using their crane and that's a small barge anyway. We had the big one here the day of the accident. Come back when that's in and you'll see what I mean." Johnson dismissed Dan's comment with a wave of his hand.

"So nothing unusual?"

"Like what? I already told you it was noisy."

"Like a gunshot."

Dan watched Johnson's reaction closely as he said the words. The man's head jerked up and he stared back, his eyes wide and fixed intently on Dan's face. If he was aware of what had happened, he was putting on a good show of being shocked.

"What the hell are you talking about? Why would I hear a gunshot?"

"We found Farnsworth's body. He didn't fall. He was shot."

For a long moment Johnson was speechless. His eyes dropped and he turned his head to look down the float. Dan had the feeling the man was trying to relive the moment, picturing whatever it was he had seen that day, running it past this new piece of information to see if it made sense. When he turned back, the belligerence was gone and his eyes were focused in the middle distance, on something only he could see.

"Nah man, that's crazy," he said, shaking his head slowly in denial. "Why would anyone want to shoot him? All he did was load and unload. And no one here has a gun anyway. Why would they? That's nuts." He shook his head again, more rapidly this time, and his voice firmed up. "Nuts," he repeated. "Couldn't have happened."

Dan watched the large man a little longer. He knew it wasn't unusual for someone to dismiss something they couldn't understand and it often meant they were telling the truth. It would take a little time to let reality sink in.

He turned to look at the other people working the farm. Two of the men he had noticed previously were now talking to a couple of divers who had obviously been down in the pens, and he could see the other two out on the floats near the building.

"Any of those guys here when it happened?" Dan nodded towards the men.

Johnson pulled himself back to the present and followed his gaze. "I guess the divers were here, but the other guys are all new."

"New?" Dan asked, his voice sharpening. "New as in a new shift or new as in new guys?"

"Both," Johnson answered. "Two of them are new guys: one started yesterday and one's just started his first shift

today. The other two have been working here for a few
months but they were off – just came back on yesterday."

"That kind of turnover normal?"

"Sure." Johnson shrugged. "At least it's not unusual. Lot of
guys figure this for easy work – all you got to do is show up
and feed a few fish right? Doesn't take 'em too long to find
out it ain't what they figured."

He gave a snort of derision and his voice took on a tone of
resignation as he recited a litany of excuses.

"Some can't take the long shifts – they sometimes have to
work ten – twelve hours plus travel time, four days one week,
three days the next through the summer. Some can't take the
rain. Some get seasick the first time they come out on the
crew boat. Some can't handle the smell. Whatever. Winter's
the worst, but in summer we get the bums looking for an
easy buck and the city kids who want a big adventure to go
home and talk to their friends about."

That was pretty much what the woman Dan had spoken
to on the phone had said when he called the barge company,
but it still didn't seem right.

"Two out of four seems pretty high to me."

It was more than high; it was suspicious, but Dan didn't
want to voice that thought. So far, he thought Reg Johnson
was telling the truth and he wanted to keep him talking.

"Yeah, maybe. Guess it would be for most jobs, but it's
what happens out here. And we might not have anyone else
quit for another few months. Kinda balances out."

Dan nodded and glanced around the farm. Another man
had come out of the building and was checking some kind of
gauge fixed to a pipe running into the water.

"How many guys do you have here?" he asked as he
watched the man return to the building.

"Depends. We usually have two or maybe three divers,
plus four regular crew, plus the system operator and a super-

visor. If we're stocking the tanks or unloading, we'll bring in more."

"And you're the supervisor?"

"Yeah, I'm one of them. Me and a couple of other guys. We switch off."

"You stay here at night?"

"Hell, no. None of us do. We all go back to Hardy on the crew boat. The security guys stay here – two of them right now but we usually only have one."

Dan looked at him.

"Why two? Have you been having problems?"

Johnson shook his head. "Nothing real serious. Some of the locals don't want us here and they've tried to come onboard and vandalize the place. Mostly crazy kids from the city wearing headbands and tie-dye shirts and shit. They come out here in the dinghy from Mom and Pop's fancy boat and give us a hard time. Then there's a few fish-huggers – environmentalists in kayaks, that sort of stuff. Some local Indian band people – they figure we're killing their wild salmon." He spat into the water again.

Dan was going to ask if any of them had been there that day, but they were interrupted by a shout and the float lurched under their feet.

"Shit!" Johnson swung around to look at the barge then strode over towards it. The crew had let go the forward line and the bow had caught the current and swung out, forcing the stern in so that it slammed hard against the edge of the float.

Dan watched for a moment as Johnson and a crewman struggled to hold the heavy vessel off, and then let his eyes roam over the farm. Had he learned anything? Not really, and he doubted that talking to the divers was going to help, but he was certainly going to look into why so many people had quit their jobs, particularly those who were working the day Colin Farnsworth was shot.

A gust of wind blew into the cove from the south and he was suddenly engulfed in the reek of rotting fish. The smell was so strong he almost gagged, and he felt his eyes start to water. On the other side of the float the divers had returned to the water and were passing up nets full of dead fish to the men on the float who emptied them into waiting plastic containers.

Dan had worked his share of homicides and he had attended more autopsies than he cared to remember. It had taken him a long time, but he had finally learned to handle some pretty overpowering odors. This was perhaps the worst he had ever known and he suddenly understood exactly what Johnson had been talking about when he said people quit because of the smell. It was so strong the air was thick with it, as if the odor itself had mass and density.

He turned back towards his inflatable and stepped over the tube and down onto the floor. The smell seemed a little less intense here, although that was probably just because the wind had lessened. Compressing his nostrils and narrowing his eyes, he reached for the key and turned the motor on. There was no way he could go and talk to the divers now even if he wanted to. They didn't seem to be diving to any great depth, but they only came up to the surface long enough to pass up their nets and Dan did not want to think about how strong the smell would be near those open totes. The sooner he got away from here the better. He was reaching for the tie-up lines when Johnson returned.

"Pretty tough to take huh?" Johnson loosed the forward line from the bollard and held it as Dan released the stern.

Dan nodded. "Yes, it sure is. Is it always like this?"

"No." Johnson shook his head. "When the fish get to this

size there's always more morts, but we just had a low oxygen event and that makes it worse."

Dan stared at him. "A low oxygen event? What the hell is that?"

Johnson turned and gestured to the building. "We have pumps in there to pump oxygen into the water. These fish are almost ready to harvest so the pens are pretty crowded. Without extra oxygen they wouldn't survive. There was a problem with one of the pumps last night. We're not sure what caused it, but it took a while to get it back online. We lost a lot."

"Do you know how many?" Dan asked. "It smells like thousands. I've never experienced anything like it."

"Few hundred for sure," Johnson answered, shrugging his shoulders. "Could even be a few thousand although I hope not."

Dan scanned the pens and tried to imagine what a few thousand salmon would look like, but failed. It was simply too large a number to grasp.

"How many fish do you have here? A few thousand seems like a lot to lose."

"We start out with a million smolt – that's the young ones the hatchery stocks us with. We've got twelve pens so about eighty thousand in each pen."

A million fish. The number was almost beyond comprehension and Dan could only shake his head. A million fish multiplied by the thirty or so fish farms in just this one small area. Where were the hatcheries that supplied the smolts? How long did it take to raise them? What happened to the fish when they were harvested? Where did they dispose of the dead ones?

His mind swirled with seemingly endless questions, but another gust of wind from the south quickly brought him back to the present.

"Guess you must get used to it after a while," he said as he turned his head and held his hand over his nose.

Johnson inclined his head. "Not really. More like you learn to accept it." He paused and stared out over the water, the rope still taut in his hand, then turned his gaze back to Dan. "You serious when you said that guy on the barge was shot?"

"Yeah," Dan said. "He was."

"Shit. That's . . . " His voice tapered off.

"Yes, it is. And we've got two other men missing. Maybe you know them? We know they worked at a fish farm around here," Dan watched Johnson closely to see how he would react to the names. "Harold Manuel and William Jules?"

Johnson only frowned and shook his head. "Manuel and Jules? Not anyone from here. They're both Native, right?"

Dan nodded.

"Don't have any Natives working here," Johnson continued. "They don't like us. Maybe on a farm up there north of Broughton. I think there's a band up there supports the industry and they might have some of their people working."

Dan nodded. He knew there was strong opposition to open-net acquaculture, but he hadn't thought about whether or not that opposition would stretch to all fish farms or to all band members. If it did, it should make locating the farm Harold Manuel and William Jules had worked on an easier task.

"How about Jimmy Fulton? You ever hear of him?"

Once again Johnson shook his head. "Not a name I've ever heard of, but you could check with the office over in Hardy. He might work on one of our other farms."

Dan thanked him, reached into his jacket, pulled out a card and handed it up. He wanted to get away before another gust of wind brought more of the smell. "If you think of anything else, give me a call."

22

The wind had picked up and was blowing from the southeast as Dan took the line from Johnson's hand and turned the dinghy away from the float. A particularly strong gust carried another wave of the miasmal smell and he glanced back, partly in sympathy with the men who had to continue working despite being immersed in the nauseous soup of decomposing fish, and partly in amazement that anyone would stay with a job that exposed them to those unbelievable conditions.

He had been wrong to think the high turnover was suspicious. In fact now he had experienced it himself it seemed incredible it wasn't even higher. Yet he could still see the men moving back and forth, seemingly unaffected, routinely emptying the nets the divers passed up into the bins, and Reg Johnson was still standing where he had left him, staring out over the water. It was a crazy way to make a living Dan thought as he started to turn away again, eager to be out where the air was fresh. His fingers tightened on the controls and he eased the throttle forward, but pulled his hand back when his peripheral vision caught movement. Johnson was no longer still.

As Dan watched, the man jerked upright and swung around to face first the building and then the far end of the float. His body twisted abruptly from side to side and he leaned forward and appeared to peer at something on the water before straightening up again and lifting his hands into the air. In other circumstances Dan would have thought Johnson had either suffered some kind of mild electric shock or was having a very animated conversation, but there was no one else in sight.

Curious and a little concerned, Dan slowed the dinghy and steered it into a wide arc paralleling the float. Johnson had seemed pretty laid back when he had been talking to him, but maybe it had all been an act. Maybe he was unstable. Unpredictable. Maybe knowing a man had been murdered almost in front of him had set him off. Hell, it could even be a medical emergency. He might be in need of help.

Dan turned the dinghy again and headed back towards the float. Perhaps the changing pitch of the motor drew Johnson's attention, because as Dan approached the man looked up and started beckoning him in with unmistakably urgent movements.

"Are you okay?" Dan asked as he slid up to the float. "You look like you have a problem."

"No, no. Not a problem. At least not exactly."

Johnson looked more puzzled than upset or ill and he turned to look at the end of the float again.

"But it could be important. You said to tell you if I remembered anything. I don't know why I didn't think of it before, but there was a big powerboat here that day. It was tied up right over there."

He pointed to the end of the float, near the hoppers, not far from where they were standing.

Dan felt the first shiver of excitement thrill along his nerve endings. It was a familiar reaction and one he welcomed. He always felt a jolt of adrenalin when there was a development in a case. He turned the motor off and stepped back onto the float, no longer bothered by the overpowering smell of dead fish coming from the open totes.

"What kind of powerboat?"

"Damned if I know." Johnson shrugged. "I'm a wooden boat kind of guy. Don't even care much for those aluminum crew boats we use even though we need them, and as for all of those plastic things – they all look like bleach bottles to me. Not much difference between them. All I can tell you is that it was big and white and had those weird smoked glass windows you can't see into."

"How big is big?" Dan asked. The smell had caught up to him and he turned his back to the wind, but it didn't help much.

Another shrug. "I'd guess at least thirty feet, maybe bigger. Maybe thirty-five?"

A white powerboat somewhere around thirty-five feet long. It was a critical piece of information, but unless Johnson could give Dan something more, it was close to useless. At this time of year there were probably a hundred boats that would fit that description cruising around the Broughtons. They filled every marina, every bay and every cove – and that wasn't even counting any that were simply moving through the area on their way to somewhere else. He needed to get more, but even as he was trying to figure out a way to stimulate Johnson's recollection of the boat, another thought came to him.

"So how come you let him tie up here? When I arrived you tried to wave me off."

"Head office orders. At least that's what I was told."

Dan stared at the man in front of him. Was he being deliberately obtuse or had he genuinely been so uninterested in the boat that he hadn't paid any attention either in it or its reason for being there.

"So it was someone from head office?" he asked. This was like talking to a child.

"No, at least not our head office." Johnson seemed unsure and he looked a little awkward, perhaps embarrassed by his lack of knowledge and the fact he had only now recalled something so obvious.

"I guess it belongs to some bigwig from one of the fish-food companies – or maybe it's someone from the company that manufactures the totes the food comes in. I'm not sure which, but it's one or the other. Something to do with the food anyway."

He pushed back his cap, scratched his head and glanced at the end of the float again.

"I wasn't working when the office called. One of the other supervisors – Don Eastman is his name – was on shift then. He said they told him there were some guys coming out on a boat and he was to look after them. I didn't know anything about it until I came back on a couple of days later – he told me when we switched off. He said the boat had already been out once and one of the guys on it told him they would be out again. Don wanted me to know because I would have to deal with them."

There was a pause and then another shrug. "Don was pretty vague about everything – who they were or what they wanted. I figured whoever called from the office didn't make it clear, or maybe Don just didn't hear what they were saying properly – that happens all the time if we've got a barge in. Like I told you, it gets pretty noisy here then."

He gave Dan a meaningful look, apparently wanting to

confirm that his earlier comments about the noise were remembered. Dan nodded his head in agreement, not wanting to interrupt Johnson's story.

"Anyway, Don told me we were supposed to let it tie up and we were to answer any questions they had. That's all I can tell you – but it was here when the barge arrived. I remember Reuben came out of the wheelhouse to check there was enough clearance behind it for him to get in."

Dan blinked and squinted his eyes to try to relieve the stinging. While he might have briefly forgotten the stench in his eagerness to learn about the powerboat, it was now at least as strong as before and he knew it carried actual molecules from the dead fish – and maybe some of the food and antibiotics they had been fed as well.

Odor was particulate and he'd learned about both the potency and effectiveness of smell after attending his first autopsy. He had been sitting in the hallway outside the coroner's office waiting to pick up some paperwork when one of the staff came by and knocked on the door. Dan heard her ask if the clothing was available for a Mrs. Something-or-other to collect – it had been an unfamiliar name and it didn't register – and he thought he heard a special emphasis on the word 'clothing'. It sounded like a private code with a special meaning and it made him curious. When the coroner finally emerged, Dan asked him about it. The man was tall, thin to the point of looking cadaverous, and even his name, Dr. Theodore Tod, had been perfect: Tod meant 'death' in German and a casting agency could not have found a more perfect fit for the role.

In any case, Dr. Tod had taken the time to tell him that they took great care with the clothing of the deceased because the family always wanted it. It carried not only the visual memory of their loved one, but also the scent that was created by the presence of particles – actual molecules - from the person who had worn them. The doctor went on to say smell, more than any other sense, was intimately associated with the part of the brain that processes emotion and so the clothes were a continuing link that provided solace and comfort to those left behind. He also said he had heard of people, usually the parents of a young child, who had kept the clothing for twenty years or more.

Dan sincerely hoped that his memory of this particular smell lasted for a much shorter period of time – twenty seconds would seem too long.

"Don't rub your eyes. It'll only make it worse." Johnson had seen his discomfort and understood the source.

"I'm damned if I know how you stand it." Dan blinked a few more times hoping it would help. It didn't. He needed to get as much information as he could and then get the hell out of there.

"So did these people ask any questions?" he asked.

"Nope, at least not to me. Didn't do anything but look at the totes and the hopper. Mostly they got in the way." Johnson's dismissive tone left no doubt as to his opinion of the visitors.

"Sounds like there were a few of them?"

"Four the first time, although there might have been more inside the boat. No way to tell. I think there was less that day the guy fell off the barge . . ." Johnson caught himself, his hesitation reflecting both an awareness of the truth and his unwillingness to acknowledge it.

He took a quick breath and ploughed on. "That day the barge was here – three maybe – but I can't be sure. Too much happening to worry about a bunch of management types wandering around and making a nuisance of themselves. As long as they stayed out of the way I didn't pay them any attention."

He pointed to the area where the boat had been. "You couldn't even see it from the other side of the float anyway."

There wasn't much more he could offer. Dan asked him if the boat had a name, but Johnson simply shrugged. He wasn't even certain if it had been flying a flag.

"Has it been back since Farnsworth was shot?"

Johnson winced as Dan said the words he had avoided using.

"Came back once for sure, but it was late, almost dark. I was already in the crew boat and heading home so the security guys handled it."

"Same security guys on now?"

Johnson turned to stare at the building at the end of the float.

"Maybe. I don't have a lot to do with them. They have different shifts than the rest of us. I only know a couple of them but they're good guys. There might be a schedule in the office but I haven't seen one. Head office could tell you."

"You never have security on during the day?"

"Yeah, if we know there's going to be a problem, like some big protest or something, but not on a regular basis." He looked around the float. "What would they do? Me and the guys can handle the kids and the yuppies."

It didn't seem likely Reg Johnson was going to be able to provide much more information and Dan could see he was starting to glance restlessly at the men on the other side of the float who appeared to have finished their gruesome task and were simply standing around talking.

Dan tried to reassure himself that he had all the information he could possibly get and that for now at least there was nothing more he could do out here, but he knew he was so desperate to get away from the smell he couldn't be objective. All he could think about was getting back to his own boat where he could stand in the shower for however long it took to feel clean again – and that was going to be a very long time.

Although he knew it wasn't true, it felt as if those airborne fish particles had somehow permeated his skin and he was sure he would never be able to get the foul stench out of his clothes. He would have to throw them away.

He glanced down at the T-shirt he was wearing. It had 'Kinda Blue" stenciled across the front together with a graphic of a trumpet. It had been a gift from Claire to celebrate their most recent anniversary. He hated to lose it and she wouldn't be happy to know he had put it in the trash, but right now it was not something he could worry about. He needed to get the hell out of there.

He stepped back down into the dinghy and re-started the motor.

"I'll probably be out to talk to you again once I've spoken to your head office." He had to shout over the noise of the motor.

Johnson had already turned his back was walking away, but he lifted a hand in acknowledgement.

23

D an spent half an hour in the shower. He lathered his skin with soap and scrubbed it so hard it was almost raw when he finally turned the water off. He had shampooed his hair three times and cleaned his fingernails, but he thought he could still smell that pervasive odor.

He knew it was mostly his imagination, but the knowledge didn't help. He had stripped all his clothes off as soon as he stepped onto the aft deck and put everything he had been wearing, even his sneakers, into a heavy plastic garbage bag. He sealed the bag carefully, tied it off and then inserted it into a second bag which he then secured down on the swim grid as far away from his living quarters as he could get it. He even hosed off the dinghy. Short of scrubbing the whole boat and spraying both it and himself with a deodorant – or maybe a disinfectant – there was nothing more he could do.

He towelled off his hair, pulled on a clean pair of jeans and a sweatshirt and stuffed his feet into a pair of deckshoes. As he started the engines he checked the anemometer for the windspeed: it was blowing from the southeast at twenty knots gusting to twenty-five. If it stayed like that it would be a rough trip back to the marina with a quartering sea for most of the way, but a southeast wind on this part of the coast inevitably meant bad weather and with the temperature already dropping it could get worse. At least he had anchored in a cove that opened to the northwest otherwise he might not have been able to leave.

While he waited for the engine to warm up he lifted the dinghy out of the water and secured it to the davits. As he listened to the winches work he thought back to his conversation with Reg Johnson. Would it really have been so noisy the day Farnsworth was killed that a gunshot would not have been heard?

He needed to hear the big barge in action and he needed to check what the weather had been like that day. If it had been blowing hard the barge would have been chafing against the float. Equipment would have been banging around and the chains on the winches would certainly rattle. Add to that the wind and the waves slapping against the hull and it might well be enough to mask a gunshot. He certainly had to admit it was a possibility. Markleson had said it had been a close contact shot fired a small caliber gun, probably an automatic, which would have kept the noise down, and Dan knew from experience that people often didn't recognize a single shot when they heard it, dismissing it as just some unidentified random noise.

On his way back through the salon to the wheelhouse, Dan picked up his notebook and pen. One man murdered and three men missing and he still had almost nothing to help him figure out what was going on. He should have shown Jimmy's photo to Reg Johnson. He had thought about it briefly when the man had mentioned crazy kids making a nuisance of themselves, but the overpowering stench of dead fish had driven the idea from his mind. Markleson had said Jimmy was supposed to have a job with the fish farms, but he had also said that Jimmy was like his grandfather and enjoyed the outdoors. Perhaps the job Jimmy had come west to do was not *on* the farms but *about* the farms.

If Dan's recollection was correct, Pete Clements, Jimmy's grandfather, was more than just an outdoorsman; he was also passionate about the environment. Dan had heard talk that a few years before, when a week of heavy rain had caused a mudslide that blocked a salmon spawning stream, Pete Clements had taken time off work to help clear the debris. He had also recruited a few of his fellow officers to join a group working with some of the schools to clear out invasive plants from local waterways and replant the littoral with native species. What if Jimmy had followed in his grandfather's footsteps? What if he had planned to work not on one of the fish farms, but with some environmental activist group fighting the fish farms?

There were many groups active in the area and one of them might very well have caught his interest. That would even fit in with Belinda's comment that Jimmy had been trying to hitch a ride out to one of the fish farms. Surely if he actually had a job lined up, his employer would have arranged transportation for him. As Reg Johnson had pointed out, the workers travelled to and from the farms on crew boats. They didn't need to beg a ride from a passing yacht. The idea was definitely worth checking out – but that too would take time. At this time of year most of the environmental groups were camped out along the shores of the inlets, some of which stretched inland for over seventy miles.

THE LIST of people Dan needed to talk to was growing, but none of them were readily available or even easily identifiable. It seemed as if each time he tried to pin someone or something down, it disappeared. It was disorienting. He felt as if he were looking at himself in one of those crazy mirrors they used to have at fun fairs his mother had taken him to when he was a kid. They had reflected a weirdly distorted image of himself – but here it was everything around him that was distorted instead. There were missing men that had never been reported missing. A drowning that had morphed into a murder. A young man who had arrived but then disappeared. A powerboat that had no identifying features.

In many ways this was rapidly becoming the strangest case he had ever worked on. In fact, now that he thought about it, pretty well all the solid information he had unearthed so far – and it wasn't much – had come from people who were not directly involved in the case at all: Roger and Sam, Belinda Travers and the old man from Banks Inlet who had contacted Walker. Other than that the only person he had been able to talk to was Reg Johnson, and even he had not been able to give Dan much that was helpful.

He checked his notes again to verify the timing. A little over a week since the first of the Banks Inlet men went missing. Five days since Markleson had told him about Jimmy, four days since Colin Farnsworth was shot, and in that time one of the guys from the barge and two of the men from the fish farm were no longer working, at least for the same employers. Tracking them down was going to be time consuming and it meant deskwork – and Dan disliked deskwork.

Deskwork meant hours sitting inside an office and hours on the phone – another activity Dan was neither fond of nor good at – trying to work around the barriers that all businesses, even legitimate ones, put between their employees and anyone trying to get information about them. It meant meeting with judges and getting court orders. It meant contacting other detachments and asking them to assign their officers and staff to something outside their jurisdiction. Something they would be unwilling to spend time on.

It was all going to take a long time and if there was any chance of figuring out what was going on and preventing even more disappearances and murders, he didn't think he had much of that. Whatever was happening had to be coming to a conclusion of some sort. This wasn't the work of a serial killer or a mad man. This was tied to some specific activity or event. It had to be. It was all too sudden – the events had all been too close together – and whatever it was, it was all somehow linked to the fish farms.

Dan punched his course into the computer, set the autopilot and opened the notebook on the dashboard in front of the screen. He would make a chart to track exactly when everything had happened: a complete timeline that included Jimmy's departure from Toronto and his arrival at Sullivan Bay, Sam and Roger's information on Harold Manuel and William Jules, and Walker's visit from the old man. Maybe it would help him see some pattern he had yet to notice. There had to be something.

He was halfway back to the marina, his conscious mind occupied with charting every detail of the case so far and his subconscious marking off the various beacons and buoys he was passing when the squawk of the VHF interrupted his thoughts.

24

"Where are you?"

He smiled as he heard Claire's voice and the tension that had been building unnoticed in his neck and shoulders suddenly eased. It had only been a few days since they had parted company, but he had missed her. He was more relaxed when she was around, more grounded. He could handle the times they weren't together because he knew they were both busy, both totally involved in their work and passionate about what they did to the point where neither of them could or would allow their personal lives to interrupt, but it was becoming harder. In many ways, her absences made him appreciate their time together even more, but there were other moments when he became aware of the emptiness he felt without her. Perhaps they should talk more often. It would be easy enough to call each other in the evening, but they seldom did.

Dan suspected both of them had become accustomed to spending time alone, immersed in their respective jobs during the day and then happy to let the evenings wrap around them as they sat in solitude in their respective coves or marinas. They both liked to listen to the lapping of the waves and the chatter of birds settling in to roost, or to simply watch night creep over the land. They both cherished those quiet evenings on the water, whether apart or together. Perhaps subconsciously they were also both reluctant to disturb that special time by using some man-made electronic device to have a remote, faceless conversation.

But right now none of that mattered. Claire had called him and it felt good.

"I'm on my way home," he answered. "Should be at the marina in a couple of hours. Where are you?" He gazed out the windscreen towards Port McNeill as his mind conjured up an image of Claire standing out on the wharf waiting to welcome him and he felt his smile widen.

"I'm sitting on the float with Willie Pete. He's given me two Dungeness for our dinner. They're huge!"

Willie Pete seemed to have found a way to lure the biggest Dungeness to the strange but simple device he had created by twisting a section of a wire coat-hanger into the shape of a hook and tying it to a piece of twine. Whenever he wanted to catch a crab he simply attached a fish head one of the anglers had discarded to the 'hook' and dropped it into the water. Minutes later he would pull it back up with one or more of the crustaceans attached. The crabs he caught always seemed to be larger than anything Dan was able to lure into the fancy trap he had purchased up at the local chandlery.

His stomach rumbled as he thought about the meal to come.

"I'll put a bottle of wine in to chill. Might even be able to find a loaf of bread in the freezer."

"Mmm, sounds lovely. Reminds me of that quote from Omar Khayyam – you know the one. Something about a jug of wine, a loaf of bread and thou."

He laughed. Talking with Claire always seemed to make the day brighter. "I can't say I'm familiar with it, but it certainly works for me. How long are you going to be in port?"

He heard her sigh and his spirits dropped a notch.

"Only a couple of days," she answered. "I have to wait for the results on some specimens I sent down to the research station, but they're usually pretty quick to get back to me so I don't think it will take long. I might be able to stretch it longer if the forecast is correct and this bad weather they're predicting hangs around. How about you? Are you on a case or just wandering?"

She knew he often took *Dreamspeaker* out to some quiet cove when he wasn't working, preferring the peace and quiet he found there to the sounds of halyards rattling, hulls rubbing against the wharf, people shouting and traffic up on the road. Port McNeill was a small town but it depended on the ocean for its livelihood and the marina was always busy.

"I'm working on a case. That's why I'm heading back in. There's no way I can get out of spending time at the office and I'm going to have some driving to do, but I should be able to spend at least the evenings with you at the marina."

He was still smiling as he put the microphone back in its cradle and he increased the revs to pick up speed. Just hearing her voice had been enough to lift his spirits and as he looked across the water towards the town that had been his home for the last couple of years an image of Claire and Willie sitting out on the float formed in his mind. He could see Claire, lithe, blonde, in her thirties, and beside her Willie, bent, grizzled and well into his seventies. Two people who had completely different backgrounds and histories and who had lived completely different lives, but who none-the-less had found enough in common to form a bond of friend-ship. Willie would be cackling as he told her one of his stories. Claire would be leaning forward to listen, her eyes fixed on Willie's face, focusing with complete attention to every word he said.

He pictured her wearing a pair of faded jeans and a T-shirt, with perhaps a flannel shirt to ward off the chill and a pair of runners on her feet. It was her normal attire, but she still managed to look graceful when she wore it, in her own way as elegant as any well-heeled city girl. It was something innate and unplanned, coming from the inside, not from the clothes she wore and Dan thought she could probably wear a burlap sack and still look good. She possessed a natural grace that allowed her to move through life easily.

She would not agree with him of course. She was still haunted by the failure of her first marriage, blaming it on what she perceived to be her poor ability to relate to people, but he had seen how people responded to her. She could talk with anyone: fishermen and scientists, First Nations folk, bureaucrats and politicians, rich and poor, old and young, without ever noticing their age or their role or their dress, only the person inside.

Perhaps it was that incredible mix of traits: the combination of intelligence and empathy, the contrast of complete confidence and humble acceptance, the quiet introspection and the open warmth that drew people to her. Whatever it was it was magic to watch, but even better to experience.

He gave a sudden burst of laughter. It was a good thing he had not said any of that out loud where someone could hear him. He sounded like a love-struck teenager – although that didn't make it any the less true.

Perhaps most people had similar contrasts, that strange dichotomy of personality traits. Now that he thought about, it seemed likely that was the case, although why he hadn't realized it until now was something he couldn't explain. He had certainly seen it often enough in the people he had interviewed: odd combinations of naiveté and sophistication. A man who controlled every second of his business life, but in private lived in complete chaos. A woman who was seen by her workmates as cold and uncaring, but who cried over a sick pet. The young punk who, when being arrested for beating an old man so severely the senior citizen had spent months in hospital recovering, had asked Dan to please care for his rabbit.

The list was endless. Dan supposed he had always been aware of it, but had never let himself think about the people he was interviewing closely enough to let it sink in. He simply put the information he received into various and separate compartments, waiting to see if one of them would give him the final piece to the puzzle, and then when he found the solution, he forgot about the rest.

So what did that make him, he wondered. A logical analyst suddenly overwhelmed by love? Now there was something to think about!

25

The sky was still dark when Dan awoke the next morning, the water silvered with light from the low moon. The forecasted bad weather had been and gone although heavy clouds were still massed to the north and the air carried the weight of rain still to come. Claire was still asleep, her smooth back resting along his arm, her round bottom curled gently against his hip. Her slow breathing was barely audible, but yet loud enough to change the normal silence and solitude of his morning into the easy warmth of companionship. Careful not to wake her, he lifted the covers and slid out of bed.

Not long after he had moved *Dreamspeaker* to Port McNeill he had been out exploring the streets of the town, familiarizing himself with his new home, when he had heard the sounds he associated with a judo dojo. He had discovered Judo long ago at the Police Academy and he had practiced the martial art for many years when he was working down in the city. Since then he had made desultory efforts at maintaining his form, but he had never found either the resolve or the discipline to return to the daily katas he had once performed. Recently, a couple of fast uphill runs to the local detachment had let him know in no uncertain terms that he was getting out of shape, a knowledge confirmed by glancing at his reflection in the salon window. Perhaps it was time to resurrect his old habits.

The sounds were coming from a detached garage squeezed between two houses high up on the hill above the town. Going closer to investigate, he found a fully functional dojo complete with floor mats. A man who Dan thought was probably Japanese was teaching two young boys the finer points of a kata. The sensei was wearing traditional judogi with a black belt wrapped around his waist and he was both very old and very small, so short that Dan doubted the man would reach as high as his shoulder. After a few minutes of watching the formal bows and the repetition of some basic moves, Dan started to turn away, not wanting to intrude, but he had been seen and the sensei called and beckoned him in.

"You wish to practice judo?" The voice was old but strong.

Dan shook his head. "Thank you, no. I'm sorry if I disturbed you. I was out walking and I heard you in here and thought I would check it out. I used to practice, but I haven't worked out for some time."

"Then now is a good time to return." The old man gestured to the now vacant mat. "What level have you attained?"

Dan had reached black belt, but that had been years ago. While he was well aware that without regular practice he would be no longer be qualified for that level, he told himself that he still did the occasional kata, still remembered all the moves and even though he had gained several pounds he was still strong and, he thought, reasonably fast – certainly stronger and faster than a man much older and smaller than he was.

"Now? I don't know. As I said, it's been a long time."

"So. We will find out." It seemed the old man was not going to take no for an answer. He gestured towards the wall where several judogi lay along a shelf, carefully folded in the traditional way with the canvas pants inside the heavy cotton jacket, each neatly tied with an obi and labelled with the size. "Please. We have all sizes."

Looking back on it now, Dan still found what happened astonishing. He was probably half the age of the old man and twice the weight and while he might have slowed down from his time at the dojo down in the city, he was no slouch. He had also had boxing training at the academy, and he had won his share of street fights. As he stepped onto the mat and bowed to the tiny senior citizen who faced him he thought he would need to take it easy on the man. It wasn't until he found himself on his back for the fourth time that he started to realize that he was going to have to call on every bit of skill and strength he could conjure up if he was not to look like a rank amateur. A minute later, lying on the mat after suffering the sixth throw, sweat streaming from every pore, he was very grateful to see his tormenter step back and bow to signify the end of the session.

"So. Now you practice, yes? You come tomorrow. Same time."

Dan simply struggled to his feet and nodded. He was breathing too hard to speak.

That had been the beginning of his return to judo. Now he worked through his katas every morning, either on the stern deck if the weather allowed, or down in the vast empty space of what used to be the fish hold and which had now been transformed into a storage area for the driftwood he occasionally collected and carved. At least twice a week he climbed the hill to the dojo to work with the sensei and to help with some of the students.

This morning he put on a pair of old sweat pants and a worn and faded sweatshirt and went out on deck. The teak was wet under his feet, and the moon was low in the western sky, dodging between patches of dark cloud left over from the night's rain, but there was more than enough light for him to work with. He lifted his face, allowed the damp night air to wash over him, and began his routine.

BY THE TIME he came out of the shower, daylight lit the cabin and the smell of fresh-brewed coffee filled the air. Claire was standing at the stove in the galley wearing one of his T-shirts and looking out the porthole.

"Good morning," he said, moving up to drop a kiss on the top of her head. "Is there enough for me?"

She reached for another cup and filled it.

"Good morning to you too. Are you heading up to the station? I wouldn't mind the walk if you're okay with company."

"I'm more than okay with company and we can stop at the coffee shop and grab a cinnamon roll on the way."

His love of cinnamon rolls was one of the reasons he had been putting on weight, but as his workouts were now keeping that under control he saw no advantage in denying himself the pleasure.

"Crab for dinner and cinnamon rolls for breakfast. Now there's a healthy diet," Claire said as she rinsed the cups in the sink. "Good thing your office is up at the top of the hill or I could end up wearing more than a few extra pounds."

Dan doubted whether that was true. Claire was one of the fittest people he knew, spending long hours each day either out on the water in her kayak, or walking the beaches checking on the health of the inhabitants of the inter-tidal zone. Whether on shore or on her boat, she rarely sat down and relaxed, seeming to spend her time in almost constant motion checking traps, testing the water temperature, identifying the tiny creatures she found in her samples, looking under rocks to see what lived there. He thought she was probably incapable of either sitting still for long periods or of gaining any weight.

It took them barely half an hour to walk the two miles up to the police station and despite the cinnamon rolls, neither of them was out of breath when they arrived there.

"What are your plans for today?" Dan asked as he slid his card into the lock on the rear door. "Are you staying at the marina?"

"Probably," Claire answered, gazing back down the hill to the ferry dock where the cars had started loading for the trip over to Sointula. "I have a bunch of reports to catch up on, but if the weather stays nice, I might go out and do a little exploring.

"Sounds good," he replied. "I wish I could join you, but I think this is going to take a while. I'll be home for supper for sure."

PORT McNEILL WAS A SMALL TOWN, and while the RCMP had a small office to match, that office housed a bigger staff than other communities the same size because it looked after a number of tiny villages and marinas scattered among the islands of the Broughton Archipelago. This morning it was crowded with the normal crush of shift change, and Dan chatted with those who had worked through the night, listening to the usual stories and complaints and sharing the banter and the dark humor that came with the job. It took a while for everything to quiet down, and for Al Rediger to appear at the front counter.

"You happen to have a desk with a phone and a computer

I can use?" Dan asked. There were only four desks and two of them were already occupied.

Al shuffled a few papers and pulled out a book before turning to glance back at an empty desk in the far corner of the room. "You can have that one." He inclined his head as he spoke. "Nyland's down in Victoria for a couple of days. He won't mind."

"Thanks."

Dan knew everyone at the detachment, but he was not part of their team and he was aware of the glances cast his way as he walked over and switched on the computer. There were disadvantages to being an outsider, a 'lone wolf' as Markleson called him, but as far as he was concerned it was the way he liked it.

THREE AND A HALF hours and several cups of coffee later he pushed back his chair, stood up and stretched his shoulders. All he had to show for his time was an address for Paulie Benko's townhouse and another for Paulie's landlord, an address for Reuben Crosbie and the name of the marina where he kept his boat, and telephone numbers for the men who had been on board the fish farm at the time Colin Farnsworth was shot, but who had since quit. He hadn't been able to get a response from any of them. One of the phone numbers had an Alberta area code, and when Dan had called it he had reached an answering machine. The other was out of service.

It wasn't much for three hours work and although he'd phoned the head office of the fish farm twice, he still hadn't been able to reach anyone who could give him the information he needed in order to be able to identify the powerboat Reg Johnson had told him about. All he had was the names of two people who might be able to help him get that information, but neither of them had been in the office when he called.

Dan nodded to the lone guy who was still working at his desk and headed back to Al Rediger's counter.

"You got a vehicle I can use for the afternoon?" he asked.

Rediger barely glanced at him before using his thumb to indicate a rack on the wall behind him. "If there's anything left, you can have it."

Dan grinned. Rediger always knew exactly which vehicles had been signed out and by whom, and he would also know the make and model of the two still in the lot.

"Either of those an SUV?" he asked. The vehicles the RCMP bureauocracy had recently ordained for the various detachments scattered around the north island – an area where rough logging roads far outnumbered blacktop highways – were for reasons no one had been able to figure out, compact sedans. Several had already gone in for major repairs, and all were a tough fit for a man with a broad, six foot two inch frame.

"Number three, but Jarvis had it last. Probably needs cleaning."

Jarvis was a recent addition to the staff, but he had already earned a reputation for his love of greasy food and his less than elegant way of eating it.

"I'll take it."

Dan took the keys, signed the book Rediger pushed his way, and headed out. He didn't go far. A couple of minutes later he sat down at a table at the Haida-Way pub and surveyed the lunchtime crowd. Although he didn't know all of them by name, he did recognize many of the faces. Almost all were local: fishermen waiting for an area to open, loggers hoping for a callout, workers from the big gravel pit up on the highway plus a smattering of government and office workers. The few unfamiliar faces were scattered amongst the government workers were undoubtedly visiting civll servants of some kind.

"What'll you have luv." His reverie was interrupted by a voice he had come to know well. Elsie Drake was a fixture at the Haida-Way. She had grown up in Port McNeill, married a fisherman and started working as a waitress two days after the wedding. With time off to deliver three children who had mostly been raised by her mother, she had now worked at the Haida for more than thirty-five years.

She poured him a coffee while he scanned the menu. "The halibut's good," she said. "Marty caught it yesterday." Marty Drake was her husband.

"Halibut it is then." Dan handed back the menu. "I don't suppose you know Paulie Benko do you?"

"Paulie? Sure. Met him a few times. Odd kind of guy. Really into ghost stories. Talks about them all the time. "Alternate dimensions" he calls it. Haven't seen him for a few days. You looking for him?"

"Nothing serious, but I'd like to talk to him. I've heard he might have left town."

"Yeah? Doesn't sound right. He might be kinda odd, but I think he likes it here. Got a job working on one of those fish farms. You might want to check with them." She turned to go then stopped as a new customer entered the room. "Hey, you're in luck. That's Tor Stromgren. He's Paulie's landlord. Owns that big block of apartments over there." She nodded vaguely towards a window. "If Paulie's left town Tor's gonna know about it. He lives there too."

She headed over to Stromgren's table, poured him a cup of coffee and pointed back at Dan. Stromgren ignored the coffee, stood up and walked over. He was tall and angular, with thinning blond hair and piercing blue eyes set in a sharp face. He didn't look happy.

"Heard you're looking for Paulie Benko?"

"That's right. You know where I can find him?"

"No, I don't, but I wish I did. The bastard's done a runner and he owes me two months rent."

26

"I love you."

Claire's declaration caught Dan completely by surprise. They were sitting in the cabin drinking a glass of red wine, a very nice Chilean Shiraz the clerk in the liquor store had recommended to him when he stopped in on his way back to the boat and he had been telling Claire about the frustrations of his day. In fact, if he were to be completely honest with himself he might even have to admit he had been whining a little – so while he was delighted to hear her say the words, he was also a little puzzled as to why she would choose to say them now.

"I love you too," he replied, putting his arm around her shoulders to pull her close. "But was it my natural charm or my list of complaints that roused such unbridled passion?"

She laughed. "Well it certainly wasn't the complaints so I guess it must be the charm." Her head rested briefly on his shoulder, but then she pushed herself back upright and looked at him. "Seriously though, it's just – you. You don't know any of these men you're looking for, but you talk of them as if they've become family."

"Well, I guess in a way they have." Dan felt surprised by her statement, but also, for some reason he did not understand, slightly uncomfortable. "It's always that way, especially with murder victims. I guess it's because you get to know them so intimately: their lives, their families, their jobs, their habits. Everything. You have to. It's the only way to solve the case. You usually end up knowing more about them than their wives or girlfriends ever would."

It was a kind of pact, he thought. A pact between the victim who could no longer speak for himself and the only person who could still speak for him. The only person who could still right the wrong that had been done. The victim shared in death what he or she would never have shared in life. Nothing was held back. Fears, hates, loves, betrayals, deceits – no matter how closely guarded in life, in death it was all provided.

"Exactly," Claire continued. "But that's not true for the other guys. I've heard a couple of them talking about the cases they're on and it seems like it's just a job to them. They could be working for any big company: names, locations, facts and figures. You don't do that. For you it's really personal."

Dan shook his head. "It's personal for the other guys too. You just heard the public talk."

"No. That's not it. I understand what they're doing and why they do it. With what they must have to deal with on a regular basis it makes sense that they would try to distance themselves from it all. I guess it's a form of self-protection. Sophie does the same thing."

"Sophie?" Dan had dismissed his initial feelings of discomfort and was starting to enjoy hearing Claire talk about what she perceived as his loveable qualities – even though he was not quite sure he possessed them all – and he didn't want to distract her, but he was unable to recall anyone he knew called Sophie. "Is she on one of the new boats on the wharf?"

"No! My friend Sophie. Sophie Collins. She's an Emergency Room nurse. You met her when we were down in Victoria last year. We had dinner with her and her husband, remember?"

Dan had a fleeting recollection of a crowded restaurant down by the water, with a small, vivacious, dark-haired woman and a very large, very quiet, fair-haired man sitting across a table from him, their faces illuminated by a flickering candle.

"She does the same thing as those guys – those officers – I'm talking about," Claire continued. "She distances herself from even the most heartbreaking traumas – even when it's a child – and that has to be so hard. I've heard her talk about accidents that involve some really gruesome injuries, and it's as if she's just talking about another day at the office. It's not that she's uncaring. It's just her way of dealing with it."

She closed her eyes as she thought about it, but then her intense gaze focused on him again. "You're a cop. You've probably seen just as much as she has. Certainly as much as those other cops have, but it's still personal to you. Even the way you say the names of those missing men sounds like you know them. Like they're old friends who you have to find. Who you have to protect."

She leaned against him and slipped her arm through his. "It's like you haven't developed that hard shell, that personal armor to protect yourself. I'm sure it makes it much harder on you, but it also makes you a very special person. That's what I love."

He stared at her, all jocularity suddenly gone. He had been going to say something witty, something about what a wonderful, loveable fellow he was, but suddenly it all seemed merely inane. She was wrong, just as Susan had been wrong when she too had called him special on that last evening together. He wasn't special. It was just a job to him too, and one he had too often not done very well. If he had been anything like the two women in his life thought he was, he would not have allowed Susan's murderer the opportunity to kill her and he would not have chickened out of calling Mike to find out whether they had caught the man suspected of doing it.

Hell, even now he wasn't doing what he should do. He shouldn't have left the office in frustration this morning when his phone enquiries were proving fruitless, and he certainly shouldn't have quit working early this afternoon after checking out the addresses he had come up with and finding no one home.

No. If he really were a special person he would still be out there, searching, digging, asking questions instead of sitting here drinking wine and discussing where to have dinner. Claire had mistaken the connection he felt with Jimmy Fulton's grandfather as an ex-cop and had applied it to everyone he was looking for – or was supposed to be looking for.

He stood up and blindly pushed his way out onto the deck, barely hearing Claire call his name. What the hell was he doing? His job was to help people, to keep them safe, but his self-indulgent avoidance of anything he didn't enjoy was actually doing the opposite. No, he wasn't special – unless you expanded the definition of that word to include especially selfish. What he really was was weak. A weak coward.

There were still a few boats coming into the marina – mostly recreational fishermen who had stayed out on the water as long as they could in the hope of catching the big one – but he wasn't aware of them. He was oblivious to everything except the need to be rid of this agony of self-doubt and fear. He had to pull himself together. He had to deal with this whole mess once and for all. If he didn't, he would lose Claire and that would be the end of everything.

Hell, there was a good chance he would lose his job too, although that would be easier to take than losing the woman he loved. He certainly hadn't been very effective on this case. He hadn't done justice to the men who were missing and who might be counting on him, and that was largely because he hadn't been focused. If he continued like this Markleson would shuffle him off to some desk job he would hate and he would have no choice but to quit.

He had no idea how long he stood there, staring into the darkness. It was Claire's hand on his arm that finally pulled him back and he looked down to see her holding out a glass of scotch. He seldom drank it any more, but he still kept a bottle the liquor cabinet.

"I thought you might like a drink," she said as she offered it to him.

He nodded slowly. "Thanks." He lifted the glass to his mouth and took a long sip.

"Do you want to talk about it?" Her voice was gentle.

He didn't answer, just shook his head as he let the whiskey burn its way down his throat to his stomach. The next time he was aware of lifting the glass it was empty.

"What was it I said that upset you so much?" Claire was still standing by his side. He wasn't aware of how long she had been there.

"Nothing," he said. "It was nothing. We should go inside."

He put his hand on her back to guide her back into the salon, but stopped before he reached the door.

"No," he said. "That's not true. It wasn't 'nothing'. It's time. I have to deal with this."

IT WAS two in the morning when he finally finished talking. He had told her everything: Susan, the murder, even what he feared had been his role in it when he ignored the threats he had received.

He acknowedged the alcoholic haze he had descended into after Susan's funeral. Described his escape from reality on *Dreamspeaker*, which he had named after the boat he and Susan had dreamed of sailing down the coast. And finally he somehow found the strength to tell her of his inability – no, his refusal – to face the possibility that the murderer was still at large. He told her all of it.

It was perhaps the toughest thing he had ever done, and when he was finished he felt drained, exhausted. Somewhere deep down he had hoped that telling her, saying it all out loud, would be the beginning of healing, but at that moment he felt as if he had re-lived every second of it all. Had experienced all of the pain and the doubt and the fear of the past four years again, compressed into the past four hours.

He didn't want to even look at Claire. He was afraid he would see disgust on her face now she knew how much of a fraud he really was.

He felt her stir on the settee beside him and forced himself to glance at her.

"Great story right?"

Even now he had to be flippant. To try and make light of it. "Well at least you now know what the guy you're sleeping with is really like," he said.

It took a few seconds for her to respond and when she did her words were so unexpected he could only stare at her in confusion, unable to understand what she was saying.

"Do you remember what it was I said that started all this?" she asked. She turned to look directly at him. "I said I love you, and I said you were special. I'm going to say it again now." She smiled. "I do love you, and you are special – and I think we both need another scotch and a stroll around the deck before we go to bed. It's late and you need to get up early and make a phone call."

27

The second body washed up on a reef off Booker Lagoon on the south shore of Broughton Island in the early hours of the morning. Only the faintest glimmer of light etched the rim of the Coast Mountains when Markleson phoned to give Dan the news and the shrill peal of the satellite phone pulled him from a deep sleep.

After his cathartic meltdown of the previous night, he and Claire had stayed up late, talking about everything and nothing, savoring a new-found closeness. Both of them were very aware that she had to leave later that same day and both of them wanted to delay the moment as long as possible.

The lovemaking that followed the talking had been slow and sensuous, perhaps the most erotic they had ever shared. Their fingertips stroked each other's skin, explored every curve and contour, lingered over hollows and valleys as they took delight in their partner's body. Their lips nuzzled and grazed as if tasting each other for the first time. Over and over again they roused each other to fever pitch and yet they fought to delay completion as long as possible.

Now, as he struggled up to consciousness, not sure what time it was but knowing that it had to be something important for Markleson to be calling him – and no one used that phone except Marlkeson – he found the two of them were still tangled together, her leg draped over his thigh, her arm across his chest, her head on his shoulder.

Unbelievably she did not seem to have heard the shriek of the phone and he tried to ease himself out of the bed without disturbing her, but she woke at his first movement.

"What's that horrible noise?" Her voice was thick with sleep as she pushed herself upright and blinked at him, her face lit by the harsh light shining through the porthole from the wharf. "Is that an alarm? Is there something wrong?"

"It's the satellite phone," Dan answered, already groping his way towards the wheelhouse. "Don't worry about it. Go back to sleep."

He heard her mutter something indistinguishable and then he was out in the companionway, the red light of the receiver pulsing in time with the shrill squeal and reflecting off the mahogany paneling on the walls. For a moment, his sleep-addled brain thought an ambulance had managed to drive down the wharf and was parked on the float, but then reality reasserted itself – although he found it hard to shake off the feeling of apprehension that had come with the image.

"Connor," he mumbled as he lifted the microphone, still not fully awake.

"Markleson. We've got another body."

Dan stared blindly out the window into the night as the words slowly sank into his brain. Why was it, he wondered, that sounds were always louder at night: the chuckle of water against the hull, the splash of a drop of dew falling from the coach roof, the voice at the other end of the phone.

"Jimmy?"

"No. They think it's a native man. Looks like he was a big guy. Long hair tied in a braid. No ID."

"So one of the guys from Tsa'wit?"

"Probably, although without any information we can only assume that's who it is. You're going to have to go out there and talk to them. We don't have any choice now."

"Who found him?" The questions came easily. They were routine, and Dan was still on autopilot, not quite able to focus on what Markleson was telling him.

"Couple from Seattle who are up here fishing," Markleson answered. "They've got an RV parked at the Quarterdeck in Port Hardy. Towed their boat up here on a trailer. They left the marina a couple of hours ago so they could be in place and ready to catch a few big ones."

"A couple of hours ago?" Even half asleep Dan found that hard to believe. "It would've still been dark as hell and they would've had to run flat out to make it to Booker's in that time. Hell, they would've been lucky not to rip the bottom off their boat on a deadhead or a rock. They'd have to be crazy to do that."

Markleson's snort of derision was loud and clear. "Yeah, well I said they were up here fishing. I didn't say they were smart or knew a lot about boating. We've already checked with a couple of their neighbors at the Quarterdeck – none of whom were happy to get woken up this early in the morning. It sounds like this is the kind of thing this pair does pretty regularly."

"So if it was dark when they got there, how did they find the body?" Dan's brain was slowly starting to function again.

"They said the wife was hanging over the bow with a flashlight, making sure they weren't too close to the rocks. There's a pretty shallow reef there. I guess the body got wedged in at high tide and when the water went down it was exposed. Whoever it is, our guys say he's been in the water a while. He's not a pretty sight and it sounds like the woman is really freaked. The coast guard is bringing her back in now. The doctor's going to meet them at the wharf."

Dan ran his hand through his hair and opened the wheelhouse door to see if the cool air would complete the job of waking him up – or at least make him feel more alert. The sky was a little lighter now and he could see movement further up the dock. It looked as if someone was loading a boat with fishing gear. More recreational fishermen heading out, these ones a little more knowledgeable, or at least more cautious, than the couple Markleson had described.

"So what do you want me to do? Sounds like you already have people at the scene."

"I do, and they'll be bringing the body in. The coroner wasn't too pleased to be dragged out of bed, but he'll be there by the time they arrive which should be in an hour or so. Maybe less. They're already on their way and they'll pick up speed with the daylight. I need you there too. Hopefully there's enough of this guy left that we can get some kind of a description even if it's just clothing, and then you can go over to Tsa'wit and see if you can get an ID."

"Ah man . . ."

While Dan was not fond of deskwork, or of spending hours on the telephone, there were two aspects of police work that he truly hated and autopsies were one of them. The other was notifying the family. It looked like he was going to be saddled with both. The fact that the family was probably in Tsa'wit only made it worse.

"You don't have to attend the autopsy. I'll get Richardson to handle that. Just get over to the morgue so he can pass on the information he gets."

Dan replaced the microphone and headed for the

shower. At least he'd been given a bit of a reprieve, but getting over to the morgue was not going to be easy. The hospital in Port McNeill was small and handled only run-of-the mill stuff. Anything more serious was sent to Port Hardy, which had a much larger facility with more specialized equipment, and where there was a morgue.

To go there by boat would take far too long. The coastline at the north end of Vancouver Island was dotted with small islands, reefs and rocks. It required careful navigation and a meandering course which added both miles and time to what on paper looked like a relatively short trip. Not only that, but the town of Port Hardy sat in a deep bay which often experienced high winds funneled in through Goletas Channel, a narrow strip of water running all the way up to the open ocean of Queen Charlotte Strait.

The only other option was to drive. By road Port Hardy was about twenty-six miles further up the coast along a well-maintained blacktop highway, but Dan didn't own a vehicle. He briefly considered the local taxi, but there were only two and both were owned by a guy who believed that no-one should be out later than midnight or earlier than seven in the morning. The taxis would not be on the road for at least a couple of hours and even then they would probably be solidly booked. That meant Dan's only option was to walk up to the station and try to convince the guy on night duty to let him have a car. There were times being a 'lone wolf' was a disadvantage.

He dried his hair, pulled on a clean pair of jeans and a T-shirt and went out to the galley where Claire was already making coffee.

"Sorry about that," he said as he slid his arms around her. "I was hoping you could get back to sleep."

He felt her shrug. "I'm an early riser anyway and it's

always good to get out of the marina before the morning rush." She turned and looked up at him. "Bad news?"

He nodded and looked away. It was bad news. He knew he was one of those people who moved through life always believing the glass was half full and if there was no body then there was still hope. With the amount of time that had passed he knew on some level the chance of finding any of the men alive was almost nil, but he still stubbornly clung to the belief that if he kept on searching he would find and rescue them. It might not be realistic – hell, it could probably be called quixotic – but it was what drove him. The news that one of them had been found dead hit him like a personal loss. A personal failure. Even worse, it forced him to acknowledge that the others had probably met a similar fate.

"They found another body," he said. "Looks like it might be one of the men from Tsa'wit."

She looked at him over the rim of her cup. "So now you'll have to go to there."

It was more of a statement than a question.

"Seems that way. I guess they'll call the band office and tell them I'm coming."

She nodded. "Are you leaving right away?"

"No," he answered. "I have to go into Port Hardy. They're bringing the body in now and they want me there to talk to the coroner. We need something to help us figure out who he was: tattoos, clothes, jewelry. Anything that will help us get an I.D. How about you?"

He knew she planned to return to Bull Harbour that morning: the results from the samples she had sent down to the Pacific Marine Institute had come in the day before. "Are you leaving right away?"

"Yes," she said. "But I should be able to come back down in a few days."

"That would be good," he said as he pulled her to him

and kissed her. Neither of them mentioned the telephone call he had planned on making.

He was halfway up the hill on his way to the station when he turned to look back at the marina. Claire had wasted no time. Her boat was already rounding the end of the peninsula that protected the harbor. Dan felt a strong pang of regret as he watched it disappear.

28

T he body had already arrived by the time Dan got to the morgue. The two marine officers who brought it in were in the reception area drinking coffee. They were still wearing their police-issue Mustang Floater suits and water glistened on their faces and dripped from their boots. They both looked exhausted.

Dan nodded towards the door of the only autopsy room. "The coroner get here yet?"

"No, but he's on his way. We called him from the dock. You're Connor aren't you? You here to observe?" The expression on the man's face portrayed exactly what he thought about that particular task. Dan didn't bother to tell him he agreed with him.

"Yes, I'm Connor and no, I'm not here to watch. Markleson's sending another guy for that. I'm just hoping for something to help me get an I.D. I've got a couple of missing persons I'm trying to track down."

The tallest of the two men gave a derisive snort. "Good luck with that. This guy's been in the water a long time. Not much of him left."

"But enough to be sure he was Indigenous, right? At least that's what Markleson told me."

"Yeah, he was Native. Still had all his hair. It was in a long braid, but that's about it."

The two men threw their paper cups into the trash and pushed their way out through the swinging doors to the parking lot. Dan watched them go, aware their parting words had caused his heart-rate to suddenly increase and his skin to feel cold and damp. Why hadn't he thought of it before? Walker was Native. He wore his hair in a braid and he spent most of his time out on the water.

Dan pushed the doors open and waved at the pickup truck the men were in as it backed out and headed for the exit. The driver slowed and rolled the window down.

"You need a ride somewhere?"

"No." Dan tried to keep his voice steady. "I was just wondering if you have any idea how long the guy was in the water? Was it two or three days or two or three weeks?"

"Hell, I don't know. The coroner should be able to tell you that, but if you want my guess – and that's all it is – I would say at least a week. Probably more. The water's damn cold right now so it would have slowed things down a bit, and he's in real bad shape."

Dan sucked in a deep breath of air. If the body had been in the water a week it couldn't be Walker. He had spoken with Walker only three days ago.

"Thanks," he said as he felt the tension drain out of his body. He smacked the roof of the cab with his hand and stepped back as the truck pulled away. It had barely disappeared around the side of the building when two cars drove in. One was a black Honda CRV and it pulled into the slot nearest the door. The other was one of the compacts the detachment was saddled with and it pulled in beside it. The coroner and Richardson had arrived. Neither looked to be in a good mood.

"They sending two of you now?"

Charlie Finlayson had a well-deserved reputation as a curmudgeon with a short fuse and a sharp tongue, but he was also well respected for his sharp eyes and attention to detail. Rumor said he had started out as a surgeon but had switched to his current profession when he got tired of hearing his patients' constant whining. One story going the rounds quoted him as saying that he preferred dealing with the dead because they were more grateful for his services than the living.

"Only got room for one of you in there," he said as he pushed past them into the hallway and opened the cupboard where the gowns, caps and booties were kept. "This is Port Hardy, not Vancouver General."

"Richardson will be in there with you," Dan answered, throwing a sympathetic glance at the other man who so far hadn't uttered a word. "I'm just here to collect any of the belongings and to try and get an I.D. then I'll be out of your hair."

"Could be in for a long wait then," Finlayson retorted. "I'll send this fella out with anything we get, but if it's as bad as Markleson said, it's going to take some time. Better make yourself some more coffee." He nodded at the almost empty coffee pot.

The two men disappeared through the double doors and Dan sat down to wait. It was not yet seven o'clock in the morning, but he could hear the pace of the hospital picking up around him as staff arrived to start their shift. Maybe he could use the time to figure out how he was going to handle the trip to Tsa'wit.

Banks Inlet was one of the smaller fjords on the coast, but it still stretched thirty miles from the ocean to mouth of the

Banks river and Tsa'wit was several miles beyond that. Dan knew the village would have some kind of dock, maybe even a wharf, but he was doubtful whether *Dreamspeaker* with her deep draft could make it. Even if she could, from what he'd heard he was pretty sure he wouldn't be welcome to tie up once he arrived. That meant he would either have to find a place to anchor in Banks or hope he could find space at one of the marinas in the area, either Sullivan or Shawl Bay. Whatever he ended up doing, he would have to go the rest of the way in the inflatable which, assuming the weather cooperated, would at least let him get in and out quickly and do what he had to do without upsetting too many people.

It would be much easier for all concerned if Walker were with him. The thought had come to him along with a surge of relief when he realized it was not Walker's body they had found.

Walker had been involved in this from the start. It was Walker the old man from Tsa'wit had approached and it was Walker who brought the message to Dan. Walker's presence would ease Dan's introduction to the community of Tsa'wit and help him locate the families of the two missing men, maybe even help them deal with the news that he, Dan, was going to have to deliver. Certainly they would find it easier if there was an intermediary between them and a white police officer.

The problem was how to find Walker. Dan now knew where he lived, but going there added many miles to what was already a long trip, and there was no guarantee Walker would be there when he arrived. Still, the more Dan thought about it, the more he thought it was what he should do.

HE WAITED WELL over an hour before Richardson stepped out and handed him a plastic bag.

"It's all there was," Richardson said. He was inhaling large gulps of the relatively fresh air in the corridor and his nose glistened with the Vicks Vaporub he had smeared on to help counteract the smell of the autopsy.

"Most of the clothes were gone. The rest is just rags, bits and pieces. Looks like the guy was wearing jeans: there's a couple of pieces of denim there, and there's the collar and part of a sleeve from a lumberjack shirt. It was red and green. There's also one shoe." He pointed to the lower part of the bag where the white tread of a running shoe was visible in the pool of water pooling on the bottom. "It's pretty torn up too. I guess he got dragged over the reef a few times before he got snagged in the rocks."

"No jewelry?" Dan asked. "No rings?"

Richardson made an unpleasant sound somewhere between a laugh and a cough.

"Hell no, he didn't have any rings. He doesn't even have any fingers." The young cop sucked in a few more deep breaths.

"Pretty tough in there huh?" Dan was glad he had been spared the job, but he could still be sympathetic.

Richardson's round face twisted into a grimace. "Worst I've ever attended," he said as he shook his head. "Unbelievable. I don't think I'll ever get that smell out of my mind."

Dan had a momentary flashback to the fish farm, but quickly dismissed it.

"So nothing that would help identify him?" he asked.

Richardson shrugged. "The only thing the good doctor found was some kind of clasp attached to the braid. He says it's made out of wood and he thinks it's a stylized Killer Whale – something like they have on their totem poles." He looked down the corridor towards the exit. "That's what took so damn long. I told him he should just cut the braid off and give it to you, but he said he couldn't do that. Said it had been important to the man who wore it and would be important to his family."

"He's probably right," Dan said, impressed by the thoughtfulness of a man who was generally known to be abrupt, if not outright difficult.

"Waste of time." Richardson was obviously not in agreement. "I told him the family wasn't going to know one way or the other – there's not going to be any open casket for this guy even if you do figure out who he was – but he refused to listen. Spent maybe fifteen minutes unbraiding before he got that thing free." He nodded briefly towards the bag. "It's right there at the top, bagged and tagged like the rest of the stuff."

He took one more breath, straightened his shoulders and turned back towards the door of the autopsy room. "Make sure you enjoy that fresh air out there. Sure isn't any inside here."

There was a tinge of resentment in the voice along with resignation. Dan couldn't blame him. He wasn't sure why Markleson had picked Richardson for the job, but whatever the reason he was certainly glad he had.

Dan put the bag into a plastic container and headed back to to Port McNeill. He felt as if he had already put in a full day, but it was not yet nine when he drove through the gates of the police compound and he still had many hours ahead of him.

He put the vehicle back in the same space in the parking lot and carefully lifted the bag holding the meager belongings of the dead man from the container. The movement of the drive had caused the various items to shift and the smaller bag holding the clasp had moved to the bottom, but with a little poking Dan managed to locate it.

Protocol and procedure demanded that he hand it all in – the same protocols and procedures he had recently spent several uncomfortable days listening to. Until the cause of death had been officially determined it was all supposed to be kept as evidence for forensics, but Dan figured the chances of being able to determine anything from clothing that had spent so much time in the ocean was probably nil. Still, rules were rules and he was about to break one.

He slipped his fingers into the bag, removed the clasp and slid it into his pocket. Even if he had been allowed to take the tattered remnants of clothing with him there was no need. He doubted there was enough of it left for the family to identify and it would only cause more pain. The clasp would be enough.

He took the clothing into the office and handed both it and the keys to Al Rediger who had now replaced the night-duty clerk at the desk. Al glanced up briefly as he felt the key in his hand, then looked back down at his puzzle.

"You think of something for "Cold wind in deep water?" he asked. "Five letters. Starts with "D"".

"Draft," Dan answered. Maybe he should take up cross-word puzzles. It could be much more satisfying than figuring out what was going on with this case.

29

It was only a half-hour walk back down to the marina, but this was one of two mornings each week that Dan volunteered to teach Judo to a bunch of local youngsters. The dojo was only a few blocks out of his way and the few extra minutes it would take to go and make his apologies would not make any real difference to his plans, nor to the man lying on that slab back in the autopsy room. While the sensei could certainly handle the class on his own and was well aware that Dan was a cop who could be called out at short notice, it didn't seem right to simply not show up if there was an option.

The door was open when he arrived, and the first of the kids was already dressed and waiting to be invited onto the mat. Sensei Ishikawa was on the floor performing an advanced kata. Dan moved towards him and stood quietly, waiting for him to finish before speaking.

"My apologies Sensei, but I am unable to assist today. I have to work on a case and it may keep me away for several days."

The man bowed in acknowledgement.

"I thank you for coming to tell me. Please be careful. I shall look forward to your return."

Dan bowed his own acknowledgement and moved back to the door where he stepped aside to allow two more youngsters in. Across the street a garage door rumbled open to reveal a dark-colored pick-up truck and beside it, an inflatable loaded onto a trailer. As Dan waited for the kids to pass him, he saw a man emerge and glance up and down the street. The man was tall and slim with dark hair tied in a neat ponytail at the back of his neck and even at this early hour he was wearing dark glasses. It was the man from the yacht, the one that the woman and dog had been on. It had to be. How many other people in this small logging and fishing community would look anything like that? How many would have that same still, dangerous quality Dan had noticed before? What the hell was he doing here? Surely neither he nor the yacht's owner would own an old house in Port Hardy?

A car pulled up in front of him and blocked his view. It disgorged two more kids to their judo class and then pulled away, but by the time Dan was able to see the garage again, the man had disappeared.

Sensei Ishikawa was helping one of the younger students tie his belt as Dan re-entered the dojo and bowed to him once again.

"There is something else?" the sensei asked.

A couple of the kids were starting to look their way now, wondering what was going on and why their lesson had not begun.

"Nothing important Sensei, but I wondered if you knew who owns the house across the street."

Ishikawa leaned past him and peered out the door.

"The blue one?"

Dan nodded.

"I believe it still belongs to a Mr. Halvorsen, but he

has not been here for a long time – three or four years I would say. I think he must be very ill, or perhaps even dead. I do not know. His son comes here occasionally, and sometimes other people I assume are the son's friends, but they keep to themselves. I have never spoken with them, but I see them loading their fishing gear into their boat. Usually the house is empty."

"Can you tell me what Halvorsen looked like?" Dan asked. The name sounded European, probably Scandinavian. Not likely to belong to a man with black hair and brown skin.

If Ishikawa was surprised by the question, he gave no sign. "When he first purchased the house, perhaps thirty years ago, he was a large man. Tall. Wide shoulders. He was very fit, very strong. He told me he worked in the forest, cutting trees, but then he had an accident and after that he lost weight and became weak and bent."

"Bent?" Dan asked, not understanding what the sensei meant.

"Hunched?" Ishikawa leaned forward and patted his shoulders to indicate what he was talking about. "Bent over."

"Ah, okay. Thank you. Just one more thing. He was white? A European?"

Ishikawa looked at him in confusion for a moment and then gave a quick nod of understanding. "Yes, of course. Both he and his wife. I believe he told me his grandparents were from Finland, or perhaps it was Sweden. I cannot remember which, but he looked Scandinavian. His hair was very pale, but not as pale as his wife's. She was English. Even when they first moved in, when she was still young, her hair was like snow and her skin was without color. She became ill and died several years before he too became sick."

Some of the waiting students were starting to push and

jostle each other and Ishikawa raised his hand to pause the conversation and turned to look at them.

"Please. You know the rules. Start your warm-up exercises. I will be with you in a minute."

He turned back to Dan. "Is that all you needed to know?"

"One more question. The son. Is he also blond?"

"Indeed. How could he be anything else?"

Dan smiled and bowed his head. "Thank you. I am sorry to have delayed you."

Sensei Ishikawa turned his attention to his students and Dan made his way back to the door. When he got there, the garage door belonging to the blue house across the street was closed and there was no sign of anyone.

THE ROAD LEADING down to the waterfront was steep, but trees and buildings blocked the view of the harbor for much of the way and it wasn't until Dan was almost there that he saw the yacht. It was anchored in the same place on the far side of the bay. He hadn't noticed it when he had left a few hours before, but it had been dark then and he had been preoccupied with other things so he might have missed it. On the other hand, he was sure it hadn't been there the night before. Not that it mattered. Its presence there now was all the confirmation he needed: the man he had seen at the blue house was the same man he had spoken to at Sullivan Bay.

Dan walked out along the wharf and down the ramp, waved a greeting to Willie Pete and climbed aboard *Dreamweaver*. A sleek white powerboat with long, dark plexiglass windows now occupied the neighboring slip where Claire's boat had been tied up until just a few hours ago. Even more confirmation. Although he hadn't paid much attention to it at the time, Dan thought it looked very much like the one that had brought the woman and the dog in to the dock a few days ago.

He let his eyes scan the full length of the float. He knew it was sixty feet, the same as the one *Dreamspeaker* was tied to, and the powerboat took up a little more than half of it. That made it about thirty-five feet, the length of the powerboat that had been at the fish farm.

It could be a coincidence: there were many boats that would fit the description Reg Johnson had given him, but something told Dan this was the same boat. If he was right, then the man he had seen both up at the house and on the big yacht now anchored across the harbor was somehow linked to the fish farm. And Jimmy Fulton was linked to the yacht.

The powerboat had a registration number on the hull. Dan opened his notebook and flipped to the page where he had written down the name and registration of the yacht, added both the registration of the neighboring boat and the street address of the blue house and then phoned the detachment.

Markleson's secretary, Maureen, had been a fixture in the Port McNeill office for almost twenty years, longer than most of the officers, and she knew all there was to know about how to work the computers and find information. She was also the wife of the harbormaster and Dan had been at their house for dinner on several occasions. With luck, that fact would work in his favor and allow him to jump to the head of the inevitable queue for her attention. She picked up the phone on the second ring. listened as he explained what he needed and then told him she would try and get him the information by lunchtime.

"Have I told you lately that you're the greatest?" Dan asked her.

"Yeah," she replied. "I think that was the last time

you were at the house, but it was right after I served the Beef Wellington so I figured that's what you were talking about."

Dan laughed. "So young and yet so cynical. How about I bring you one of those big Banks Chinook salmon when I get back."

"And I guess you'll expect me to cook that too?"

"Well, it will taste a whole lot better if you do it."

It was her turn to laugh. "You're probably right – and Donny can cook it on the BBQ anyway. Talk to you later."

Donny was her son, and he had made the BBQ his domain.

Dan hung up the phone and started the engine. While it warmed up he took out the camera he had purchased a few months back to take pictures of Claire, climbed back down to the dock and took photos of the boat in the neighboring slip. A quick stop at the fish farm would not take him far out of his way. He could show the pictures to Reg Johnson and see if he could get confirmation that this was the same boat that had been out there that day.

The computer screen lit up and he scanned through his charts until he found the one he wanted. It didn't take long to punch in the GPS waypoints that would guide him first to the farm and then on to Knight Inlet. After he talked with Reg he would use the rest of the day to try and find Walker.

It didn't seem likely Walker would be at his cabin during the daylight hours and Dan figured the best chance of locating him was probably to anchor as close to the entrance of the cove as possible, somewhere *Dreamspeaker* would be very visible when the man returned to his home. While he waited, Dan could search the nearby shoreline in the inflatable in the hope that he would come across Walker's small canoe out on the water.

It was all guesswork. Although Dan had called Walker a friend for over four years, he had never known how the man actually survived. All he knew was Walker had returned to his traditional ways, and those ways had to include catching and preparing his own food.

This was salmon season, the time when the big runs of sockeye and coho and chinook returned to the rivers to spawn. It seemed logical that Walker would be spending most of the daylight hours out on the water fishing, but he would have to take his catch back to his campsite well before night fell: hia only only way to preserve his catch for the coming winter would be to dry it or smoke it.

Dan's plan was far from perfect, but it was the best he could come up with. If he didn't succeed in finding Walker, he would just have to go to Tsa'wit alone the next morning.

He spent fifteen minutes plotting the course and punching it into the computer before releasing the lines and easing *Dreamspeaker* out of her slip. As soon as he was clear of the breakwater and could see there was no other marine traffic headed his way he set the autopilot, went back to the galley and started a pot of coffee.

He was already tired. The emotional turmoil of the previous evening had left him drained, and even though the mental anguish it had started with had ended with physical pleasure, it had all taken its toll of his resources. While just thinking about the lovemaking with Claire brought a smile to his lips, it didn't alter the fact he had managed to get only four hours sleep before the phone woke him.

Food would help. It had been a long time since he had last eaten and he was hungry, but a proper meal would have to wait at least until he had passed Haddington Reef and was out of the major traffic lanes. For now, coffee and a snack bar would have to do.

The shrill ring of the radiophone interrupted his coffee making. He could easily get to hate that sound he thought as he lifted the microphone from its holder and flipped the switch, but it was probably Maureen with the information he had asked for.

"Hi Maureen," he said. "That was quick."

"Maureen?"

It wasn't Maureen. It was Claire.

"How are you?" she asked.

Such simple words, but coming from her they sounded like a caress.

"A hell of a lot better now I can hear your voice," he answered, and it was true. Even when he couldn't see her, just talking to her made him feel good. "I saw you leave. I was halfway up the hill when you turned the marker."

"No point in hanging around," she answered. "I figured I would get an early start so I went up to the wharfinger's office to pay my moorage right after you left. Good thing too. If I hadn't I would have missed the drama."

"Drama?" he asked, his imagination immediately creating vivid scenarios peopled with burning boats and screaming people.

She laughed. "Nothing too exciting, but you remember that woman and her dog? Well that big powerboat – the one we figured came from that yacht we saw – came in around the breakwater as I was letting go the lines. I waited until they passed because I didn't want to cut them off. The woman was standing out on side deck so I waved to her and said something about it being a nice morning to walk her dog – and she burst into tears!"

"Did you see the dog?"

"No sign of it. Isn't that a bit strange?"

"Yeah, I guess so." Dan wasn't sure what to say. "Was she alone?"

"No. She had that same guy with her. He said something to her – I couldn't hear what, but it sounded angry - and she went inside."

Dan was suddenly much more interested. "Was this the guy with the long hair?"

"Yes, that's him. Those people are odd."

Definitely odd, Dan thought. And maybe much more than odd, although how the woman and her dog fit in he had no idea.

HE HAD ALMOST REACHED the fish farm when the phone once more interrupted his thoughts. Again he lifted the microphone expecting to hear Maureen's voice and again he was disappointed. This time it was Markleson's harsh growl travelling across the airwaves.

"Where are you?"

"On my way back to the fish farm. I've got a couple of photos I want to show the supervisor there. Maybe get an ID on a boat that was tied up there when Farnsworth was shot."

"Well we sure as hell need something, and we need it in a hurry. I got Doc Finlayson's report on my desk a couple of minutes ago. Looks like the guy he had on the table this morning was shot with the same gun."

30

The dark-haired man, whose name was Eric Lasalle, closed the garage door and joined his partner in the kitchen.

"You see that guy over at the judo place watching us?"

Karl Halvorsen took two beers from the fridge and offered one to Lasalle.

"Didn't see no one. Why?"

"He's a cop. He came out to the yacht when we were over in Sullivan Bay. Wanted to talk to Melissa."

Halvorsen shrugged. "So what'd the princess do? Lose an earring or something?" He still stung from his one meeting with the woman and his tone left no doubt as to what he thought of her.

Lasalle didn't answer. He had an instinct for trouble, and this cop was beginning to set off major alarms.

"We're going to have to find another guy to fill the bags. The man isn't happy with how long this is taking."

Halvorsen's heavy face took on a sulky look.

"We got the shipment out to the Betty Jean on time! Ain't

our fault Steiger marked up the wrong bale and it got sent to the wrong farm."

"It doesn't matter whose fault it was," Lasalle snapped. "It happened. Now we need to speed things up. Masterton called last night. He's flying back up on Tuesday and then he wants to take the yacht back down south. That only gives us four more days to get the rest of the stuff out there, and I need to spend some of those days on the yacht. If I don't, the crew's going to start asking questions, and we could be in trouble."

He moved to the window and used a finger to part the drapes just enough to see out onto the street. It was empty. The cop was gone.

"I'll contact Steiger and get him to tell Anderson to send over someone from the farm again. They've got another Indian guy working there. I saw him when we were out there and he's the same as the other one: doesn't live in town and brings his own boat in from some reserve way the hell and gone up some inlet. If he doesn't show up no-one will worry about it – those guys are all unreliable anyway."

Lasalle pulled a cell phone out of his pocket and started dialing. "We'll do it the same as before. Steiger will call you to go pick him up from the wharf when he gets there and you bring him back here and put him to work."

"Ahh man," Halvorsen whined. "That takes forever. We shoulda just kept the first guy. We would've had it all done by now."

Lasalle went still. When he turned back his eyes were cold. "Yes. Indeed we should have – and we would have if you hadn't screwed things up and let him get out on deck."

"That was an accident – and we coulda just brought him back here anyway. Nobody saw him. You didn't have to shoot him."

"Really? And I guess you could have kept him quiet? He

was already screaming his head off. We had people on other boats looking at us. What would you have done? Maybe asked him to join you for dinner and a drink?" Lasalle's voice dripped sarcasm. "Good thing one of us has a brain. I'll do the thinking here. You just do as you're told."

He slid a small Beretta 1919 semi-automatic out of a holster on his belt and checked the clip. "Nobody's ever going to find that guy anyway. Both him and the one from the barge are long gone. If they're ever found – which I doubt – there's not going to be enough left to identify. All those whales around here will take care of that."

'I don't know, man." Halvorsen's fleshy face had taken on a hang-dog look. "I don't think those things eat anything but fish and seals and stuff. If anyone finds one of those guys, the cops are going to start looking real close at the farms – and people on the farms have seen us."

"You seen any reports in the paper about anyone finding a body?" Lasalle snarled. "Of course not – but then you don't read the paper do you? How about the TV? You hear anything on the news? They're gone. Forget about them."

He looked at the sullen man standing in front of him and wished for perhaps the hundredth time he could work alone, but Masterson hadn't given him a choice. If there had, Lasalle certainly wouldn't have picked Karl Halvorsen. The man was pathetic, but they needed him – at least until the job was finished.

He worked to moderate his tone. "We'll get this other guy to package up the rest of the stuff and then we're done. You don't even have to be here except maybe to bring something to feed him. You can help me deliver the bags when they're ready. We'll both be out of here in a couple of days and you'll be laughing all the way to the bank."

The words seemed to cheer Halvorsen a little, but he still

didn't look convinced. "So if we get another guy, what'll we do with him when he's finished?"

Lasalle's smile would have sent chills down the spine of anyone seeing it, but he had turned away.

"One more body isn't going to make any difference," he said.

31

The air carried the rich, ripe scents of summer: trees and grasses heavy with seed, dens and burrows crowded with young, the littoral thick with roots and berries. The bright shoots of spring had turned to a dense green and bears ambled along the beaches, turning over rocks and scrounging the last few traces of herring roe off drying strands of kelp.

It had been a good year for the herring and Walker had collected his winter supply of roe well over a month ago. The spawning fish had filled the coves, releasing so many eggs the clear water had turned a milky white and the kelp fronds had been blanketed with them, six or seven layers deep on a single strand. The cedar and hemlock branches he had anchored along the shore had been covered with such a heavy load of spawn they had been almost unrecognizable, more like white tree skeletons than the graceful green fronds he had submerged only weeks before. He had filled his canoe with them and taken them back to his cabin where he hung them up to dry.

Today he was more interested in catching another

salmon, but his mind kept returning to the man he had met in the cove near the fish farm, and to the dog the man had rescued.

Walker might live a mostly solitary life now, but there had been a time down in the city when he had met plenty of odd characters, and in the almost three years he had spent in jail he had come across more than a few troubled misfits. Some of them had been loners and others were simply lonely, but none of them even came close to Arne Hjorth. Arne's looks alone were strange enough to set him apart.

The man was so pale he could hardly be called white. It was more like a complete lack of color although he certainly wasn't albino: his eyes were an electric blue, startling in such a pale face. He was also excruciatingly thin, although not what Walker would describe as emaciated. The bones and sinews and muscles were all there, almost visible beneath the weathered skin, but they somehow gave the impression of strength rather than weakness – or maybe it was simply endurance.

But apart from all of that there was the anger. Walker could sense it burning inside the man, shining from his eyes, spoken in his words, expressed in every movement. Walker had known many angry men in his time, but none had come close to this. In Arne it seemed contained, fed, focused. It flashed like fire every time the man looked at the fish farm anchored a few hundred yards away from the entrance to the cove he was living in.

And then there was the dog. It too was strange and certainly nothing like any other dog Walker had ever come across, but that wasn't what occupied his thoughts either. It had taken him a long time to figure out just what it was that bothered him, but finally it had come to him. It was the relationship between the two of them: the odd-looking man and the wounded animal.

Walker had never allowed emotion to play a role in his life, at least not since his pride led him to those long years of incarceration, and the thought that an animal, any animal, let alone one like this with dirty matted hair, could possibly inspire the kind of emotion he had seen in Arne was hard for him to believe. All it took was one glance at the dog to change Arne completely. The fire of his anger disappeared, snuffed out in an instant. The hardness in his eyes softened and they seemed to change color, the blue deepening as anger changed to what Walker could only believe was love.

Love was an emotion Walker had never allowed himself to even dream about. He didn't need it in his life. Hell, he hadn't even had a friend until Claire and Dan had come along. Besides, who would love a crippled ex-con who lived in a crude shelter at the end of some God-forsaken inlet?

Walker shook his head to clear it. What the hell was the matter with him? That was self-pity talking and he didn't need that either. He was fine as he was. He liked the life he had created – but the transformation he had seen in Arne still lingered. If a relationship with a dog could inspire such . . . happiness? contentment? . . . then what more was possible with a human relationship?

Enough! The dog was hurt and needed help. That was probably what had roused such caring and concern in the man who had rescued it. Walker was letting his imagination run away with him and by doing so he was missing the real issue.

He knew Arne figured the injury must have happened when the dog scraped against a sharp rock or a submerged tree branch as it was trying to swim to shore, but Walker wasn't so sure. When they had first started talking about how the dog was thrown in the water, Arne had mentioned hearing a sharp noise he thought might have been a gunshot. He dismissed the idea almost immediately, brushing it off as ridiculous, but although Walker didn't say anything at the time, he did not agree. The wound the dog had sustained was a long straight furrow along its shoulder, exactly the kind of wound that a bullet would make.

Walker spent some time helping Arne to bathe that wound with warm salt water heated in an old pot over the fire. He had also given him some of the poplar resin he always carried with him. It was how he treated his own wounds so he figured it should work for a dog the same way and before he headed his canoe back out into the channel he promised to bring some more.

If he was right, the dog and its wound was something he needed to share with Dan Connor. Dan was out there at Walker's request looking into the disappearance of the two men from Tsa'wit, both of whom had been working on one of the fish farms. Walker figured Dan would be very interested in knowing that someone with a gun had been on one of them too. It didn't take detective skills to think that there just might be a link.

He turned his canoe and moved a little further out from shore. It was time to get back to fishing. He had always felt a kinship with the salmon. They had been the sustainers of his people for thousands of years, but he knew from experience they only offered themselves to him when he was in the right frame of mind, at peace with himself and cleansed of all conflict and doubt. He thought perhaps his mood moved through the water somehow, transmitting the state of his spirit to the fish, and if he hadn't achieved the proper balance they would turn away. He did not think they would come to him today.

Earlier that morning, before he left his cove, he had caught a few small squid in his dip net. They were hardly enough for a meal, but perhaps he could use them to lure a halibut onto his line. Halibut were bottom dwellers, surging upwards only to eat, and squid were one of their favorite meals. If he could catch one of them he could afford to head back to his cove earlier than usual, but it wouldn't be easy.

Often they were too big for him to pull up. He knew of a couple of fishermen back in Y'alis who caught a four-hundred-and-fifty-pound halibut up north near Dixon Entrance, big enough to sink a much larger vessel than his tiny canoe. Other times they were too deep for his line to reach, although occasionally he found one as shallow as twenty or thirty feet. In any case it was certainly worth a try. If he could catch one of the huge fish it would give his winter food stock a large boost as well as providing him with a meal when he got home.

He felt the current grab his canoe and he let out his line. There was no hurry. He could take his time and let the ocean calm his spirit. If he hadn't got a bite after seven or eight passes he would head back to shore where he could wait for the ocean to work its magic on him. All he had to do for that to happen was to sit still and listen until he was quiet enough to hear the sound.

It would be almost subliminal at first, as the vast expanse of the Pacific approached the land and felt the sea-bottom start to rise beneath it. There would be a soft groan perhaps, born far beneath the surface. The sound would be felt rather than heard as the weight of the water was forced up, pushing against the air above, arching higher and higher until it could no longer maintain its form. Then the sound would become a roar as wave after wave crested and surged against the shore only to dissolve back into the ocean with a last sibilant hiss.

The rhythm of the ocean never failed to sooth him, and when it had erased the questions and doubts from his mind he could return to his home and try for a salmon up near the mouth of the river.

He caught a halibut on his fifth pass. It was a small one, less than three feet long and probably no more than twenty-five pounds, but it took him over half-an-hour to pull it up to his canoe. It took another twenty minutes of hard work to drag it into the boat without either losing it or tipping over. That was followed by yet another struggle as he fought to stow the awkward shape in the bottom of the hull under one of the thwarts.

He allowed himself to rest for a few minutes before turning the canoe south. It was time to head home. The physical effort had worked to clear his mind and he no longer needed the solace of the ocean to calm his soul. He would get back earlier than usual, but he had caught more than enough for one day and he had work to do back in the cove, preparing the fish for drying and smoking.

32

Dan pushed the engine revs as high as he dared. Markleson's phone call had increased his already overactive sense of urgency to an almost unbearable level. Everything about this case frustrated him. The best he had been able to do so far was to develop a few random ideas, none of them more than vague, disconnected guesses that had not a shred of substantiation. Somehow he needed to get some solid information, some definite facts to work with, but even after all this time, he still had nothing concrete, nothing that would give him a place to start. Even the normally reliable Maureen had failed to get back to him with the information he had asked her to get.

He exhaled his breath in a harsh snort of laughter. It didn't really matter how long she took. He was going to be tied up with other things for the next couple of days and wasn't going to be able to do anything with whatever information she might come up with anyway. All he knew for sure was when he got back to Port McNeill after his trip to Tsa'wit, he wanted to find some reason to get aboard that yacht. Even better, he wanted to find something he could use to keep it from leaving the area, at least until he had searched it from one end to the other.

He turned into Nicholl Passage and watched as the fish farm Reg Johnson worked on came into view. He was still too far away to be able to make out any activity, but there was definitely no sign of either a barge or a white powerboat anywhere in the vicinity. In fact, there was no sign of anything tied to any of the floats. He checked the radar, but it too had nothing to show. Except for *Dreamspeaker* the passage was deserted.

He shoved his hands into his pockets and his fingers touched the bag containing the clasp the coroner had removed from the braid. In some strange way, even though Dan had never seen the man, had not even seen his body when they brought it in, the clasp brought him to life. It created an image in Dan's mind of someone proud, strong, and hardworking, and it seemed impossible that this image, this person who appeared so vital, could have been found lifeless out on the rocks . . . surely that couldn't have been only been this morning?

Dan thought back to the phone call that had pulled him out of sleep. It seemed as if several days had passed since he sat in the hallway outside the autopsy room, but when he instinctively checked his watch he was forced to acknowledge it had only been a few hours.

He took the bag out of his pocket and held it up to the light. The clasp was small, no more than three inches in length and perhaps an inch and a half at its widest point which formed the dorsal fin of a stylized killer whale. Even viewed through the plastic the detail was incredible and the workmanship top quality. Whoever had carved this had been an artist.

Dan turned it over and checked the back. It appeared to be completely smooth except for three tiny shaped protruberances obviously designed to prevent it from slipping once it had been put in place. On the lower left corner there was a mark of some kind, but it was too small for him to determine if it was a flaw in the wood, a scratch or even initials, although it would be hard to imagine a tool small enough to create those. In any case he was sure that if the man who had been wearing it had been its creator, he would be well known in the village and therefore easy for the people there to identify.

As he placed the bag into the waterproof pack he used in the inflatable, Dan suddenly recalled the bandana he had found with the cedar bracelet attached. It too had been decorated with stylized killer whales. Could it have belonged to the same man?

Dan slowed *Dreamspeaker* and let her drift up to the float. It would take too long to anchor and launch the dinghy and his business with Reg Johnson was not going to take long. He had closed all the portholes and doors as soon as the farm came into view in case there had been another 'event' that brought with it the same smell as last time, and before he left Port McNeill he had put on his oldest jeans and sweatshirt. That way he wouldn't feel so bad if he had to dispose of them later.

With the camera secure in his pocket, he slid open the door and took a cautious sniff. This time there was only the scent of living fish. It was stronger than he had experienced the few times he had come across a big school at sea, and it was mixed with something he couldn't quite place – antibiotics maybe as there was a faint medicinal quality to it. It was certainly less than appetizing, but not really unpleasant. He jumped down onto the float and wrapped the lines around the railing. Reg Johnson joined him before he completed tying the knots.

"Didn't take you long to come up with more questions."

Johnson seemed more relaxed than he had been on Dan's previous visit, which tended to confirm that he had been telling the truth about his ignorance of what had gone on, but which could also be because he was not being subjected to the odor of rotting fish. Dan suspected that would be enough to make anyone up tight.

"I'm still working on those," Dan replied. "What I need you to do right now is look at some photos."

He pulled the camera out, switched it on and scrolled through until he found the shots he had taken of the white powerboat.

"Any of these look like the boat that was here the day Farnsworth was shot?"

Johnson looked at him oddly. "You saying the office doesn't know who these guys were?"

Dan shook his head. "I haven't talked to them yet, but I need to make sure I have the right boat."

Johnson didn't look convinced, but he nodded, took the camera from Dan's outstretched hand and squinted at the image that appeared on the screen. After several seconds he handed it back and shook his head.

"Sorry. I don't want to disappoint you, but I'm just not sure. It could be, but like I said, they all look pretty much the same to me."

Dan scrolled to the next image. "How about this one?"

Again Johnson studied the screen, and again he handed it back with a shake of his head.

Dan was bringing up the last shot he had taken when he heard the phone up in the wheelhouse once again demanding his attention. He thrust the camera back to the supervisor.

"Just keep scrolling through. There's a few more there," he said as he swung himself back up onto the deck and ran forward to grab the microphone.

"Connor," he snapped. Surely Markleson couldn't have more bad news for him.

"Dan?" Maureen's soft voice was a welcome relief and he felt himself relax a little. "I have that information you asked for. Sorry it took so long. It's been a little crazy around here."

"I thought it was always crazy around there," Dan joked. "At least that's what you tell me."

"Not like this." There was a somber tone that caught Dan's attention. "We've got another kid dead from an overdose. Only thirteen years old. He went to the same school as Nathan."

"Another? How many are there?" There was no joking now.

"This is three – and there's one adult as well – although she wasn't really much more than a kid either. Doesn't really sound like a lot when you read the numbers coming in from Vancouver, but for a small community like this . . . it's really awful. All the kids know each other. Hell, most of the adults know all of them too."

Dan thought he heard a catch in her voice.

"Are you alright?" he asked. "How's Nathan handling it? Is he okay?"

Maureen sniffed and then her voice evened out.

"Yeah, I'm okay, and Nathan is with his dad. Larry took him to work with him today. Said he needed help fixing up the dinghy float and Nathan always enjoys working with him on stuff like that."

Another sniff. "Anyway, you got your notebook ready?"

She had done even more than he had asked. She had checked the registration numbers on both the yacht and the launch – he really couldn't bring himself to call it a dinghy any longer – and they were both registered in Vancouver to a Donald S. Masterton. Masterton's address was in Shaughnessy, which didn't surprise Dan as he knew Shaunghnessy was one of the wealthiest suburbs in that city with tree-lined streets curving past elegant multi-million dollar mansions. A man who owned a house there should be able to easily afford a yacht the size of the one Dan was interested in.

A phone call to Masterton's house had been answered by a housekeeper. The woman said Masterton was not at home and would probably not return for several days or maybe even weeks. Another call to the Royal Vancouver Yacht Club had been a little more rewarding. The office there confirmed Donald Masterton was indeed a member and his yacht, the *White Lightning,* was normally moored on one of their docks however it was currently absent from its berth.

Of more interest was the information that Masterton did not operate the boat himself. He had both a captain and a crew. While no list of the crew was available, the captain's name was on file in case of emergency. Maureen said the office had been reluctant to give it out, but had finally been convinced by the threat of a subpoena. The captain was one Daniel Vienza and, when not on duty, his residence was listed in a floating home community in Steveston, an area of Richmond.

Maureen had not stopped there. When a question to the manager at the Yacht Club about a possible female passenger on the yacht had met with no success, she asked a friend of hers who worked in the Richmond RCMP detachment to do a little checking. The friend had not been able to come up with an answer, but in turn referred the question to yet another contact in the Vancouver Police department. That contact had made a few discreet inquiries and discovered that while Donald Masterton was not currently married, and had in fact only recently divorced his third wife, he did indeed have a female friend who often accompanied him when he took his yacht out. Her name was Melissa, and Melissa was known to have a dog, a purebred Afghan hound, which she insisted on taking with her everywhere she went, including aboard Donald Masterton's yacht. Melissa's last name and address had yet to be confirmed, but Maureen's contact was working on it. Maureen had also put in a request for background information, including criminal record checks, on both Masterton and Vienza, although so far she had heard nothing back.

"Maureen, you are the absolute best," Dan said, smiling for perhaps the first time that day as he stared out through the windscreen. "I am going to have to catch at least two of those big Chinook salmon to pay you back for this."

"That and a couple of bottles of Malbec should just about do it."

The sadness had not completely left her voice but she sounded stronger and her sense of humor was definitely coming back. Her love of the Argentinian wine was well known to all of them, both at the Port McNeill detachment and at the marina.

Dan replaced the microphone and headed back outside, his mind racing. Melissa might be exactly the key he had been looking for in order to get onboard *White Lightning*. It was a key he wasn't sure how he could use yet, but he would thing of something.

He climbed back down to the float to talk to Reg Johnson again.

"Sorry about that," he said as he took the camera back. "Anything there that looks familiar?"

Johnson shook his head. "Not really. Certainly nothing I could swear to. The windows look like they're the right shape, but the rest of it . . . "He spat into the water. "Like I said before, they all look alike as far as I'm concerned."

It was disappointing. Dan had hoped for more, but the information Maureen had given him balanced it out. As soon as he had finished at Tsa'wit he woud track down Masterton and his yacht and find a way to get aboard.

Thanks for your time," he said to Johnson. "I know there's not much there. I was just hoping there would be something that would jog your memory. If you think of anything later, you've got my card. You can phone me."

Johnson nodded and unwrapped the line as Dan climbed back onboard.

"Only thing I can think of that might help is the dog," the man said as he pushed *Dreamspeaker* away from the dock.

33

Dan was already halfway to the wheelhouse when he heard the words, but he spun back so fast he almost fell. "The dog? What kind of dog?"

"Ah man, I can't give you a breed or anything. It was just that one time. We were heading back into town and it was already getting a bit dark, plus we were quite a ways away by the time I saw it, but it was pretty big – kinda tall anyway – and it looked weird. It seemed to move funny. Sorta bounce as it walked."

"So are you sure it was a dog?"

"What else could it have been? It was just this shape that jumped off the boat onto the float. I only saw it for a few seconds anyway. Probably don't help you much, but it seemed kind of an odd thing to do you know – bring a dog out to a fish farm – and you said to tell you if I thought of anything else."

"No, that's great." Dan heard the apology in Johnson's voice and tried to reassure the man. The dog might be the best information he had received so far. "It all helps. I don't suppose you could you make out a color? I know you said it was getting dark, but you could still see it?"

"Yeah." Johnson thought about it for a moment. "It was sort of pale, but I don't think it was white. Gray maybe? Or light brown?"

There was nothing else he could add.

For the first time in the last couple of weeks Dan felt a hint of optimism. He finally had something concrete to link at least some of the disparate pieces of the case together. It might not be enough to take to a prosecutor or even to impress Markleson, but it was something. If nothing else, it gave him a direction to follow. Now if he could just find Walker...

FINDING WALKER PROVED to be no challenge at all. Instead of the difficulty Dan had feared, it proved to be the easiest thing he had done that day. Once he reached the cove where Walker made his home, Dan spent almost an hour searching for a good place to anchor. It had to provide a secure holding ground and also be a place where he would be seen by Walker on his return from whatever fishing or gathering expedition he had been on.

Dan found the perfect place just off the entrance to Walker's cove. Protected from the wind and with a depth of thirty feet, it had more than enough room to swing in a rising tide. With the anchor set, Dan went aft and started to lower the inflatable, but a sound caught his attention and he looked down to see Walker's canoe slide up to the stern grid.

Dan eased the inflatable back onto the davits and went to the gate.

"I was just going to look for you. Isn't it kind of early for you to be quitting for the day? I figured you would be out fishing much later than this."

Walker gestured to the fish lying in the bottom of his canoe. "Caught a halibut a couple of hours ago. Gotta get it back to the cabin and cut it up." He looked up at Dan. "I know I told you where I lived, but I didn't really expect to see you this soon."

Dan shook his head. "This isn't just a friendly visit. I need your help with something."

Walker stared at him for a moment and then looked away. When he turned back he had a look of resignation on his face.

"Does this have anything to do with the men from Tsa'wit?" he asked.

Dan nodded. "Yes, it does. At least with one of them."

Walker turned away again and stared out over the water. After what seemed like a long time, he spoke without looking back.

"You need to come to my place. I have to clean the fish."

The words were difficult to hear, almost lost in the sound of the wind and the waves. He let go of the stern grid and dug his paddle into the water, sending his tiny craft surging.

Dan watched him go, then climbed back up and released the dinghy again. He suspected he might be in for a long night and he hoped he was up to it. He was already exhausted by the events of the past two days.

WALKER BARELY ACKNOWLEDGED Dan's arrival at his cabin. He was seated on a log that rested high on the beach, his canoe drawn up beside him and the halibut spread out in front on a mat woven from what Dan thought was cedar bark. To either side Dan could see drying salmon. They were split and stretched on stick frames or hanging in strips from ropes strung between the twisted arms of driftwood roots. The roots had either washed up or been dragged up high on the shore and below them the sweet, pungent smell of smoke rose from a low fire. From the look of the glowing embers, it had been burning all day.

"You lose any of this to bears?" Dan asked as he looked around the tiny cove with its serried ranks of drying fish. "Seems like it would make a pretty tempting meal."

Walker shook his head and gestured behind the cabin to where sheer rock walls formed a narrow crevice that channeled a steady trickle of water down onto the sand. The walls curved around the cove, wrapping it in a towering embrace before stretching out into the ocean on either side. The entrance was so narrow Dan had almost missed it when he came in.

"Had a young one swim in once, but the fire chased him off." Walker placed another strip of the white flesh onto a pile that had already reached over eight inches high.

Dan sat quietly and watched him work. The place both fascinated and awed him. It was tiny and in many ways crude yet it was also unmistakably a home. The cabin, really more of a lean-to, was fashioned from driftwood logs leaned against a heavy central frame created from a forked branch. Moss chinked the cracks between them.

The floor was raised, probably on more logs, although a thick bed of branches hid them from view and woven mats lay on top. What appeared to be several heavy wool blankets were piled against the back wall and a stack of neatly folded clothing filled a corner. Baskets woven from either cedar bark strips or spruce root hung from protruding knots in the logs, and several braided ropes were looped over the smooth nubs of branches broken and then worn smooth by months or even years in the ocean.

"You want me to put another piece of wood on the fire?" Dan asked.

Walker gestured to a large pile of branches and Dan

leaned over and picked one up. It was heavy and obviously had not been allowed to dry.

"You always burn green wood?" he asked.

"Depends. Green alder makes more smoke, but it burns fast. Arbutus burns longer so I don't have to worry about the fire going out when I'm not here. I change the mix to suit the need."

Dan looked around the tiny cove. There were a few straggly bushes growing up near the rock wall but there wasn't a tree in sight.

"Driftwood?" he asked, although he couldn't see much of that either.

"No. There's plenty of trees in the next cove." Walker nodded towards the east and reached for another piece of fish. "You want to tell me why you need my help or are we going to sit here and talk about bears and wood all night?"

Dan gave a short bark of laughter. "Straight to the point as usual." Picking up a piece of wood from the stack, he turned it in his hands and avoided looking at the man he was talking to. "We found another body. We think it might be one of the guys from Tsa'wit."

Walker continued to cut up the fish, not saying anything.

"He was Native," Dan continued. "A big guy. He had a long braid." He threw the wood back on the pile and fished in his pocket for the bag that held the clasp. "His braid was tied with this." He held it out for Walker to see.

For what seemed to Dan a very long time Walker remained still, both his knife and the fish apparently forgotten in his hand as he stared at the bag Dan was holding out to him. Finally, just as Dan was about to pull it back and return it to his pocket, Walker put his knife down on the ground and reached his hand out.

"Did they cut his braid off to get this?" he asked as he turned the bag gently from one side to the other.

"No," Dan answered. "The coroner refused to do that. Said that it was important to the man who wore it."

Walker nodded. "Smart guy for a white man."

"How do you know he was white?" Dan asked, a little stung by the comment.

"Don't have too many Native coroners," Walker answered. "Not exactly a popular occupation with our people." He held the bag up to the light and studied it. "You see that mark on the back?"

"Yes," Dan answered. "I wasn't sure if it was made deliberately or whether it was just a scratch. It's too small to really make out without a magnifying glass."

"It's deliberate. It's the signature of the carver."

Dan's heartbeat picked up. "Do you know who that is? Is it someone from Tsa'wit?"

Walker shook his head. "Perhaps. I don't know all the carvers there, but something about this looks familiar." He looked at Dan. "That's what you need me for, right? To go to Tsa'wit with you?"

"Yeah. It's going to be hard on them to lose one of their people. Even harder for the family to hear it from a white cop. I figured if you were there too it would make it easier on them."

Walker nodded slowly. "They know you're coming?"

"I figure my boss will have called them to let them know."

Walker passed the bag with its clasp back. "You planning on taking the big boat?"

"Not all the way," Dan answered. "I'm not familiar with that area, but I doubt I could get that far upriver even if I wanted to – and I don't. I think it would be better if I arrived in a small boat. The inflatable will work fine and it might be less threatening that way." He shrugged. "It's probably just my attempt at amateur psychology, but that's what I figure."

For the first time since Dan had arrived in the cove, Walker laughed, although there was a hollow tone to it.

"Not bad for an amateur." He picked up the last piece of fish and quickly cut it into thin slices. "Be better if we went in my canoe."

Dan looked at him, trying to guage whether he was serious or not. It was in many ways an excellent idea and one that would certainly ease his introduction to the people of Tsa'wit, but he wasn't sure whether Walker really meant it. While Walker was so at home in the tiny vessel it seemed at times that he and the canoe were a single unit, it wasn't Dan's favorite form of transportation – a fact Walker was well aware of – and Tsa'wit was a long way away.

"Depends on how far you're thinking we should go in it," he said.

Walker's smile grew wider. "Not into long canoe trips?" he asked, his voice sounding innocent.

"To tell you the truth I'm not into any trips right now," Dan answered. "It's been a long day and if I don't get a few hours sleep I'm not going to be in any shape to do anything tomorrow, including talk to people who have lost one of their own."

"Yeah." Walker nodded as he piled the fish onto a rough board. "You look like hell."

"I feel like hell, and tomorrow does not promise to be any easier than today." Dan stood up and stretched. "I need to get back to the boat. How about we leave early tomorrow morning – my kind of early, not your kind of early." He was familiar with Walker's penchant for being out on the ocean long before dawn and had no intention of joining him. "I can load the canoe onto the grid and then we can launch it again when we get somewhere near the mouth of the river."

Walker didn't answer right away and Dan thought he was

going to disagree, but finally he nodded. "Yeah. Then we can come back here through Retreat Passage."

"Okay, I'll see you in the morning. We'll leave once it's full light out." Dan put a heavy emphasis on the "full light" part and then turned to leave. He was halfway down the beach when Walker's words sank into his tired brain and he turned back. "Wait a minute. Why would we come back through Retreat Passage? It's way out of our way."

"Yeah, it is," Walker agreed. "But there's someone there you need to talk to."

34

Whenever Dan looked back on the events of the following day, he always felt a sense of wonder mixed with both gratitude and sorrow. It was an odd combination of emotions for a day that had started with dread and was filled with challenges, but it was the way it ended that would forever haunt his dreams.

Walker arrived long before the sun appeared, and was already sitting out on the stern deck when Dan went out to check the weather.

"How the hell did you get up here without waking me up?" Dan asked, staring at the man who was leaning back comfortably against the seat cushions as if he had no care in the world.

"Must have been my innate grace and athleticism," Walker answered, his face expressionless.

Dan stared at him for several seconds then went over and looked down onto the swim grid. Walker's canoe was sitting there firmly attached to the hooks Dan had installed to hold it. How the man had managed to lift it up out of the water without help was – and knowing Walker, would forever remain – a mystery.

"I must have been more tired than I thought. I never heard a damn thing. How long have you been here?"

Walker shrugged. "A while."

"A while" was obviously all Dan was going to get and he was not about to waste any more time trying. He went back inside and started the engine, then let it warm up while he returned to the galley to start a pot of coffee. It was the way he started every day and coffee was the one thing he knew Walker would accept from him.

By mid-morning they were in Banks Inlet and had arrived at the mouth of the river, but it took a long time for Dan to find a safe place to anchor and it was well past noon by the time they got the canoe back in the water and started upstream. Two hours of hard paddling brought them within sight of the village, but they couldn't see either a wharf or a float until they rounded a curve a good half-an-hour later. By that time Dan's arms were so tired he could barely lift his paddle and he didn't think there was a part of him that didn't ache.

He wasn't even sure he could stand as his knees seemed to be locked in place, but he knew he had to move. A group of people were coming down a path from the village led by an elderly woman with long gray hair. At first glance she reminded him of his grandmother. It wasn't an entirely good memory. His grandmother had been a stickler for both appearances and manners and Dan had many times been the recipient of her sharp tongue. He could hear her now telling him he needed to step out of the canoe with some appearance of confidence, if not with grace, but instead he could only manage to crawl out onto the float and he found himself staring at the woman's knees.

He pushed himself upright, inwardly cursing his ignominious arrival, and heard her speaking to Walker. As he tried to make out her words, Dan realized she was speaking in her own language and Walker was replying in a similar fashion. It was a language Dan had never heard spoken before and he was both surprised and confused. If he couldn't understand what they were saying it put him at even more of a disadvantage.

He finally managed to straighten up and look around. The woman was still standing quietly beside him, her face serene as she watched him struggle. All Dan could think of doing was to offer an apology.

"I am so sorry Grandmother. Please forgive my awkwardness. I don't mean to intrude. My name is Dan Connor."

Grandmother? Where had that come from? This woman was not his grandmother. Had he just insulted her?

All he could do was hope she didn't speak or understand English because she would probably think he was a complete idiot. He was certainly babbling like one. *"Great way to start Connor"* he chided himself.

The woman did not appear to notice his stupidity, or to be offended. Instead she inclined her head, smiled and held out her hand.

"Welcome to Tsa'wit Dan Connor. Walker tells me that you have news for us. I have sent my sister's grand-daughters up to the village to ask our chief to join us."

Dan glanced behind her to see two young girls running back along the path towards the houses he could see scattered between the trees.

"I think perhaps it would be better if we went to the beach." The woman gestured to the gravel shore that edged the river. "The logs there are comfortable to sit on and Walker could pull the canoe up close to them."

Walker had been sitting quietly in his canoe ever since they arrived, and it was only as he looked down at him now that Dan realized he had been so caught up with his own concerns he had not given a thought to the difficulty – perhaps the impossibility – of Walker being able to climb out onto the float. What the hell was the matter with him? He was too old to be acting like some flustered teenager just because he was in an unfamiliar situation. He had a job to do. A difficult job perhaps, but one he had been trained to do, and the people here deserved he do it well. Walker too deserved his consideration. The man was only there because Dan had asked him to help.

"Of course," he answered, grateful that she had taken the lead. "Thank you – but I don't know your name?"

She laughed. "I rather liked 'grandmother', but if you prefer you can call me Rose."

They walked along the float together and by the time they stepped down onto the gravel shore Walker had already moved the canoe over and run it up onto the beach. Dan took the bow line and tied it to one of the logs as Walker lifted himself out of the little vessel and made his way slowly up to join them.

It wasn't just the Chief who came down to greet them, it was the entire village – or so it seemed to Dan who watched with mounting dismay as a crowd of people emerged from the houses and made their way down the path. Children of all ages, mothers with babies in their arms, older folks assisted by younger ones, and one frail and bent old man wearing a black and yellow woven cape and a cedar headdress who was assisted by two younger men.

This surely had to be the "old man" who had spoken to Walker, but Walker had failed to mention he was also the Chief. Dan had expected to meet him, but he had no idea of the protocol required to greet a Chief properly and he watched helplessly as the entourage approached.

He needn't have worried. The old man made his slow way

down to where Dan stood, a welcoming smile on his face, and held out his hand just as Rose had done. His handshake was surprisingly strong considering the years etched on his face.

"Dan Connor," he said in a thin, rasping voice that reminded Dan of a rusty pump but which, like his hand-shake, was stronger than Dan had expected. "You are welcome here. I thank you for coming. I am told you have some news for us."

Dan didn't so much nod as bow his head. Something about this old man commanded instinctive respect.

"I believe I do, but I'm not sure, and if I am right, then the news is not good," he said.

"Bad news is better than no news," the old man said. "We are thankful for anything you can tell us. Please. Tell us what you know."

Dan reached into his pocket and pulled out the clasp. He placed it on the palm of his hand and held it out.

"We found the body of a man in the water yesterday." He tried to keep his voice low so that only the Chief would hear him. "We don't know his name or where he came from, but he was wearing this on his braid."

The chief looked at it for several moments before he reached out and picked it up. He turned it over and looked at the back for several moments more and when he spoke there was both sadness and a kind of reverence in his voice.

"This is the work of one of our people. His name was William Jules. We called him Billy. He always wore this on his braid. He has been missing now for over two weeks."

He looked at the clasp again. "May I give this to his mother?"

Even though it was technically evidence and should have been turned in, Dan didn't hesitate. He would deal with any repercussions later and the clasp belonged here, with the family.

"Of course – and please tell her how sorry I am."

The old man turned and handed the clasp to Rose. She in turn walked over to two women who were standing together at the front of the crowd. She said something and then placed the clasp into the hands of one of them. The woman looked at it, held it to her chest and closed her eyes.

The old man turned back to Dan and smiled. "Thank you," he said and gestured to the logs where Walker was sitting.

"I might have something else."

Dan held out the bandanna and the cedar bracelet he had found. He had removed the roll of plastic bags, but the bracelet was still tied to the scarf. "Do you know if these also belonged to William Jules?"

A murmer ran through the crowd, and this time the woman to whom Rose had given the clasp stepped forward. She reached out and touched the bracelet with her fingers, bent her head to look at it more closely, then straightened up and looked at Dan with eyes that held an infinite sadness.

"This too belonged to my son," she said. "We called him Billy."

Dan placed both bandanna and bracelet gently into her hands. "I am so sorry," he said.

The woman turned away and the crowd followed her down onto the beach. As they moved forward Dan noticed for the first time that people had brought baskets of food and were placing them on top of the logs and along the side of the float. He could see the unmistakeable color of dried salmon and leaves of black seaweed covered in roe, as well as oyster and mussel shells and stacks of fry bread.

Had he interrupted a ceremony of some kind? That would make this an even more unwanted visit, but surely this could not be for him. There was no way they could have known he was coming, and even if they had, it didn't seem likely they would hold a feast like this in his honor. He must have arrived at the start of some festival or event. He started to protest but caught Walker's warning gaze and thought better of it. To refuse this invitation would be rude.

The Chief confirmed he had made the right decision as he led the way to a seat on the logs.

"I think there may be things you want to ask us, and perhaps things we wish to ask you, but all that can wait. You have come a long way. You must be hungry. Please join us."

The rest of the afternoon passed in a blur. People came up to him, introduced themselves, thanked him and offered him more food than he could possibly eat. Instead of feeling like an unwanted outsider, it seemed he had become a welcomed guest – which didn't make sense considering he was not only an intruder into their community, but also the bearer of bad news. Still, he was not about to question it, and by the time the women shooed the children away so that the adults could talk, Dan was feeling very relaxed.

It was the Chief who asked the first question.

"You said you found Billy in the water. Did he drown?"

Again protocol said that Dan should not answer, but again he decided that he should give them the truth.

"No. He was shot."

His statement was met with a stunned silence.

"Do any of you know where Billy was working?" he asked, looking around the group. "We need to find out who did this."

"Some fish farm," one of the men offered. "He said it was up near Tribune somewhere."

Another man chimed in. "It was the same one Harold was working at. Harold got him the job."

"But you don't know which one?" Dan asked.

The men looked from one to the other, but all shook their heads.

"So you're not opposed to the fish farms?"

Dan still had not established which of the bands supported the industry, or which companies they worked for.

It was the Chief who answered.

"We do not like them, but there are not many jobs around here for my people. In the old days we did not need jobs. We built our houses from trees in the forest. We gathered berries. We ate clams and mussels and oysters. We had the salmon and the herring . . . "

He gestured towards the wharf with its array of now empty baskets. "But the trees have mostly been cut down, and we are not allowed to take those that remain because the government says they do not belong to us. The roads the logging companies built have destroyed many of the places where we picked berries."

He nodded towards the ocean." There are fewer salmon now, and many of the oyster and mussel beds are poisoned. To survive, we must buy from the towns and for that we need money."

Dan nodded his understanding. "So Harold and Billy took jobs on one of the farms. Do others from your band also work there?"

"No. Harold and Billy were the first." The old man looked at the people gathered around them, his face troubled. "I think they might also be the last."

35

The flow of the river and the ebbing tide made the return trip both faster and easier, but it was still late when Dan hauled anchor again. He was pretty sure that by the morning, his shoulders and arms would be too sore to perform even the most basic kata and he felt both physically and emotionally exhausted by the events of the past couple of days.

"So you really think it's important I meet this guy?" he asked Walker. "It's going to be dark by the time we get back to your place even if we don't stop along the way."

"Yeah," Walker answered. "I do."

Dan sighed. "Has he got a name?"

"Arne. I think he used to be a fisherman. He's got an old fish boat tied up in there."

"And he lives in this little cove, which is so small it doesn't show up on the charts and which I can't take this boat into." It wasn't really a question. Walker had already told Dan the location, and he never provided a more detailed explanation.

"Yeah."

"So how do you figure I'm going to be able to get in there

to meet him?" Dan fought to keep his voice neutral. There were times when dealing with Walker's reticence tested the limits of his patience, and this was one of them. "There's nowhere to anchor."

"Tie up to the fish farm."

"There's a fish farm there?" Dan didn't know why he should be surprised. There were farms everywhere in the area.

"Across the channel."

Dan shook his head. "I can't tie up to a fish farm. They don't allow it."

Walker gave him an odd look. "You're a cop. Tell them it's police business."

It was an obvious solution, although not something Dan particularly wanted to do. It felt like a misuse of power, but on the other hand he was too tired to come up with something better.

The security guard appeared before he had tied up the first line.

"Sorry mate. Private property. You can't tie up here." The accent was a laid-back Aussie drawl, but there was nothing laid back about the man who spoke. He had the build and attitude of a bar-room bouncer.

"Police," Dan answered. "I need to check out something up there in the channel and I don't have time to find a place to anchor. I won't be long."

"Police huh. Doesn't look like any police boat I've ever seen." The man was standing very close to the swim grid, effectively blocking Dan from stepping off.

"Guess there's a first time for everything," Dan answered. "How about you call the Port McNeill detachment and check it out. I'm sure you can find the number."

The man stared at him with narrowed eyes. After several seconds he made his decision.

"You got any ID?"

Dan reached into his pocket, pulled out his wallet and badge and held it out.

"Dan Connor huh? You're a detective?"

"Yes, I am, and this is police business."

"Huh." The guard scratched his head and turned to look out over the float. "How long you gonna be?"

Dan breathed a sigh of relief.The question was as good as an invitation and he really didn't want to have to wait for a phone call. It was already almost dark and he wanted this day to end so he could get some sleep."

"An hour or so should do it. Maybe less."

The man stared at him some more before he stepped back and moved away from the grid.

"Guess it's okay. Move her up a bit and you can use those bollards over there." He pointed higher up the float.

"Thanks." Dan stepped onto the float and wrapped the lines to the posts the guard had indicated.

At Walker's insistence they used the canoe again. He figured Arne would be less upset if he saw at least one familiar face in a familiar vessel come into the space he had claimed as his own. If he saw an inflatable with a stranger aboard the man might clam up completely.

"So what's this guy's problem?" Dan asked as he forced his aching muscles to work the paddle.

"Doesn't really have one," Walker answered.

"Okay." Dan's patience was wearing perilously thin. "So you think I should talk to him because . . . ?"

Walker glanced back at him, read the fatigue in Dan's drooping shoulders, and decided to take pity on him.

"You can quit paddling. You're not helping much anyway."

"Gee, thanks." Dan lifted the paddle back into the canoe and flexed his shoulders. "So tell me about this guy."

"Not much to tell. He's a loner, kinda like me I guess. Doesn't like people too much and he sure hates fish farms. Keeps watching that one we just tied up at. I think he might be planning to do something to it."

Dan stared at Walker's back.

"That's it? You think he's going to try and take out a fish farm? Hell, even if he is, he's not going to tell me – and you know I couldn't do anything about it even if he did."

"No, that's not it. We'll be there in a minute and you can figure it out for yourself." Walker dug his paddle into the water and turned the canoe into an opening so narrow as to be almost invisible. He emerged on the other side in a tiny cove with a small beach on the far side where a campfire glimmered.

"Arne?" Walker had stopped paddling and was letting the canoe glide forward. "It's Walker. Okay if I come in?"

A shadow moved in front of the fire and gravel crunched under a foot.

"Walker? That you?"

Walker steered the canoe in closer.

"Yeah. Came by to see if you're okay."

As the canoe slid up onto the shore, the shadow moved closer and Dan could make out the skeletal figure of a man standing immobile a few yards away, apparently frozen in fear.

"I've got a friend with me. His name's Dan."

Dan was too busy taking in the odd sight of what appeared to be a living scarecrow to notice Walker's sudden conversional skills.

"How's your dog?"

It took a second for the words to seep into Dan's brain. A dog? There was no dog anywhere in sight. What the hell was Walker talking about? It seemed no matter where Dan went a dog kept cropping up. It was crazy, but even as he was trying to figure it out he saw the man become animated. Walker's words had obviously got a reaction.

"She's doing better. You want to see her?"

"Sure." As Walker started to lift himself out of the canoe he turned towards Dan and spoke in a quiet voice. "Come with me, but don't say anything."

"Jesus, Walker! What the hell is going on here?" Dan kept his voice to barely a whisper.

"You'll see."

Dan followed Walker's laborious progress up the shore to where a crude shelter had been formed from a couple of branches and an old tarp. There was a pile of tattered blankets and rags underneath, and as they got nearer they could hear a low growl.

Arne gave a high, cackling laugh. "She don't like people any better 'n me!" He reached a hand into the blankets and lifted them up to reveal the form of an animal, although only the black nose and eyes and the bared teeth identified it as something other than a pile of twisted string and rope. "That stuff you gave me sure works good."

"Got some more for you here." Walker held out a small package Dan hadn't noticed him bring. "You want to let Dan take a look? He's real good with animals."

Arne swung around to stare at Dan, his eyes wild. "She's mine. You can't have her!"

"Whoa! No problem." Dan put his hands up and took a step back. "Just wanted to help." What the hell game was Walker playing?

Arne's eyes slid back and forth and finally settled on the pile of rags. "She got hurt bad," he said as he reached out his hand and touched the dog's nose. "But she's going to be okay. That stuff Walker gave me is real good."

He glanced back at Dan as if assessing him for any threat

he might pose. Presumably he was comfortable with what he saw.

"You can look," he said as he took a step aside. "She won't hurt you."

Dan had no idea what he was supposed to do, but it was obvious that for some reason both Arne and Walker wanted him to look at the animal. It had now stopped growling and was watching him approach. He reached his hand down slowly and touched the matted head.

"Check out her shoulder." Walker's voice caught him by surprise. "Arne figures it was a stick, but he might have heard a gunshot just before he pulled her out of the water."

Dan's head swiveled around to look at the man who had finally made it up to the shelter and had taken a seat on one of the rocks beside the fire. "A gunshot?"

"Yeah. Said there were some people over on the farm and they threw the dog off the float and then tried to shoot her."

Dan turned to Arne. "That right? Someone shot at her?"

"Ah, I don't know." Arne's whole body squirmed, arms and legs undulating like the tentacles of an octopus. "Maybe, but it was just a noise. Why would anyone shoot a dog?"

It was a good question and one Dan would very much like to answer. He turned back to the dog and leaned down again, sliding his hand over the head and down towards the shoulders. As the hair slowly parted another thought started edging into his mind and he glanced back at the dark nose and the eyes that were following his every move. Could this be the same dog he had seen on the wharf that day? The dog from the yacht? It would be a hell of a coincidence, but the face was the right shape, and if the hair was cleaned up and groomed . . .

His hand found a rough bandage and he carefully lifted it up to reveal a long, red gash that sliced across the skin. The wound had been deep, but it was showing signs of healing – most likely the result of the alder sap Walker had provided.

"You think she's okay?" Arne asked, his voice eager as he peered around Dan's shoulder.

"It's healing up pretty good," Dan answered, hoping he sounded more knowledgeable than he felt. "She walking around at all?"

"She stood up yesterday!" The man sounded like a child at Christmas.

"That's great. Looks like you're doing fine." He pushed himself to his feet. "You pulled her out of the water? How exactly did she get here?"

Arne's whole demeanor changed and his face took on a look of pure hatred.

"Some people over there," he nodded in the direction of the fish farm, "threw her off the float. I guess she can't swim too good and the current pulled her over this way." He pointed to the rocks that ran out from the entrance. "I grabbed her when she was going by."

"They had her on the fish farm over there?" Dan was having trouble taking it all in. None of it seemed to make sense, but perhaps it was because he was so tired.

"Well not on the farm exactly. She was on a fancy boat. It came there a few times. Guess she did something they didn't like – jumped down onto the float or something. I heard them yelling and then one of them kicked her real hard. I heard her cry out." Arne's face transformed as he looked back down to where the dog lay. "I think the man that kicked her must have told the other man to throw her off." He turned his gaze back to Dan. "They didn't want her any more so she's mine, right?" The child-like tone was back as he pleaded with Dan to agree with him.

Dan looked helplessly at Walker. What could he say? If what he was thinking was right, then the dog belonged to

Melissa, the woman on the yacht, but Arne was so attached to the animal he was never going to give it up willingly. Even if he did, how would they get it into the canoe? He shook his head and then nodded. "Yeah, she's yours."

Arne's smile lit up his face.

36

The security guard was less than happy when Dan and Walker got back well over an hour later.

"Must have been something pretty major to take that long," he snarled as Dan lifted the canoe back onto the grid. "Kinda odd I haven't seen any other boats."

Dan ignored him. He had too much on his mind to spend time soothing ruffled feathers. "Thanks for your help," he said as he freed the lines and let *Dreamspeaker* drift out.

He had slowly dragged more information out from Arne, enough that he could at least piece together a reasonable understanding of the story. It seemed the dog had arrived on what Arne described as "a big, white, fancy-boat" that he had seen at the fish farm on more than one occasion. There had been several men aboard every time, but no woman – at least that Arne ever saw – and they never stayed long. Although he couldn't be sure, Arne said he figured maybe the men got angry at the dog for sticking its nose into a fish-food bale. He thought the bale might have been damaged because it had been left sitting on the float. It had all happened three days ago and the "*fancy-boat*" hadn't been back since.

"Still think it was a waste of your time to talk to him?"

Dan and Walker were anchored in Knight Inlet at the entrance to Walker's cove. The two men were sprawled along the benches on the aft deck drinking a couple of bottles of the Green Tea Claire had left in the fridge as they watched the stars and planets wheel overhead.

"What? Oh no! No. That was … "

Dan couldn't quite figure out just exactly what the whole evening had been, but it certainly hadn't been a waste of time. He had completely forgotten about his tired shoulders and his lack of sleep and now felt more wide-awake than he had in days.

"I just can't put it all together," he said. "That dog he has there has to be the dog I saw over at the marina in McNeill: there can't be two like that around here. And that means the powerboat Arne saw must belong to the yacht – but what the hell would they be doing at that farm?" He shook his head. "The boat Reg said was at the other farm on the day Colin Farnsworth was shot had a dog on it too, so that has to be the same boat."

"Well we know they shot the dog." Walker's laconic voice floated across the deck. "Maybe they shot this other guy too."

"Yes." Dan stared out over the water as he thought about the wound he had seen. "I've been thinking the same thing – and that means they probably shot Billy Jules as well. Too bad we haven't found any of the bullets so we could get a comparison."

He swallowed the last of the tea and stood up. "You want to stay the night? I think I need some beauty sleep before I pay that yacht a visit tomorrow."

As Dan had expected, Walker refused his offer of a bed and after helping him offload his canoe, Dan headed for his bunk. He felt too wired to sleep, but he had to try. He needed to be alert if he was to finally get aboard the *White Lightning*, but after a couple of hours of tossing and turning he gave up and started the engine. He was back at the marina well before the sun came up. The yacht wasn't there.

He was on his second cup of coffee when Markleson called him and told him to come up to the station. The walk up took him longer than it should have, but the brisk morning air refreshed him and the two men spent over an hour discussing everything they had come up with so far.

"You think it's enough to get a search warrant?" Dan asked.

Markleson shook his head. "Not likely. We don't have a single witness who can identify that powerboat as being the one that was at either of the farms, and we have nothing to tie this "dark-haired" guy you keep talking about to anything. Hell, we don't even have his name. No judge is going to issue a warrant on what we've got so far."

"But what about the dog? It has to be the dog from the yacht." Dan ran his hand through his hair and leaned forward in his chair. "Maybe we can use that."

"How? You said yourself the wound is not definitive. It could have been a sharp rock or a floating tree branch and it's already starting to heal. Besides, this guy – Arne? – Arne sounds more than a little weird, so there's no way he's going to be able to testify to anything. He's not even not convinced what he heard was a gunshot." Markleson reached for his lighter. "We've got nothing," he said as he tried to relight his pipe. "It's all speculation."

Dan leaned back and tried to wave away the clouds of smoke being blown his way. "Why the hell do you keep doing that to yourself?"

"Damned if I know," Markleson answered between fits of coughing. "Guess it's because it feels good."

"Well it sure as hell doesn't sound or smell good," Dan answered. "Maybe you should try using those patches."

"Already did. Didn't do a damn thing." Markleson cleared a space on his desk to put the pipe down. "Anyway, I gotta try and work through this pile of bureaucratic good news so you need to get the hell out of here and keep digging. We've still got two other guys missing."

Dan stood up. "Thanks for reminding me."

As he was closing the door he heard Markleson's voice trail after him. "Maureen and Rediger will help you if you need them. Just don't tell them I said so."

After spending so long in the smoke-filled office, the air outside seemed blessedly fresh as Dan looked down the hill to where the Sointula ferry was ploughing its way across the water. Without a warrant, he knew his chances of getting aboard either the yacht or the big powerboat it used as a dinghy were slim. He also knew Markleson was right; without the name of the dark-haired man he had nothing to follow up on. Still, if he was going to be able to do anything he needed to find where the yacht was and he figured his best chance was to contact marinas in the area – although that didn't guarantee anything. A yacht that size could be many miles away.

He checked his watch. He hadn't been to the dojo in a couple of days and the early class would be starting soon. He wanted to talk to Maureen as soon as she got to work and ask her to check the marinas, but he had time to go help with the kids before she arrived. That would make him feel good both mentally and physically and he could check out the blue house again while he was there.

The dojo was a fast ten-minute walk away, just far enough to clear the last of Markleson's smoke from Dan's lungs. As he changed into his judoka, he stared at the house across the street. It looked deserted. The front yard awas unkempt, the driveway empty, and curtains were drawn in every window, yet he had a feeling that there was someone inside. Perhaps it was his imagination but he thought something was going on in there and he very much wanted to know just what that something was.

An hour later, the judo class over, showered and back in his street clothes, Dan crossed the street. He walked up the weedstrewn path, climbed the steps and knocked on the door. There was no answer, but the feeling someone was inside was even stronger than before. He had heard no sound, and he hadn't seen movement, but the house didn't feel empty.

He rapped on the door again, louder this time.

"Police. Anyone home?"

Again there was no answer and Dan stepped back down onto the path and followed it around to the back.

The house was old and built of wood, but it sat on a basement and there were two small non-opening windows cut into the cement. Although they were dirty, smeared with years of neglect, they were presumably put there to let in light and Dan bent down and scratched at the filth in an attempt to peer in. It was useless. He couldn't see anything but his own distorted reflection. It looked as if they had been painted over with black paint.

Frustrated, he returned to the front. This time he banged on the front door with his fist, but still the house remained silent.

37

M aureen was already at her desk when Dan got back to the office.

"Good morning beautiful," he said, as he leaned his elbows on her desk.

She gave him a skeptical look. "Sounds like you're getting ready to ask another favor," she said. "And I don't see any of those big Chinook salmon you promised me."

Dan laughed and threw his hands up in the air. "Right on both counts – but the salmon's coming, I promise. A bottle of Malbec too."

She raised her eyebrows. "Hmm. Guess I'll give you the benefit of the doubt. So what's the favor?"

He gave her the list of marinas. "Could you call these and see if the *White Lightning* is tied up or anchored off any of them?"

She scanned the list. "Doesn't look like too much of challenge. What do you want me to do if I locate it? Where are you going to be?"

"Right here." Dan nodded towards the computers sitting idle on the empty desks in the room behind her. He knew

Markleson had asked the detachment to put as many bodies out on the street as possible to try and find the source of the drugs that were killing local kids. It looked as if they had cooperated.

"I've got to try and figure out which aquaculture company owns which fish farm," he said. "It's going to take me a while."

She nodded. "I'll let you know if I come up with anything."

Dan started to walk away, but thought of something else and turned back.

"You've lived here for a long time haven't you?"

"All my life," she answered. "Same as Mark. We met in high school. Why?"

"You ever know some people called Halvorsen? They used to own a house up there on the hill. I think he was Scandinavian and she was English?"

"Karl and Penny Halvorsen? Sure. My mom used to visit Penny when she first got sick, although that was years ago now. Why?"

"I saw someone at their house a couple of days ago. I think it was a guy who may be linked to these missing men and to the murders as well – but I can't figure out what he was doing there. He's off the *White Lightning*."

"What did he look like?" Maureen asked. "I think their son inherited the house when Karl died and he looked a lot like his dad." She turned back to her desk. "Too bad Victor wasn't like Karl in other ways as well."

Dan started to ask her what she meant but the phone rang and he had to wait while she handled the call.

"It sounds like you don't like Victor Halvorsen very much. Any particular reason?"

She was writing a message so he couldn't see her face, but he could see her head nodding.

"Victor was a bully. Probably the meanest kid in school and not too bright. He was big, built like his dad, and he liked to pick on the little kids. Used to threaten them and steal their lunches. Mark said he took money from them too. I never saw that, but I wouldn't be surprised. I *did* see him beat up a little kid once. Took his bike and threw it in the creek."

"Sounds like a real jerk," Dan said. "Was he blond like his dad?"

"Victor? Yes. Very. His hair was almost white – but I'm not sure whether he still owns the house. I haven't seen him for a while." She glanced at Dan. "Does that sound like the man you saw?"

"No," Dan answered. "That guy has dark hair – but there may have been someone else there as well."

38

Harold Manuel was pretty sure he was going insane. He had spent three days - or maybe it was four, he had lost track of night and day – down in this hellhole and he was tired, hungry and more alone than he had ever been. Bright fluorescent lights glared down twenty-four hours a day and although he had thought about trying to break them, the idea of being left in complete darkness was even worse than trying to sleep in the relentless light. Bare cement walls kept out all sound and he couldn't even hear the footsteps of his jailer the few times he had come down the stairs with a tray of what tasted like canned mush.

The first time he came, Harold had been locked into his cell for more than a day without food or water. He was hungry and thirsty – but he was also angry, angrier than he could ever remember. He heard the click of a lock being turned and saw the wooden door swing open to reveal the man who had brought him there.

The guy was carrying a tray with a plastic bowl and a bottle of water on it. As he reached down to slide the tray through a slot near the bottom of the inner door, Harold tried to grab him through the bars, but he failed. The man simply stepped back out of reach and pulled the tray back with him. No words were spoken, but the smirk on his face as the wooden door closed behind him spoke volumes.

It was at least eight hours later when the same man returned with what looked like the same tray. This time Harold simply sat on the bed and watched him, his eyes dull and resigned. He no longer had the energy to try to escape even if he had wanted to.

The man slid the tray through the slot and nodded towards the table. "You finished bagging those yet?" he asked.

Harold shook his head. He hadn't even started and he didn't want to. He knew what the pills were. Knew what they did. They were one of the reasons his people had put their community off-limits.

"Better get moving." The man was already turning to leave. "You don't get anything more to eat unless there's a whole bunch of them done when I come back." The slamming of the door cut off the last of his words.

Harold did as he was told. He put the pills into the bags. He had tried not to, but in the end his hunger and thirst won out. He worked slowly, hating what he was doing, but knowing he had to at least do enough to ensure he got another meal – although it was hard to call the swill he had been given a meal. To a man who had spent his life eating food fresh from the sea this crud was barely edible, but at least it eased the ache in his belly.

He cried, something he hadn't done since he had been small, the tears streaming down his cheeks as he dropped the pills into the bags and watched them fall to the bottom. As his fingers reached again and again into the container he wondered if these would be the ones that hooked one of his people. If it would be what killed one of his family. Because of him.

When he finally collapsed on the hard mattress, he beat his fists against the cement so hard they bled.

The faint scratching at the window came with a surge of hope, but he no longer trusted his senses and he couldn't be sure he was really hearing anything. The window was too high for him to reach and it was blocked off with a piece of wood. Even if he dragged the bed over and stood on it he wouldn't be able to see anything. The only thing he could do was shout. He knew no sound would penetrate the door to reach whoever might be upstairs, but if he really was hearing someone outside, then there was a chance they would be able to hear him too. He shouted as loudly as he could, but his throat was dry from lack of water and it sounded more like a hoarse croak. It didn't matter anyway. When he stopped to listen again, the scratching had stopped.

39

The house across from the dojo was still owned by Victor Halvorsen. Dan had confirmed that fact as soon as he got back to the office by phoning the municipal office and asking them to check their tax rolls. The city clerk informed him that Victor Halvorsen had inherited the house from his father who had died a little over four years previously. He also said Victor paid his taxes on time and there was no lien against the property. It had never been registered as a rental nor had a complaint of any kind ever been recorded against it.

Another call, this one to the electric company, revealed the house was hooked up to electricity although the monthly usage was low. The monthly electricity bill was always paid on time.

The phone company was next and they confirmed the house had phone service. As with the taxes and the electricity, the account was current. It seemed Victor Halvorsen was both organized and solvent.

A final call to the Motor Licencing Department down in Victoria informed him that Victor Karl Arthur Halvorsen, with an address in Port McNeill, was the owner of a blue Ford 150 pick-up truck.

It had been a blue pick-up truck Dan had seen in the garage and he now had little doubt that Victor Halvorsen not only owned the house, but was also living in it. That information helped, but he also knew Victor Halvorsen had white hair like his parents, so it still didn't explain how the dark-haired man fit in.

Dan enlisted Maureen's help again to help him get information on the owner of the yacht and his captain. A few clicks on the computer and he discovered Donald S. Masterton – the "S" stood for Stephen – owned a company that sold plastic wrapping. The company was based in Vancouver, but the product was purchased from China. According to the website, Masterton Plastics could provide pre-formed wrapping for any number of uses including, Dan suspected as he looked at the various items pictured, fish food bales.

A click on the heading "About Us" identified Masterton as both the founder and the Chief Executive Officer of the company and a photo showed a heavy-set man well into his fifties, with short-cropped graying hair and a thin-lipped mouth. Something about the eyes made Dan think the taut skin stretched across the broad cheekbones and heavy jaw was the result of surgery rather than genetics, but it didn't matter one way or the other. This was not the dark-haired man.

Another entry into the search engine brought up a webpage for the Yacht Captains Association and provided a link to a Captain Daniel Vienza, who had his own website complete with photographs. Those photos showed a man dressed in a white uniform consisting of a tailored jacket with gold buttons and some kind of epaulettes, sharply creased pants, and a white cap. Each one had him standing in the wheelhouse of an obviously large yacht, his hands on the wheel and a confident smile on his face. Not much hair was visible, but what could be seen was at best a grizzled mid-brown as was the impressive beard.

Daniel Vienza appeared to be well into his fifties, and he looked as if he was considerably shorter than average. As his uniform jacket stretched tightly over a round paunch, he was likely heavier than average as well. His contact information gave an address and phone number in the Vancouver suburb of Steveston. This had to be the Captain of the *White Lightning*, but he too was not the dark-haired man who had been both on the yacht and at the house.

Dan tilted his chair back and stretched out his legs. As he did so his hand brushed against his pocket and he felt the roll of plastic bags he'd found out on the rocks stuffed into the cedar bracelet. He had removed it before his trip to Tsa'wit and now he pulled it out and held it in his palm. Why would Billy Jules would have put it there?

"It was a gift from his grandmother," Jules' mother had said, her fingers stroking the finely woven strands. "She was the last traditional cedar bark weaver in our family. She gave this to him when he became Hamat'sa. He never took it off."

But Jules *had* taken it off. He had deliberately and carefully tied it onto a bandana that he had also commonly worn, and stuffed the roll of plastic bags tightly inside. There had to be a reason.

Dan stared at the plastic for ten minutes and then stood up and walked down the hall to Markleson's office.

"Those undercover guys you asked for up here yet?" he asked.

Markleson looked at him over the rim of his coffee cup. "Yeah, but they say it's going to take a while. They need to establish themselves. Get familiar with the territory. Let people get used to them. All they've found so far is some dumb kids and a couple of low-lifes with a few pills for sale. No sign of anyone further up the chain. Why?"

"I want to show them these and see if they look familiar." Dan held out the roll of bags.

Markleson frowned. "Are those bags? Where the hell did you find them?"

"In the water over near Tribune. They were wrapped in a bandana that belonged to Billy Jules. He's the guy those people from the Quarterdeck found on the reef."

"You think Jules was drug related? I don't recall the coroner saying anything about finding any drugs in his system." Markleson shuffled through the piles of papers on his desk in a search for the coroner's report. He didn't find it and reached for his pipe instead.

"Ah hell, I don't know," Dan answered. "I'm just grasping at straws here, trying to figure out why he put these in a bracelet his mother said he never took off. He had to be trying to send a message of some kind."

Markleson poked at the package with the tip of a pen, found the end of the roll and peeled a bag off.

"You thinking they were using these to package drugs?" he asked.

"I'm not really thinking anything. I just remembered you talking about a sudden increase in drug-related deaths, and Maureen saying a kid her son knows had died from a drug overdose, and I wondered if there was any link. I thought if I ran it past the undercover guys maybe they would have some idea about whether these could be the kind of bags the drugs came in."

The two of them stared at the bag for a while. Markleson had laid it flat on the desk in front of him. It was about four inches wide and maybe six inches long.

"Looks pretty big to be used in a drug deal," It was Markleson who broke the silence. "Pretty fancy too. The kids

– hell even the adults – tend to buy one or two pills at a time. Go down an alley, hold their hand out with a twenty or a fifty in it, the seller drops a couple of pills or a twist of powder in their palm and it's all over. I don't think any of them are going to worry about packaging anything in a plastic bag."

Dan nodded. "How about the next step up?"

"What? Oh, you mean whoever's getting the pills to the local dealers? Yeah, maybe. Our guys haven't found any trail to those yet, but that's what they're looking for. Follow it up the line to whoever's bringing it in and find the main distributor."

The two of them looked at the bag some more and then Dan reached out and picked up the roll again.

"Is there any way you can set up a meeting between me and one of the undercover guys?"

Markleson tipped his head in a gesture that said neither "Yes" nor "No."

"I can ask, but I don't know if they'll want to do it. It might be too much of a risk. I can't talk to them directly anyway. I'll have to go through Victoria and it might take time."

Dan stood. "Well, give it a try. Right now it's the only thing I can think of."

40

Elsie was standing outside in the parking lot smoking a cigarette when Dan stopped by the Haida-Way for lunch.

"Taking a break before the rush?" he asked as as he headed towards the door.

She nodded and blew out a cloud of smoke. "Yeah. It's already crazy in there. I've been here since six this morning and it hasn't slowed down any since then."

Dan stopped as a thought occurred to him.

"Does Victor Halvorsen ever come here to eat?"

Elsie ground her cigarette out on the pavement. "That asshole?" She turned towards the entrance. ""S'cuse my French. Yeah, once in a while." She nodded towards the dining room. "You coming in? He's in there now if you want to talk to him."

They entered the restaurant together and she nodded towards a table. "That's him over there by the window. Glad he's not in my section. Miserable bastard's too cheap to tip."

She disappeared into the kitchen and Dan looked across the room to where an overweight man wearing a blue ballcap and a T-shirt sat hunched over a half-finished meal. The T-shirt might once have been white, but was now a dirty gray and the ballcap was frayed along the brim. Even though the restaurant was rapidly filling up, the tables next to Victor Halvorsen were all empty.

Dan threaded his way through the crowd and pulled out an empty chair.

"Victor Halvorsen?" he asked.

The man glared at him from under heavy brows. "Who the hell are you?"

The high-pitched voice combined with the moon face and the heavily muscled chest and arms pointed to Victor being into some serious steroids and bodybuilding.

"Dan Connor," Dan pulled out his wallet and laid it on the table. "I need to ask you a couple of questions."

Halvorsen's eyes narrowed as he looked at the police credentials. "You're a cop? What the hell you hassling me for? Go get your own goddamn table."

"You own a house here Vic?" Dan ignored the questions. "Up there on Alder Street?"

"None of your goddamn business if I got a house! Who cares? Owning a fuckin' house ain't illegal."

"How about a blue pick-up truck?"

"Go to hell."

"How about a boat trailer?"

"I got nothin' to say to you."

Dan sighed and leaned back in his chair. "That's too bad, Victor. I was hoping we could have a nice chat over coffee, but if you would rather we go over to the station, we can talk there instead. It's your choice."

"Yeah? Well I got my rights." Halvorsen went back to eating, mumbling between mouthfuls of the huge burger and fries crowding his plate. "You gotta charge me with something before you take me anywhere, and I ain't done nothing wrong so what are you gonna charge me with, huh?"

He straightened up, raised his voice and lifted his chin to indicate he wanted everyone in the restaurant to hear what he was saying. "I got witnesses too, and they all know me. You want them to see you try and drag me out?"

Dan smiled and put his elbows on the table as he leaned forward and put his face close to Victor's. "I really don't care whether they see me or not Vic. It might upset a few of these good folks, but I doubt it. I think most of them would be pretty happy about it. You don't seem to have a lot of friends – at least not in here."

"I got plenty of friends!" Halvorsen was looking down at his plate again, sawing frantically at his burger, his knife clutched tightly in his fist as it screeched against the plate.

"Really? That include the guy that was there at the house with you a couple of days ago? Wears his hair in a ponytail?"

It was a guess. Dan had no idea whether Halvorsen had been in the house at the time or not, but knew the guess had worked when he saw a fine sheen of sweat appear on Halvorsen's forehead.

"What guy? I don't know no guy wears a ponytail!"

"Sure you do Victor. Dark hair? Slim? Looked like you two were putting your boat back in the garage."

Halvorsen's face changed, took on a furtive look, and he answered with a forced laugh. "That guy? He ain't my friend. He was just some guy I picked up when I was out fishing."

"Fishing?" Dan could see a damp stain spreading across the gray t-shirt. "Pretty early in the morning to be back from a fishing trip wasn't it? Where'd you go?"

The knife was clattering now, and Halvorsen put it down. "Ahh, I just went out to the reef, but nothin' was biting so I came back in." He words came in fast, bursts.

"That's too bad." Dan leaned back. "Lot of salmon out there. You'd think the reef would've been a good spot."

"Yeah." Halvorsen glanced at him nervously, trying to see if he was serious. "Usually catch a bunch out there. Must've been an off day or something."

Dan nodded. Halvorsen was scared. He could smell it. Fear was oozing out of the man's pores, but fear of what? He hadn't been nervous until Dan had started asking about his friend.

Dan leaned forward again and kept his voice casual. "So you just found this guy out on the reef?"

"What?"

Halvorsen had let his guard down enough that Dan's question caught him by surprise.

"Oh no! No. Hell, that would be crazy man. He wasn't on the reef. No way. He – ahh – he was on the wharf. Down there by the ramp."

"On the ramp? Was this when you went out? Must have been pretty dark."

Dan watched Halvorsen closely. He didn't want to ease off, but the man looked as if he was about to have a heart attack. His face was flushed a bright red and veins pulsed at his temples and throat. Even his eyes were unnaturally bright.

"Yeah. No." Halvorsen's fists were clenching and unclenching as he appeared to search for the words to make his tormentor leave him alone. "He was there when I came back. Wanted a ride so I gave him one, that's all." His eyes found Dan's, almost pleading with him to believe what he was saying. "No harm in that, right?"

Dan shook his head. "No harm at all." He smiled. "So where was he going?"

Halvorsen looked at him, a look of utter frustration on his

face. His mouth moved, but no words came out. Instead he rammed his chair back and headed towards the door.

He was moving so fast Dan barely heard what he said as he pushed his way past the now-crowded tables.

"Eric said you were going to be trouble."

Dan watched him go. Eric. It wasn't much, but it was the start he had been hoping for and he planned on making sure Eric was right: he was going to be trouble. He smiled and beckoned to the waitress for the bill.

41

W *hite Lightning* was tied up in Sullivan Bay. Dan got the news when he returned to the office, along with the information that the owner had flown out two days before and was not expected back for several days more.

"I left a message with their office to let us know when he got back and to ask him call us. Told them it was important." Maureen had her finger poised over a flashing phone console. "And Al Rediger wants to talk to you." She pressed a button and spoke into her headset, leaving Dan to go in search of whatever information Rediger had for him. He found the man surrounded by boxes and sorting through a stack of folders.

"Maureen said you've got something for me."

Dan watched Rediger deftly spin a sheet of paper through the air to land inside one of the boxes.

"You could do pretty well in Vegas as a dealer," he said,

He had been thinking of a card dealer when he said it, but saying the words out loud took him in another direction.

"Do you have a list of our known local drug pushers? I'm talking about the small timers, not the big boys."

Rediger looked at him. "If you mean the punks that sell on the street, I don't have a list, but I can give you a few names. Might not help you much unless you happen to know them. Most of them are either bums or kids and they don't have a record – yet. At least not for anything serious." He reached for another folder and opened it. "Markleson put you on that drug business too?"

Dan shook his head. "No. This is still with those missing men, but I think the cases might be linked somehow." He frowned, and then asked, "You got anyone called Eric on your list? I don't know his last name."

Rediger thought about it for a minute then shook his head. "Nope. No Eric."

"How about Victor Halvorsen?"

"Halvorsen? He's an asshole, but I've never heard anything about him being involved in drugs – although I can't say it would surprise me. We've had him in here more than a few times for fighting, and we've had several complaints about him threatening people, but nothing ever stuck. Why? You hear something?"

"No. At least nothing I can really put my finger on, but I think he's involved in something a little more serious than fighting. Only problem is I don't know what."

"Well, putting him away would make a lot of people happy." Rediger reached under the stack of files and pulled out the book he used to record all phone calls from the public. "You got a call from some woman at the MacKay Barge Company up there in Hardy. She said to tell you Reuben Crosbie is back in town. Said he'll be taking the barge out tomorrow."

Dan squeezed himself into the only remaining car and drove to the office of the barge company. To be able to talk to

Crosbie was a bonus. He had been thinking that the barge captain might have disappeared the same way as his crewmember Paulie Benko had.

The woman behind the desk looked exactly the way she had sounded on the phone: round, matronly and outgoing. If she wasn't somebody's mother Dan thought she certainly should have been. Dan introduced himself and asked her if she knew where he could find Crosbie. He had stopped at Crosbie's house on the way in, but there had been no one at home.

"He's probably down at the Quarterdeck. It's where he keeps his boat when he's in town so he spends a lot of time there.." She laughed. "I don't know why he doesn't sell that house of his. He's never there. I think he sleeps on his boat!"

Dan thanked her and started to leave, but stopped as another idea crossed his mind. "I don't suppose you know what kind of boat he's got do you?"

She laughed again. "Everyone knows what kind of boat Reuben has. It's his baby. My goodness, it's all he talks about – that and fishing!" She pointed to a photograph hanging on the wall. "That's him there."

The photograph showed a middle-aged man wearing a heavy-knit sweater and jeans standing on the side deck of a wooden trawler."

"He says it's a Monk 36 if that means anything to you. Can't say it does to me, but then I'm not really a boat person," the woman said. "I know it was built back in 1941 because it has a brass plaque up in the wheelhouse – I saw it when he invited Mark and me to go out with him one day – and he's restored it himself. Done a really nice job if I do say so myself. All that lovely woodwork ... "

Dan interrupted her chatter. "So it's a wooden boat?"

"Oh my goodness yes! He spends hours sanding and

varnishing. You'll see for yourself when you go over there. It's
... "

"Thanks for your help." Dan cut her off in mid-sentence.
She reminded him of his mother and he didn't like doing it,
but he knew if he didn't he would be there for at least
another half-hour of chatter.

The Quarterdeck marina was easy to find and it seemed
everybody knew Reuben Crosbie and his boat. The first
person Dan talked to pointed it out right away.

"Nicest looking boat we've got here."

It *was* nice. White-painted hull, oiled teak deck and
varnished wood trim. It was a boat Dan would have been
proud to own although there was no way he would want to
do all the work required to maintain it. Even the bronze
ship's bell gleamed.

Crosbie appeared within a few seconds of Dan knocking
on the hull.

"Help you?" he asked.

He was larger than he had looked in the photo, with
wide, athletic shoulders and a heavy chest.

"Nice looking boat," Dan said as he held out his credentials. "I've got an old Frostad but she doesn't look nearly as
good as this."

"Takes a lot of work," Crosbie answered as he waved Dan
aboard. "So what can I help you with?"

"You were driving the barge when Colin Farnsworth went
overboard?"

Crosbie nodded his head. "Yeah. One of the worst damn
days of my life. I still can't figure it out – hell, we weren't even
using the crane right then and Colin was one of the fittest
and most agile guys I ever had working with me." He
gestured to the cabin. "You like something to drink? I don't
keep any booze aboard but there's plenty of other stuff."

"No thanks. So what do you think happened?"

"Hell, I don't know. Like I said, they'd finished unloading the palette, although the hook was still hanging out there. All I can think of is somehow he stepped back into it and hit his head. It happened so fast I don't think anyone saw it."

"Was Paulie Benko out there with him?"

"Paulie? Yeah, he was there. Marge says he's done a runner. She tell you that?"

Dan nodded. "Seems like it. So was there anyone else around when it happened?"

"Yeah, there were three guys in some fancy powerboat. Looked like a SeaRay or a Maxim. Probably a SeaRay. I think they call them Sports Coupes or something. It was tied up right in front of me beside the hoppers."

Dan pulled his camera out of his pocket and held it out. "This look like the same one?"

Crosbie scanned quickly through the photos. "Looks like it, but I couldn't swear to it. You don't see a lot of them up here though, so if you took these shots here, it probably is."

"So were any of the men who were on that boat near Colin when he fell?"

Crosbie scratched his head. "I guess so. I was checking the controls so I didn't actually see it happen. Heard the yelling and when I looked he was already gone and everyone was milling around looking down where he fell."

The scene he was painting didn't quite fit the scenario Dan had pictured from the other information he had received.

"So was everybody on the float or on the barge? I was told Farnsworth fell off the barge."

"Probably a little of both," Crosbie answered. "You ever seen one of the big barges up close? There's metal rungs go down the side at both ends. Paulie said Colin had started to climb back up – had his foot on a rung anyway – and then there was a bang and next thing you know he was gone. The hook from the crane was hanging right there so I figure he must have hit it with his head and the bang was the hook hitting the side of the barge."

It was certainly plausible, Dan thought, and it would explain why no one had mentioned a gunshot. Under the circumstances it would have been the last thing anyone would have thought of.

"You know what the guys in the powerboat were doing there?"

Crosbie shrugged. "I asked Reg – he's the foreman out there – when I first arrived. Had to ask him to check if we had enough room behind it to get onto the float. He said it was some guys the office had sent out. Something to do with the food totes. I think one of them might have been damaged because it hadn't been put into the hoppers like they usually do."

There was nothing else Crosbie could add and with a couple more stops still to make, Dan took his leave. He was halfway down on the float when another thought came to him and he went back and found Crosbie still out in the cockpit bent over a locker. He stood up at the sound of Dan's voice.

"You forget something?" he asked.

"Yeah, maybe. I was wondering where those guys were when you first arrived."

"The guys on the powerboat? I think they were all on the float standing near the tote. It was right across from where they were tied."

"That the tote you said was damaged?"

"Well, I don't know that for sure, but I can't think why else they would leave it there."

It was a question Dan was going to be sure to ask Reg Johnson, but right now he had one more for Crosbie.

"Did Farnsworth go over to that tote at any time?"

For the first time, Crosbie looked confused. "I don't know. I can't say I actually remember him doing it, but he probably did. I mean it was right there and Colin was always checking things out, always trying to make sure things were okay. He might have figured he could help pick it up or move it while he was waiting for our stuff to come down. That's the way Colin was. He was a really good guy, always trying to help out."

"Okay, thanks," Dan said. He shook Crosbie's hand and climbed back down on the float. It had taken him a long time, and he still couldn't be sure, but he thought being a good guy might just have been what got Farnsworth killed.

42

Three-thirty in the afternoon and many miles still to go. Dan stopped by the police station to return the car and then went into the Haida-Way to get a cup of coffee and a piece of their home-made lemon pie. The pie was so good he briefly thought about buying a whole one to take back to the boat, but decided against it. He wasn't going to have a chance to eat it for a while. After he had spoken to Sensei Ishikawa he was going to head over to Sullivan Bay and that meant using the inflatable rather than *Dreamspeaker*. He needed speed, not comfort.

He knew the Sensei didn't have a class until later in the afternoon after the schools got out and Dan didn't want to disturb him before then so he lingered over the coffee, but he still arrived early. Both the blue house and the dojo were quiet when he got there and to kill some time, he walked around the block, checking out the houses that bracketed or backed onto Halvorsen's. Most were older homes, probably built back in the forties or fifties when logging was a booming industry, and mature hedges and gardens provided a solid barrier between them. It was unlikely anyone living in them would be aware of what was happening in a house beside or behind them.

By the time he got back to the dojo the doors were open and Dan went in, removed his shoes and bowed to the tiny man.

"I did not expect you here today." Sensei Ishikawa returned the bow then continued to check the judoki lining the shelves. "You have solved the case you were working on?"

"I wish I could say yes, but I'm afraid not," Dan answered. He picked up a small tunic and searched for a matching pair of pants. "In fact I'm working on it now. I am here to ask a favor Sensei. I can't stay."

Ishikawa was silent for a moment, and then turned to look at Dan. "This favor is something to do with your case?"

Dan nodded. "Yes."

There was no hesitation. The Sensei indicated his agreement with a slight bow. "Then I will be happy to do it. What is it you need?"

"We think that the people in the house across the street are somehow involved. We need to talk to them, but no one answers the door."

"You are talking about the son of Mr. Halvorsen?"

"No, although he's probably part of it. There is another man we are particularly interested in. I was hoping you might call me if you see him."

"That is all? It is simple! I will be happy to do this."

Dan bowed. "Thank you, Sensei."

He gave Ishikawa a description of the man he now believed was called Eric and a card with the phone number of the detachment and turned to go. "Please be careful Sensei. Don't be too obvious. We think this man is dangerous. He may have shot two people."

THE SEAS WERE RELATIVELY CALM as Dan steered the rigid-hulled inflatable towards Sullivan Bay, but even so the jolting as the boat bounced across the water jarred his spine. Braced against the console, Dan could only hope no wind developed before he got back to McNeill. If it did, it would make what was already going to be a difficult trip much more dangerous.

He had seen the white launch – the SeaRay or whatever it was - when he was leaving the Quarterdeck marina after talking to Reuben Crosbie. It had come in around the outer floats of the neighboring commercial fisherman's marina and tied up to the fuel dock. Dan had been sitting in his car writing up notes of his interview and the fuel shed blocked his view of whoever was in the boat's cockpit, but the shape had been unmistakeable. He put his notebook down and leaned back in the seat. Moving or leaving would draw attention to his presence there and he certainly didn't want to put Reuben Crosbie at risk.

It took maybe twenty minutes to fuel the boat. When it was done, Dan watched the man working the dock roll the fuel hose back up and release the forward line and the SeaRay drifted over to the visitor's float. Two men stepped out and he recognized them instantly: Halvorsen and his buddy Eric. They split up at the head of the ramp with Halvorsen going over to the marina office while Eric headed straight towards the parking lot.

The car wasn't big enough for Dan to slide down in his seat so all he could do was slide down low, bend his head down over his notepad and hope he wouldn't be noticed. It worked. Eric headed straight for a blue pick-up truck parked one row over and climbed into the passenger seat. Halvorsen joined him a few minutes later and the truck headed out.

Now, as the inflatable took a particularly hard bounce off the top of a wave, Dan was hoping the two men were still out on the road somewhere. If he could speak to any of the crew on the yacht without Eric being around, maybe he could finally learn who the man was.

WHITE LIGHTNING WAS BACK in the same berth it had been when he and Clare had visited the marina. As Dan once again walked across the empty deck to the open doors he could hear voices speaking and recognized the sound of a television. Someone was watching the news.

He rapped on the glass and two faces turned towards him. One was Captain Daniel Vienza, the man he had seen wearing the uniform on the Yacht Captain's website. The other was much younger and was dressed in navy blue shorts and a white polo shirt with *White Lightning* embroidered on the pocket. Vienza reached for a remote and turned down the sound while the younger man approached the door.

"Sorry," he said as he rested his hand on the door. "This is a private yacht. You're not allowed to be here. You're going to have to leave."

"I'm looking for Eric," Dan answered, ignoring the direction. "He said to meet him here. Is he around?"

The man relaxed a little and shook his head. "Sorry. He went out a while back. I don't know when he'll be back. You want to leave a message?"

Dan shook his head. "I really need to talk to him. I don't suppose you know how I can contact him do you?"

"Not me. The Captain might though." He turned to Daniel Vienza. "You got a number for Eric? This guy's a friend of his."

Something about the way he said the words made Dan think that Eric was not someone either man held in high esteem.

Vienza shifted on the leather settee and pulled a wallet

out of his pocket. He extracted a business card and held it out. "Here you go. Not likely I'm ever going to need it."

Dan glanced at it and slid it into his pocket. "Thanks. Sorry to bother you."

He started to turn away, then stopped. "By the way, did Melissa ever get her dog back?"

The young man rolled his eyes. "That's something we don't talk about, at least not when Mr. Masterton's aboard. Biggest fireworks display I've ever seen. Even your buddy Eric almost got caught in the fallout."

Dan waited until he was back in the inflatable to look at the card. Eric LaSalle. Import and Export. Richmond. B.C.

43

The days were already starting to shorten and it was well after dark when Dan got back to *Dreamspeaker*, but in spite of the long hours he had been putting in, he didn't feel like sleeping. There was too much adrenaline pumping in his veins. He was close. He could feel it.

He switched on the computer and plugged LaSalle's name into the search engine, found the website for the business, but no photo of the Lasalle himself. Not that it mattered. Dan already knew what the man looked like.

He looked at the card again. Import – Export. That could explain the connection between LaSalle and Masterton. LaSalle's company might bring in the plastic products Masterton sold and if the two men were business associates rather than friends, it might mean Masterton was clean – although not necessarily. There were still questions to be answered, but tomorrow, when Maureen and Rediger were back in the office, he would get them to help him fill in a few more of the gaps.

He took a beer out of the fridge, and sprawled out on the settee. Added a little Charlie Parker to mellow out his synapses and closed his eyes. Maybe if he thought about Claire...

He woke to the sound of someone banging on the hull. Light was streaming through the windows and a quick glance at his watch told him he had slept for almost six hours. He stood up and ran his hands through his hair. If he didn't get a haircut soon he would have to start wearing it in a ponytail like Eric. The thought galvanized him into alertness. Today just might be the day he closed the case.

"Coming," he yelled as he slid open the doors to the aft deck and walked over to the railing. Willie Pete was standing out on the float.

"Willie?" Dan couldn't remember Willie ever visiting him before. "Everything okay? You want to come aboard? I'll put on a pot of coffee."

Willie hesitated for a minute, and then smiled. He had long ago lost all his front teeth and the smile showed wizened gums. "Okay. Coffee sounds real good."

In spite of his age, Willie was remarkably nimble and it took only seconds for him to scramble onto the stern grid and climb the ladder onto the deck.

He cackled as he peered into the cabin through the open door. "Pretty fancy in there! I better stay out here. Might dirty it up."

Dan laughed. "Come on inside Willie. It's more comfortable in here."

Willie ignored the invitation and settled onto one of the bench seats on the deck. Except for the difference in age Willie Pete and Walker had a lot in common Dan thought as he poured the coffee.

He carried the cups outside, handed one to Willie, and sat down beside him.

"Anything I can help you with Willie?"

"Nope. Not a damn thing," Willie answered. "But I've got something for you."

Dan raised his eyebrows in a query. Willie often gave him a crab or a fish, but that was usually later in the day. This morning the man had nothing in his hands.

"Had a visitor last night," Willie said, obviously pleased by the reaction he was getting. "Never seen him before, but he knew who I was. Said he come to see you, but you weren't here."

"Did he tell you his name?" Dan couldn't think of anyone who was likely to come down to the float and give Willie Pete something to pass on to him.

"Nope. Kinda scruffy looking guy." Willie looked down at his own clothing and cackled again. "Maybe even scruffier than me! Tall. Skinny. Long hair. Looked like he hadn't washed it in a while."

Dan frowned. There was no one he knew who would fit that description. "Native? White?"

"White guy," Willie said. "Lot younger than me. Maybe even younger than you, but it was kinda hard to tell."

"So what did he give you?"

"He gave me this." Willie slid a grimy hand inside the old sweater he was wearing and pulled out an envelope. "Said he'd heard I was a friend of yours. Said you'd know who it was from."

The envelope looked almost as tattered as Willie who was watching Dan eagerly, waiting for him to open it. As he looked at it Dan suddenly had a hunch about what it contained, and who the man had been.

"Oh yeah, I know who it was. It's just an address I needed. Thanks for bringing it over." Dan laid it down on the bench beside him and moved the conversation in a different direction. "Listen, I don't suppose you know anyone who could sell me a couple of big Chinook salmon do you? I promised a friend I would get some."

"Might do. Might do," Willie said. "Gonna have to ask around though. You gonna be here tonight?"

The fishing regulations for aboriginals were different then those for non-natives and while they applied only to a food fishery, Dan knew that if you had friends within that community it was possible to find someone willing to sell any fish they deemed extra to their needs.

"Should be," Dan answered. "Let me know the price."

Willie gave another of his cackles and stood up. "Sure will. Thanks for the coffee."

"No problem. Any time."

DAN WAITED until Willie had disappeared back up the dock before he opened the envelope. If it was what he thought it was he didn't want Willie asking questions about it, and he certainly didn't want the 'kelp vine" to get wind of it.

44

Dan opened the envelope and removed a plastic bag with a piece of paper enclosed. The bag looked exactly like the one he had given Markleson and the message, written in pencil, said, "Got this from a mutual friend. It looks right."

The information didn't come as a surprise, but Dan was pleased to get confirmation of his suspicions. Drugs. That was the message Billy Jules had been trying to send when he stuffed those bags into his bracelet. Somehow, somewhere, Jules – and probably Harold Manuel as well– had run across the path of a drug dealer. Probably someone well up the chain because it hadn't been just a single bag, it had been a whole roll.

But why had Billy been killed? He had to have known his life was in danger before he tied the bags into the bandanna. Certainly before he took off the cedar bracelet that was so important to him. Had he been involved with his killer in some way and tried to cheat him? From what Dan had learned of Billy, it didn't seem likely. It seemed more probable he had seen something he shouldn't have and tried to run. Either way, Dan still needed to figure out where he had gotten hold of that roll of plastic bags.

He poured the last of the coffee into his cup and thought about what he should do next. *White Lightning* was sitting at the dock in Sullivan Bay and with Masterton away she would probably be there for a few more days. Not much he could do there but wait. The SeaRay he had seen at the Quarterdeck could be anywhere by now and even if he could track it down again it was unlikely he could get aboard it without a warrant. There probably wouldn't be anything incriminating on it anyway. They'd have to be pretty stupid to use something that obvious to carry or store drugs and he didn't think Eric was stupid- although he wasn't so sure about Halvorsen. That left the house and the fish farm – and Sensei Ishiwaka was keeping an eye on the house.

Dan washed up the cups, locked his boat, jogged up the hill to the detachment and asked Rediger for a vehicle.

"How long you gonna need it for?" Rediger asked.

"I'm not sure. Three or four hours maybe. Why?"

"Figured you'd want the SUV, but Richardson has it booked for this afternoon." Rediger filled in a couple of squares on the crossword he was working on.

"I promise I'll have it back in plenty of time." Dan grinned and lowered his voice. "And if I don't you can tell him it was an emergency and give him one of the cars."

Rediger looked up from the paper. "Yeah, right. That should make him happy."

Richardson's nickname was Streak. He was built like a fence pole, tall and skinny. He weighed about half what Dan weighed, but was four or five inches taller and he claimed the only way he could drive one of the compact cars was to either to use his knees on the pedals or glue them to his ears.

Dan laughed and lifted the keys to the SUV off the board. "Thanks Al. I'll be in Hardy if anyone needs me."

He had printed off the list of farms in the area, but it wasn't enough. He needed to know which company owned them. Maureen was certainly capable of finding out, but she was busy and it would take her more time than Dan could afford.

THE PARKING LOT behind the barge company office was almost full when he pulled in, but the only person in the office was Marge, the woman he had spoken to before. She looked up as the door opened and smiled a welcome.

"Detective Connor! How nice to see you again. Did you manage to talk to Reuben? He's working today, but I think he just left."

"Actually I came to see you," Dan said, pulling a chair over to the desk. "Do you think you could give me a couple of minutes of your time?"

"Well of course!" She beamed her matronly smile. "What can I help you with?"

Twenty minutes later he had not only a list of all the companies, but also the names of the people he needed to speak to in the three he was most interested in. They were the ones with farms in the Tribune Channel area, including the one Arne was watching.

Using Marge's name made things much easier. Charlene, a large woman with bright red hair who worked behind the reception desk at the first office Dan visited gave him a very cool reception when he first arrived, but relaxed as soon as she heard he had been referred by her counterpart at the barge company.

"Marge? How's she doing? I haven't had a chance to talk to her for a while."

"She's fine," Dan answered. "She said you could probably

help me get some information about someone who was working on a fish farm. His name's William Jules."

Charlene frowned. "Jules is a pretty common name in the Native community around here. Is he Native?"

Dan noted her use of the present tense and nodded. "He is."

"Well he wouldn't be with us then," Charlene replied. "The Native people around here don't like us, and they won't work for us. Are you sure he works on a fish farm?"

"That's what I was told," Dan said.

"Well the only place I can think of where you might find him is Knudsen's. They have quite a few Native workers. They're a family-owned company, so they're more familiar with the local Native people, and they're pretty small. They only have a couple of farms out there by Tribune. Their office just is down the road. You could check there."

Dan thanked her, climbed back in the SUV and drove three blocks to where a sign announced the location of Knudsen Aquaculture Enterprises. A large Quonset building served as a warehouse, and the office was at one end. Several men were using a forklift to offload plastic-wrapped totes of fish food from a large flatdeck truck that was parked in front of the open doors. Dan watched fthem for a few minutes before going in.

Two people were working behind the desk, a young woman with white-blonde hair, and an older man wearing jeans and a sweater. Both were looking at something on a computer screen. The man turned his head as Dan approached.

"Help you with something?"

"I'm looking for Sonya," Dan said, checking the name on the list he had been given. "Marge down at the barge company said I could find her here."

"I'm Sonya." The young woman peered up short-sightedly at him.

"Hi Sonya." Dan ignored the man, who was looking at him impatiently. "I'm looking for information about a man called William Jules. I think he might have worked for you."

The man straightened up slowly. "And you would be ...?'

"Dan Connor." Dan took out his ID and held it out for the man to see. "And you?"

The man peered at the ID and then took a close look at Dan's face. "Matti Knudsen. I manage the office." He pointed towards the young woman. "This is my daughter, Sonya. So you're looking for Billy Jules?"

Like Charlene in the previous office, he spoke in the present tense and again, Dan didn't correct him.

"I am. Do you know happen to know where I could find him?"

"Wish I did," Knudsen replied. "I'm looking for him too. He hasn't shown up for work for over a week and we need everybody we can get right now. Got nearly a million fish ready to move."

"Sounds like a pretty major operation." Neither Knudsen nor his daughter had shown any signs of nervousness or discomfort and they both seemed unaware of Jule's death. "How about Harold Manuel or Jimmy Fulton?"

Knudsen's laugh didn't sound as if he found anything particularly funny in the question. "You a baseball fan?" he asked.

"What?" The sudden change of topic was confusing.

"I was going to say you're batting zero, but maybe you've struck out would be better. Doesn't matter anyway. If you're not a fan you probably wouldn't get it either way. Manuel's another one that's gone AWOL He hasn't shown up either. A lot of people round here will tell you it's one of the hazards of hiring Native workers, but up to now I've had no problems.

Both of them have been real good workers and very reliable so this is an unpleasant surprise."

"How about Fulton?"

"Can't say that name rings any bells." Knudsen turned to his daughter. "You got a Jimmy Fulton listed in there?" He turned back to Dan. "Sonya does the payroll. She's got the names of everybody that ever worked for us in that machine."

Sonya swung her chair back around and pressed a few keys on the keyboard. The screen changed color and lines of information started to scroll down. After a couple of minutes she started the whole process again and then spoke over her shoulder to the two waiting men. "No one by that name, or by James or John Fulton either."

"Okay. Thanks." Dan was becoming more and more convinced that Jimmy Fulton was not part of the same investigation, and once he had figured out what had happened to Jules and Manuel, he was going to start looking in a very different direction.

"You seem pretty interested in these guys. Have they done something we should know about?" There was genuine concern in Knudsen's voice although it was probably more directed at the security of the business than anything personal.

"Not that I know of," Dan answered. "They were both reported missing by their families a few days ago."

"Been more than a few days for Jules, at least as far as we're concerned," Knudsen said. "More like a couple of weeks. You think they're together?"

Dan looked at him. "I hope not. We found Jules' body out on Booker Reef a few days ago. He'd been shot."

His statement was greeted by a stunned silence.

45

A framed navigational chart took up most of the wall behind Sonya's desk. It had been enlarged to show only the Broughtons, and colored squares indicated the location of the various fish farms. Knudsen and his daughter watched silently as Dan moved around the counter to look at it more closely.

"Can you show me exactly where the farm Jules and Manual were on is located?" he asked.

"Sure!" Dan's question snapped Matti Knudsen back to reality. "We've only got three. There are two up here off North Broughton, near Sullivan Bay." He indicated two small orange squares before running his finger down until it was pointing to a spot near Minstrel Island. "The other one's down here in Tribune. That's where they were."

Dan leaned over and studied the chart more closely. It showed very familiar territory. He had been up and down every one of the channels marked on it many times and he knew exactly which farm Knudsen was pointing at. It was the same one he and Walker had tied up to the night they had gone to visit Arne.

He stepped back, picturing the other farm he had visited, where Reg Johnson had told him about the big white Sea-Ray.

"You hear about Colin Farnsworth?" he asked.

"The kid that had the accident on the barge? Yeah. That was terrible. Reuben said he was a really nice kid." Knudsen shook his head.

"You know Reuben?" For some reason the information surprised Dan, although it shouldn't have. Port Hardy was a small town and it made sense that people who worked in the same industry would all know each other.

"Sure. Known him most of my life, and we use those barges all the time."

"I talked to him yesterday. He said he thought there was a damaged tote of fish food sitting on the float. That happen often?"

"Once is too damn often," Knudsen grimaced. "That stuff costs a lot of money, and we've got to bring it in from Vancouver."

"Has it happened to you?"

"Yeah. Twice."

"Recently?" An idea was forming in Dan's mind. It was linked to the odor of dead fish he had experienced at Reg Johnson's farm.

"Yeah. Why?"

"Just wondering. Does the food have a strong smell?"

Knudsen laughed. "You could say that. It's mostly made from fish oil and fish meal, but the new pellets aren't as bad as they used to be. I can get you a sample if you want."

Dan shook his head and smiled. "I'll pass thanks."

"Good choice." Knudsen laughed again and nodded. "Well I'm really sorry to hear about Billy Jules. He was a good man. I hope you catch the guy that did it." He glanced towards a door on the other side of the room. "Anything else I can help you with? I've got a couple of calls I need to make."

"I don't want to keep you, but there is one more thing," Dan answered. "I was wondering of you've had any visitors out at that farm recently?" Dan watched Knudsen closely for any sign of a reaction to the question, but the man seemed barely interested.

"You mean tours? Nah. Some of the big companies offer them, but we don't have the staff."

"How about investors or business partners? Maybe people from some of the companies you deal with from who want to check things out?"

Knudsen shook his head. "This is a family business, just me and two of my brothers. We don't have any investors or business partners. Someone from one of the companies might have been up, but you would have to ask Bob Steiger about that. He's in charge of operations. I'm just the office guy."

"Steiger around?"

"Should be. Probably out on the dock or in the warehouse."

"Mind if I talk to him?"

"Fine with me, but you might want to wait until they're finished unloading the truck. He's checking the totes as they come off and that takes time. It makes the drivers mad – throws off their schedule – but we have to be sure we don't get any more damaged ones."

"Sounds like you're talking about pretty major damage."

Knudsen nodded. "Enough that it makes loading the food into the hoppers difficult and the supervisors out there get really pissed. It's more than just a little rip. It's like a goddamn hole's been punched in the side. It means they can't use the equipment to lift them up and dump them. If they do, half the food gets wasted. They have to do it by hand."

"So you think the damage happens on the truck?"

"Could be. That's what Steiger's checking. If it's not there then it has to be on the barge."

Dan glanced over at the chart again.

"Do you happen to know if the farm where Farnsworth had his . . . accident had a damaged tote? Reuben said he thought it did, but he wasn't sure."

"Haven't heard, but I wouldn't be surprised. A lot of us use the same trucking companies and the same barges as well."

There was nothing else he could offer.

OUT IN THE YARD, Dan leaned against the hood of his SUV and watched the totes coming off the truck. A man – perhaps the driver because he looked seriously impatient - jockeyed the totes onto a pallet, attached a hook to the straps and used the winch to swing it over and lower it to the ground. Another man, this one not much more than a teenager and with the same white hair as Sonya, operated a forklift, moving the pallets inside the building. In between the two activities, a third man whom Dan figured had to be Steiger, walked around checking each one.

Steiger was short and solid with a skull covered with gray-brown stubble and a rough beard that looked as if he hadn't shaved for a couple of days. To Dan's eyes, the inspection he was giving the totes seemed cursory, but then any damage of the type Knudsen had described would be pretty easy to spot.

The last tote disappeared into the warehouse and the driver climbed into the truck, slammed the door and turned on the engine without speaking to either of the other two men. Dan pushed himself up off the hood of his vehicle and walked over to where Steiger stood writing something on a clipboard.

"Bob Steiger?"

The man narrowed his eyes and stared at him. "You talk to the office? This yard is off-limits."

"Matti Knudsen sent me out. I need to ask you a few questions."

"You're a cop?"

Dan hadn't shown him any ID, but it was probably a fair assumption. "Yes. Knudsen said you would be the one to ask about any visitors going out to the farms."

Steiger's face changed and took on a furtive look. "We don't allow visitors." His tone was brusque and his eyes refused to meet Dan's. The man was nervous,

"Not even people from the companies you deal with?"

Steiger's eyes slid sideways and Dan could see his hands clenching and unclenching. "No way. Not unless they've got work to do out there."

"So no one from the company that supplies the food went out to look at the damaged totes?"

A sheen of perspiration had appeared on Steiger's face. "I already told you. No visitors." He started walking towards the warehouse. "I gotta go. I've got work to do."

Dan watched him for a few seconds then went back to his car and started the engine. As he drove through the gate he looked at the rearview mirror. Steiger was standing in the warehouse doorway watching him.

D an was halfway back to the office when his phone rang. He reached into his pocket and fumbled it out. He hated cellphones and barely knew how to use one, but Markleson insisted he carry one whenever he was off the boat.

The ringing stopped before he had figured out how to answer it and he stabbed at the redial button as he pulled over to the side of the road.

"Connor," he mumbled.

"Rediger. You got a message from a Mr. Ishikawa. He says he's got some information for you."

Ishikawa! The sensei had come through for him.

"I'll be there in about ten minutes. How long ago did he call?"

"Just finished talking to him."

Dan threw the phone onto the passenger seat and swung back onto the highway, the big tires on the SUV spraying gravel as he pushed the accelerator almost to the floor.

He made it back to the office in record time, put the car back in the lot and headed inside to the desk. "You got a number for Ishikawa?" he asked Rediger as he handed him the keys.

"On the slip," Rediger replied, handing Dan a printed message form in return." Before you go, you got a word for "Chance occurance on the sea floor". Five letters. Starts with "F".

"Fluke," Dan answered as he headed for a phone.

ISHIKAWA ANSWERED on the second ring.

"Sensei, this is Dan Connor. I got a message that you had called."

"That is correct." As always the sensei was unhurried and courteous. "I wished to let you know that I believe the man you asked me to watch for was there at the house with Mr. Halvorsen a short time ago."

"Mr. Halvorsen?" The formal title momentarily was momentarily confusing. Dan had only heard it used before to refer to the older man, Karl's father.

"Indeed, and I believe it was his truck they arrived in. It is a blue pick-up. I have seen Mr. Halvorsen drive it several times before."

"Do you know if they are still there?" Dan asked.

"No. They left almost immediately. They seemed to be in a great hurry. It was a little strange." Dan could almost see the old man shaking his head.

"Strange in what way, Sensei?"

There was a pause which Dan found familiar. The sensei always chose his words with great care, deliberating over each one to ensure his meaning was precise and clear.

"They parked in the driveway and opened the garage door. They did not enter the house. There is no direct access to the house from the garage, only a door to the basement. I know this because both my wife and I visited there many times before Mr. Halvorsen became ill."

"Perhaps they had forgotten something in the basement. Or maybe they were dropping something off?" What Dan had heard so far was interesting, but it hardly qualified as strange.

"Perhaps, but Mr. Halvorsen was carrying a box of pizza. I recognized the box and it had the name Pizza Express written on it. They took it to the basement, but returned almost immediately without it. Why would you take a pizza down to the basement and leave it there?"

It was a very good question, Dan thought. Why indeed.

"So they came back without the pizza, and then what?" he asked.

"The man you asked me to watch for had a bag with him. He must have collected it from the basement because he did not have it when he went in. He carried it out to the pick-up and then they both got in and shut the garage again."

"And they left right away? They took the bag with them?"

"Indeed."

"Did you happen to see what kind of a bag it was?"

"It was very similar to the ones many of my students use. It was dark blue and it had the word Adidas written along the side. It looked full."

Dan thanked the sensei and hung up the phone. If only other witnesses were as precise and careful with their reports, his job would be much easier.

He went back to Rediger's desk. "Markleson in?" Dan asked. "I need to see him."

Rediger was still working on his crossword puzzle and didn't look up. "Far as I know. He was a while ago, but he doesn't always share his schedule with me."

"Okay. Thanks." Dan headed down the hall.

MARKLESON WAS on the phone when Dan opened the door, but he beckoned him in and pointed to the chair in front of his desk.

"So what have you got?" The growl was even rougher than usual. "Better be good news. That was the hospital. Got another woman in there with an overdose. They're not sure she's going to make it. If she doesn't, it makes four deaths in a week."

Dan leaned forward. "I think if we can move quickly, we might be able to find the guy who's distributing it."

Markleson had been reaching for his pipe when Dan started speaking and his hand froze in mid-air as he heard the words.

"The distributor? You're talking about the drugs?"

Dan nodded.

"So how the hell does a big-time drug distributor become part of your investigation into a couple of missing guys?"

"A couple of missing guys and two murders." Dan didn't want to spend any more time than he had to explaining. That could come later.

"I can give you all the details, but first I need you to get our guys out to look for a blue pick-up truck. If we can find it quick enough, the two guys in it are going to have enough drugs with them to get them sent away for a good long time."

"You're going to have to give me a bit more than that," Markleson said. "I can't just call up the detachments and order them to put their guys out on a search without giving them a reason."

"Okay, here's the thing." Dan sucked in a lungful of air and ran his hand through his hair as he thought about where to start. "Remember that guy we talked about last time I was here – long, dark hair but I didn't know his name?"

Markleson nodded.

"His name is Eric LaSalle, and he's friendly with Karl

Halvorsen. The two of them are in this together. LaSalle either brings the drugs into Vancouver himself – he's in the import-export business so it's possible – or he has a supplier there. It doesn't matter. Either way he has the drugs put into bales of fish food that get shipped up here to the farms. The bales are marked somehow and a contact here – I think it's a man called Steiger who works in the yard at Knudsen's – either removes the drugs or more likely makes sure the marked bales are delivered to a certain farm. LaSalle comes up here on a yacht owned by one of his business associates, collects the drugs, and re-packages them. The re-packaging is done in the basement of Halvorsen's house."

Markleson stared at him. "Can you prove any of this?"

"Some, and some of it is still just guesswork, but if I'm right, they're out there right now with an Adidas sports bag full of whatever drug they're selling. If we can catch them with that, we can clear it all up at the same time."

"Both those two murders you're looking into are tied into this?" Markleson's hand was already moving towards the phone.

"I think both Farnsworth and Jules saw something they weren't supposed to see. Farnsworth for sure. Jules might be something different, but I'll explain that after you've made the call."

It took almost ten minutes for Markleson to contact the detachments and get them to organize the search and when he had finished he called Rediger and told him to make sure he kept everyone focused on finding the truck. Now the two men were sitting quietly, both working on a fresh pot of coffee while the waited to hear the results of the search.

"So tell me about Jules and this "different thing". I assume it's also linked to the drugs?" Markleson reached for his pipe again.

"Yeah." Dan could finally picture the various scenarios in

his mind. "I think he was taken – bribed, kidnapped, I'm not sure – but coerced in some way, and forced to help move them. Either he escaped, or they didn't have any more use for him, so they got rid of him."

"You keep saying "they". You talking about Halvorsen, Lasalle and Steiger or are there more?"

"Well Steiger would have had to contact somebody to get Jules involved. It doesn't seem too likely either LaSalle or Halvorsen could have done it – they wouldn't have known him – and both Jules and Manuel worked on the same farm. I think one of the supervisors over there might be tied up in this so I got a list from Matti Knudsen. A guy called Anderson was on shift when both Jules and Manuel disappeared"

Markleson nodded slowly. "So what about Manuel? You think he's floating out there somewhere too and just hasn't been found yet?"

Dan shook his head. "I think Manuel's still alive. At least he was about an hour ago. I don't think they would feed anyone they didn't plan on keeping alive for a while longer."

47

The call they were waiting for came in twenty minutes later. The blue pick-up truck had been seen coming out of Quatse River campground with two men in it. When it was stopped, the officers had found a blue Adidas bag with "suspicious contents" in the back seat. The two men were currently being taken to the Port Hardy police station for questioning, as was a local Port Hardy man who was already known to the police and whose car had been closely following the pick-up. A search of the pick-up had turned up a Beretta 1919 25 automatic.

"So have we got enough for a warrant on Halvorsen's house now?" Between the waiting and the three cups of coffee, Dan was so wired he could barely sit still.

"Yeah, but let's wait until we get official confirmation on what they find. If it's what we think, we can get all the warrants we want, and if Manuel is in that basement, it sounds like he'll be okay where he is for now. "Markleson paused and frowned. "How the hell do you know they fed him?"

Dan grinned. "The neighbor is a friend of mine, Mr.

Ishikawa. He's my judo instructor. He lives right across the street. He saw them take in a box of pizza and come out a couple of minutes later without it. I phoned the pizza place down there in the mall. They confirmed Halvorsen had just picked up a pepperoni pizza."

Markleson gave a chuckle. It grew into a laugh and after a few moments Dan joined in.

"Goddamn!" Markleson wheezed as he slapped his hand on the desk. "If this all works out it'll be the first case I ever heard of that was solved by a box of pizza!"

The two men were still laughing when Maureen stuck her head in the door. "You might want to switch your phone back on." She nodded towards Markleson's command phone where a solid red light announced an open line. "Port Hardy's trying to reach you. They say they think the local drug problem might be solved."

TWO UNIFORMED COPS, plus two men in Hazmat suits and a plainclothes guy who fit the description of Willie Pete's visitor met Dan and Markleson outside Halvorsen's house.

"You want us to take the house or the garage first?" one of the uniforms asked Markleson.

Markleson stabbed his thumb towards Dan. "Ask him. He's in charge of this one."

"We need to get into the garage," Dan answered. "There's a door going down to the basement. Take it easy down there. We think there might be a hostage."

The group organized themselves, Hazmats in the middle with their sensors ready, the two uniforms on either side and the plain-clothes guy standing a little behind. Dan and Markleson followed them. Someone produced a couple of jacks which they inserted under the door and less than a minute later they were all standing inside the empty garage.

There were no windows, but they could make out a solid metal door set in the far end of the inner sidewall.

"Locked," one the men said as he tried the doorknob, and another stepped forward and clamped an electronic device over the locking mechanism.

A set of steep stairs led down to another door, this one made of heavy wood and held shut with three sliding bolts. The two Hazmat men moved forward to open it, moving their sensors up and down and running them along the walls. Once inside they moved towards yet another door just a few feet ahead, this one made from heavy wrought iron.

Although the air smelt stale, there was a faintly astringent quality to it and the Hazmat team indicated that the rest of them should wait until they finished checking it out. Their bulky suits partially blocked Dan's view, but ahead of them, he could see a bare cement floor and walls a long fluorescent light fixture set into the ceiling. It glared a harsh light down onto a white plastic table that held a jumble of plastic bags and containers. The floor beneath it was sprinkled with a dusting of white powder and the same powder outlined a meandering trail of footprints that disappeared out of sight.

The Hazmat team finished their testing and stepped back to let one of the uniformed cops open the door. He stepped in, glanced around then turned and beckoned Dan forward. Sitting on a thin mattress on an old iron cot, an open pizza box beside him, was a man with braided hair. He was staring at them, his body drooping in despair, but his face showing the first signs of hope.

"Harold?" Dan asked as he walked towards him, his hand outstretched in greeting.

48

Harold Manuel sat out on the aft deck as *Dreamspeaker* made her way towards Banks Inlet. Several times Dan had offered him food or drink, but Harold only shook his head and smiled, his eyes fixed on his surroundings. Occasionally his gaze moved from the shoreline and the trees to follow the flight of a soaring gull or the wandering flight of a butterfly, and sometimes he seemed to focus on the flash of a silver fin, but the smile never left his face. After three attempts to engage him in conversation, Dan gave up. It felt somehow sacrilegious to interrupt such an intense and private communion with the natural world.

Dan anchored *Dreamspeaker* in a cove near the mouth of the river and lowered the inflatable into the water. As he stepped into the dinghy and reached up to release the hooks, a hand stretched past him to take the line. It was the first time Harold had moved since they left the marina.

Twenty minutes later they rounded the point and the village came into view. The shoreline looked nothing like it had the last time Dan had been there. Then it had been empty except for a couple of small runabouts. Now it was covered by boats of every size and shape imaginable. Dragged up onto the beach, tied out in the shallows, lined up along the float Dan could see canoes, kayaks, skiffs, runabouts, and even a few small fishboats. The news of Harold's rescue had obviously spread. It looked as if the entire population of even the most remote Native community in the Broughtons had shown up to welcome Harold Manuel home – and they had used anything that would float to do it.

It wasn't until Dan got almost to the float, which was as crowded with people as the shore was crowded with boats and which looked to be in danger of sinking under their weight, that he saw the lone figure sitting up on the drift-wood logs, a canoe drawn up beside him. Walker had come to join the celebration too.

IT WAS LATE the following day when Dan anchored off Walk-er's cove, just above Siwash Bay in Knight Inlet. He was as tired as he had ever been, but also exhilarated. Harold Manuel was alive and well and back with his family. The sense of relief and the satisfaction of putting the men who had brought death and sorrow to so many behind bars buoyed Dan up even though he hadn't slept for over twenty-four hours.

The celebration in the Tsa'wit longhouse had gone on all night and lasted until well into the morning. Dan lost track of the number of people he was introduced to and how many hands he shook. He also lost track of how much he had eaten although he was sure that his hands had never been empty and the galley was now filled to overflowing with gifts of salmon and halibut and venison – far more than he was ever going to be able to eat. There was also a button blanket cape hanging in his closet and a cedar bracelet on his wrist. They had both been given to him by the chief in a ceremony that took place after many hours of drumming and dancing, Although Dan had not asked, he suspected the cedar bracelet was the same one Billy Jules had been wearing when he had been found out on the reef. It, like all the rest of the gifts, was an honor he had not been expecting and he felt humbled by it all.

"You heading back over to McNeill?" Walker's voice broke into Dan's reverie.

"Yes. I've got to get back to work. There's still one more man to find."

Walker gave him a questioning look and Dan realized he had never told him about Jimmy Fulton.

"He's a white guy. Just a kid really. Told his folks back in Toronto he had a job lined up on one of the farms, but no one's seen him."

"You think he's like Harold and Billy? Those same guys had him working on the drugs?"

"No. In fact I'm not sure he's really missing at all, but I've got to find him. I've know he loves the outdoors and his grandfather's a bit of an environmentalist so I'm beginning to wonder if he might have joined up with some activist group. I've heard they have some places round here where they set up camps. I don't suppose you've seen any of them have you?"

Walker lowered himself into the canoe they had just swung, off the stern grid. "Seen a couple," he said. He took the rope Dan handed him but continued to hold onto the grid. "You got a description of this kid?"

"I've got better than that. I've got a photo. If you want to wait a minute I'll go get it."

When Dan got back with the photo, Walker stared at Jimmy Fulton's face for several seconds, and then he smiled. "Should be pretty easy to find. He's about two miles up the inlet, in Escape Cove. I talked to him just a couple of days ago. Seems like a nice kid."

After the long days of frustration, two good men murdered, three kids dead from overdoses and a young woman in a coma, to finally find Jimmy happy and healthy was somewhat of an anti-climax. Dan knew he would still have to pay him a visit, simply to confirm that he was actually there and to see if he could persuade him to at least give his parents and his grandfather a call, but there was no rush now. He had no doubt that Walker's identification was valid. The man's power of observation was incredible: he could pick out a black bear cub in a jumble of black rocks at a distance of half a mile. If he said he had seen Jimmy, Dan had no doubt he was correct. It was finally over. The case was closed – except for one thing.

He waved good-bye to Walker and then went up to the wheelhouse and picked up the phone. It was time. He knew the number by heart even though he hadn't dialed it for a long time and as he waited for the familiar voice to answer he stared out the window at a pair of otters playing on the shore.

"Mike Bryant".

How often had Dan heard that same name spoken in that same voice? A few years ago, when he had been working on the anti-terrorist squad down in Vancouver, he and Mike had talked almost daily, both on and off the job. After Susan's murder, it had been Mike who helped him find *Dreamspeaker*, and who organized the other guys to help convert her into the boat she was today. It had been Mike who had offered him a couch to sleep on when he had drunk himself into oblivion day after day, and almost two years later it had been Mike who had cajoled and prodded him back onto the force.

"Mike, it's Dan Connor."

There was a pause and Dan could almost hear the smile.

"Dan! Good to hear your voice. It's been a while."

"Yeah. Too long."

"I hear you're doing good up there. Just closed another case."

Dan shook his head. It seemed the police-vine worked at least as well as the kelp-vine. It has only been two days since they picked up Halvorsen and Lasalle and discovered Harold Manuel in the basement of Halvorsen's house.

"Yeah, although I should've figured it out a lot sooner."

"Still your own worst critic huh?"

"Maybe, but the truth is I let something distract me, and it's something I need to deal with."

"Anything I can help you with?"

Dan heard the change in tone. Mike knew exactly what he was talking about, but he was going to let him get to it his own way, just as he had let him get to it in his own time.

"Yeah, at least I hope so. I need to ask you a question. It's something I should have asked a long time ago, but for some reason I just couldn't bring myself to do it – avoidance maybe, or just plain cowardice. I guess I figured that if I didn't ask about the guy that murdered Susan ... "

He took a deep breath as he said the words, but made himself continue. "I guess I figured if I didn't talk about it, didn't hear about it, I wouldn't have to think about it. It was stupid, and it didn't work, but it became a habit. I guess the shrinks would call it a mental block."

His harsh bark of laughter was directed at himself. "Anyway, I guess I've grown up a bit. It's time."

There was a long pause, and when Mike spoke again, the smile was back in his voice.

""I wondered when you would get around to it. I don't suppose Claire's got anything to do with this new-found confidence?"

"Could be. She's an amazing lady." Dan's voice held an answering smile. "So what's the answer? You ever catch the guy?"

"We did. Twice. He managed to get off the first time, but we nailed him again. He's serving fifteen years in Kent."

Dan eyes blurred, but his laughter echoed around the bay. He might be tired, but this was going to be a perfect day: Harold Manuel was home, Jimmy Fulton was safe and Claire would be waiting for him at the marina.

ACKNOWLEDGMENTS

My thanks to Trevor Isaac, Collections Manager at the U'Mista museum on Yalis (Alert Bay) for his help and support in the writing of this book. Also to Haida cultural ambassador Aay Aay Hans, and to Jags Brown and James Cowpar for their patient and gentle teaching. Sanford Williams, Nuu-chah-nulth artist and all around good guy guided me on part of the journey that this series has become, as did Bruce Manuel, wise counselor at the En'owkin Centre, Penticton. To all of you, Haaw'a. Gilikas'la. Thank you. I am humbled by your strength, your learning and your passion.

Thanks also go to Lynne Stonier-Newman, Jim Tipton, Victoria Schmidt, Robert Drynan, Carol Bradley, Herbert Piekow, Antonio Rambles, Mel Goldberg, Carol Bradley, Janice Kimball, Margie Keene and Sally Asante for their patient guidance. I could not have done this without you.

To the 'Namgis, Tlowitsis, Mamalilikulla, We Wai Kai, Kwikwautinuxw Haxwamis, Sto:lo, Ahousaht, Musgamagw Dzawada'enuxw Nations who, together with others, are fighting to protect the waters of the west coast, and to Alexandra Morton for her tireless battle to save the wild salmon, thank you all.

- And to all my relations –

本 **Shogun Press**